Re:ZeRo
-Starting Life in Another World- Ex

5

The Tale of
the Scarlet
Princess

Jorah

A count in the Volakian Empire. Takes Priscilla as his wife with full knowledge of her true identity.

Serena

A high countess in the Volakian Empire. Goes by the sobriquet "the Scorching Lady."

Characters

The only ability Subaru Natsuki gets when he's summoned to another world is
time travel via his own death. But to save her, he'll die as many times as it takes.

Prisca

One of the children of Emperor Dreizen
Volakia. Draws the Bright Sword in order to
participate in the Rite of Imperial Selection,
which will determine the next emperor.

Arakiya

A young dog-girl who serves Prisca.

The Hornet

The queen of the coliseum where fights are conducted on the Volakian Empire's sword-slave island. Takes immense pleasure in battle.

Ubirk

A male prostitute on the sword-slave island.

Orbart

Number Three of Volakia's Nine
Divine Generals. A seemingly
laid-back and easygoing old man.

Lamia

A member of the Volakian Royal
Family. Half sister of Priscilla and
Vincent and participant in the Rite
of Imperial Selection.

Miles

Volakian spy.
Like an older brother
to Balleroy.

They stared at each other, a brother and sister with an unbridgeable gulf between them, their reunion reeking of blood. But they were both smiling.

"Of course I am, Brother. And just imagine how much better I would be if your head were to fall from your shoulders right here and now."

"I'm glad you made it, Prisca.
I hope you're well."

Re:ZERO -Starting Life in Another World-

The only ability Subaru Natsuki gets when he's summoned to another world is
time travel via his own death. But to save her, he'll die as many times as it takes.

CONTENTS

Crimson Shadow
First published in Monthly Comic Alive *Nos. 161, 162, and 164*

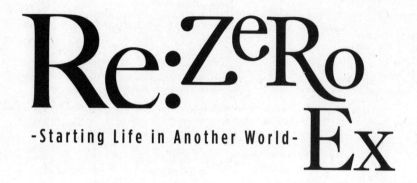

Re:ZeRo Ex

-Starting Life in Another World-

VOLUME 5

The Tale of the Scarlet Princess

TAPPEI NAGATSUKI
ILLUSTRATION: SHINICHIROU OTSUKA

NEW YORK

Re:ZERO -Starting Life in Another World- Ex, Vol. 5
Tappei Nagatsuki

Translation by Kevin Steinbach
Cover art by Shinichirou Otsuka

This book is a work of fiction. Names, characters, places, and incidents are the product of the author's imagination or are used fictitiously. Any resemblance to actual events, locales, or persons, living or dead, is coincidental.

Re:ZERO KARA HAJIMERU ISEKAI SEIKATSU Ex5 HIIROKITAN
©Tappei Nagatsuki 2021
First published in Japan in 2021 by KADOKAWA CORPORATION, Tokyo.
English translation rights arranged with KADOKAWA CORPORATION, Tokyo through Tuttle-Mori Agency, Inc., Tokyo.

Yen On
150 West 30th Street, 19th Floor
New York, NY 10001

Visit us at yenpress.com
facebook.com/yenpress
twitter.com/yenpress
yenpress.tumblr.com
instagram.com/yenpress

First Yen On Edition: October 2022
Edited by Yen On Editorial: Ivan Liang
Designed by Yen Press Design: Andy Swist

Yen On is an imprint of Yen Press, LLC.
The Yen On name and logo are trademarks of Yen Press, LLC.

The publisher is not responsible for websites (or their content) that are not owned by the publisher.

Library of Congress Cataloging-in-Publication Data
Names: Nagatsuki, Tappei, 1987– author. | Otsuka, Shinichirou, illustrator. | Steinbach, Kevin, translator.
Title: Re:ZERO starting life in another world ex / Tappei Nagatsuki ; illustration by Shinichirou Otsuka ; translation by Kevin Steinbach.
Other titles: Re:ZERO kara hajimeru isekai seikatsu ex. English
Description: First Yen On edition. | New York : Yen On, 2017.
Identifiers: LCCN 2017036833 | ISBN 9780316412902 (v. 1 : pbk.) | ISBN 9780316479097 (v. 2 : pbk.) | ISBN 9781975304263 (v. 3 : pbk.) | ISBN 9781975316013 (v. 4 : pbk.) | ISBN 9781975348540 (v. 5 : pbk.)
Subjects: | CYAC: Science fiction. | Time travel—Fiction. | BISAC: FICTION / Science Fiction / Adventure.
Classification: LCC PZ7.1.N34 Ref 2017 | DDC [Fic]—dc23
LC record available at https://lccn.loc.gov/2017036833

ISBNs: 978-1-9753-4854-0 (paperback)
978-1-9753-4855-7 (ebook)

1 2022

LSC-C

Printed in the United States of America

CRIMSON SHADOW

1

The warm sunlight slipped past the blinds and touched the sleeper's cheek.

"Mm… Mmm…" The emerging voice had yet to deepen with age. It had a neutral timbre, not obviously masculine or feminine, and its owner looked every bit as innocent as they sounded, exuding a certain unsavory attraction.

Murmuring and tossing gently on the bed was a lovely young man. His pink hair was disheveled from sleeping, and his skin was as white as milk. He looked to be ten years old, give or take, and much like his voice, his angelic appearance made it impossible to tell whether he was a boy or a girl.

His name was Schult, and the poverty he had been born into would have been the death of him if not for his powerful luck.

"Ahhh…" Schult sat up on the white sheets and yawned, rubbing his eyes. They were as red as rubies, which only enhanced his beauty. One might say he possessed a certain purity that approached perfection. However, such observations were very much at odds with Schult's opinion of himself.

"Gah, I'm still thin as a rail." He stopped rubbing his eyes as his consciousness caught up with reality and instead started pouting as he plucked at his upper arms. The source of his displeasure was simple: No matter how hard he tried, his arms and legs never seemed to get any manlier. All the training he underwent seemed to have no discernable effect on his body.

Last night, for example, he had diligently practiced swinging his wooden sword before going to bed, and yet here he was, arms still soft as wool. Worse, a faint ache lingered in his muscles—another reminder of how pathetic he was.

In truth, that pain was a sign that the boy's innocent wish was gradually coming true, but he didn't know that. Instead, Schult recalled the advice Al had given him once.

"Master Al said that pain is a sign that something is wrong. He also said that I should rest until the pain goes away."

Schult's training regimen, which he had devised based on what Al had told him, consisted of one day of sword practice followed by five days of rest. Naturally, expecting to see much improvement on a schedule like that was downright silly. That was, in fact, part of Al's plan, but that was another thing Schult didn't realize.

Not all of Al's plans originated with his own immaturity, however...

"Schult, you're awake?"

"Oh!"

Schult jumped, turning on the bed; someone else was in the room with him. She sat in a luxurious chair, her long legs crossed elegantly. Only a sheer set of sleeping clothes covered her voluptuous, feminine form. Her crimson eyes were focused on the book that rested open on her knees. To Schult, she looked like she could have been the work of the most skilled painter in the world; he could almost swear that she was glowing, radiant.

"Good morning, Lady Priscilla," Schult said.

"Mm. You look as lovely as ever this morning, Schult. And I praise how it felt to hold you last night."

"Th-thank you, milady," Schult said, enchanted. The woman—

Priscilla—nodded generously. Schult found the approving words immensely gratifying and yet embarrassing; it was a complicated feeling.

He understood that his role was to handle odd jobs for Priscilla and to serve as her bed warmer—but he often wished he could repay his enormous debt to her in a more substantial way. That was both how he truly felt as well as his deepest wish.

"*Staaaare.*"

"What's this? You seem to be looking at me especially closely this morning. Is something the matter?"

"N-nothing, Lady Priscilla. You're still the most beautiful person in the world! And I'm so happy to be able to serve you! But..."

"But what?"

"I wish I could be of more use to you, Lady Priscilla, but I haven't the strength. I wish I could swing a sword like Master Al..." As he spoke, Schult was reminded of the listless, floppy feeling of his own arms.

He didn't have to be as strong as Priscilla's knight, Al, or even her private forces, the Redmongers. His only wish was to protect her from even one of the threats and challenges she faced on a regular basis.

"When the moment comes, Lady Priscilla, I'll be your shield... Oh, but my body is so small. You could hold me up in front of you to shield yourself from— Ow! Yow!"

"That is enough frivolous blathering. *I* will decide how I use *my* possessions. When did you become so high-and-mighty to think you could give me orders?" Priscilla, who had stood up almost without Schult realizing it, managed to stroke and tug on his ear at the same time.

Leaning against her palm, Schult said, "I c-certainly didn't mean to..." He looked this way and that. "Ngh... But if I can't be your shield, then how might I serve you, milady? Oh, I know! I can cling to you and be your armor!"

"This is not a matter of what piece of my equipment you can replace. Schult, I neither expect nor need you to be my sword, nor my shield. The best thing you can do is to continue serving as my pillow."

"Just your pillow, milady…?" His head drooped; her words were merciless. It was painful to hear so clearly that the person he owed everything didn't consider him one of her warriors, even if he had realized it long ago. His flimsy arms were to blame. Or maybe it was his sticklike legs.

"Hmm." Priscilla watched Schult grimly appraise his own body, then crossed her arms, emphasizing her generous chest. "If you cannot simply continue serving as my pillow, I would rather you read a book than swing a sword. Yes, that would be much more to my benefit."

"A book, milady? So if I read a book, I can become your shield?!"

"No, you cannot. Don't forget your place."

"Sorry, milady…"

As the hopeful light that briefly shone in his eyes went out, Schult was quick to regret his overenthusiastic assumption. Priscilla flashed him an amused look, then indicated the room with a wave of her arm. They were in her bedroom, but her bed wasn't the only furnishing. Shelves full of books lined the walls. Priscilla's mansion—which stood upon the Bariel estate—was packed with these bookshelves, host to a collection of books as large as any in the kingdom. Her husband Lyp had been quite a collector himself, and once Priscilla had taken over the estate, she bought up what seemed like every book she could find. She was no casual reader. This was nothing less than the usurpation of knowledge.

"There are times when knowledge can do more to save your life than a shield or sword," she intoned.

"Wha?"

"It's a maxim, attributed to some ancient sage. I'm more or less in agreement with it, but I think it's still one step short of the truth."

"Meaning, uhh…"

What Priscilla said was difficult for Schult to understand, and he struggled to follow her line of thinking. Of course, she didn't adjust anything for his benefit. Priscilla always moved at her own pace. It was the collective desire to see her bracing figure leading them forward that kept all her followers enthralled.

If they didn't run as hard as they could, they would never catch up with the woman who stopped for no one.

"___"

"Knowledge is the omnipotent staff," Priscilla said. "A sword or a shield—what use are they when you have no need of them? Can a sword make your fields more fertile? Can a shield heal a sick man? Can either of them enrich your life? They can do none of these things. Knowledge, and knowledge alone, is like a staff that you can lean on in every circumstance. As for me, I stand and walk under my own power. Naturally, that is not to say I never stumble."

"B-but it hurts when you fall..."

"Yes, it is far from pleasant. You may be injured. You may bleed. However..."

"Oh! If you have a staff, you won't fall!" Schult cried as he raised his hand, finally grasping Priscilla's meaning.

She let her expression soften in apparent satisfaction and patted Schult's head again. Gently this time, charmed by his understanding. "That is why you should set yourself to reading books—if you wish to be not my sword nor my shield nor my pillow, but my staff."

"Y-yes, milady...! Oh, but...I don't know how to read..."

"Ask Al to teach you. He has too much time on his hands, besides. And despite all appearances to the contrary, he's quite a talented teacher. If he can't manage to put letters into your head, I'll simply cut off his *other* arm."

"A very grave responsibility! I'll try my hardest to learn—for Master Al's sake!" Schult sat up straighter, spurred by the thought of how awful Al's life would be without either of his arms. Just as Priscilla nodded in acknowledgment, Schult's gaze happened to fall on one book in particular. It was the volume that now sat on the chair Priscilla had occupied until a moment before. It had a red cover worked with gold. Schult remembered seeing this one before. Only he, who served as Priscilla's pillow every night, knew that it was her favorite book, the one she read without fail upon waking every single morning.

"Lady Priscilla, what book is that?"

"…That one? That is not a book for reading. Rather, it's…full of reminders, let us say. I doubt it would interest you even if you could read it."

"'Reminders,' milady?" Schult tilted his head, not entirely sure what that could mean.

In response, Priscilla took the book in hand, running her fingers along the cover. "Were you to read it, I doubt anything in it would benefit you. What a reader seeks from a book varies from person to person. Simply feeling the heart leap at a dramatic story is one of the pleasures of reading."

"—? But your staff, Lady Priscilla…"

"Even I do not read *only* to learn. Hmm…" Priscilla sat in her chair once more, then opened the book across her knees and scanned the contents. "You amuse me. Schult, I shall read to you for a few minutes."

"*You* read to *me*, Lady Priscilla? Oh! I can't wait!"

"Heh. Your guileless reactions continue to charm me. In any case… Yes, let's see…"

Priscilla looked at Schult, who sat bolt upright on the bed, and then she began to speak. Schult, grasping this undreamed-of chance, listened raptly. The voice that filled his ears seemed soft and billowy, like a tender song.

Her story began as it seemed every story must: "Once upon a time, in a certain place, there lived a lovely, sweet, beautiful young woman…"

2

This lovely, sweet, and beautiful young woman wore a resplendent dress.

"＿＿"

The dress, red as blood, fluttered as she walked along. A discernible youth hung about her even though her back was straight and her posture impeccable. From her eyes, almond-shaped and crimson, to her skin, as pale and as delicate as porcelain, to her finely sculpted facial features, everything about her seemed to shine; these were portents of her great and terrible future.

Six servants attended her as she proceeded down the red carpet with supreme self-assurance. When she passed through the great doors that stood open at the end of the carpet, she was greeted with a luxurious dining hall and nine more servants.

Once she reached the centermost seat of a long table bedecked with a white cloth, one of the servants pulled out a chair for her, and the preparation for her meal began. A cart full of eating utensils was wheeled in to supply the girl's place setting. She was the only one actually using the dining hall; everyone else was present merely to facilitate her meal.

As the dishes were being readied, the girl rather abruptly turned to the servant standing at her side and said, "What are my plans for today?"

The servant bowed with utmost respect and replied, "Milady's room is prepared for your studies once you've finished dining. Also, Master Vincent requests that you have lunch with him."

"My studies, hmm? I hope this meal isn't as bland and uninteresting as those lessons. But you say my elder brother is here; that's good news. I've been waiting to avenge the humiliation of my earlier loss at shatranj."

Where the servant spoke quietly and humbly, the girl was haughty. She nodded; the servant made no remark on her condescending attitude but took a single step backward, still bowing, and rejoined the line of attendants.

Approving of the carefully observed decorum, the girl said, "Very well," and faced forward once more. While she had been talking to the servant, her meal had been laid out, and the first course, a steaming hot soup, sat before her.

"If you'll permit me, milady."

"Mm."

Just because the food was ready didn't mean she could simply start eating. Instead, one of the servants stepped forward and, after humbly asking for permission, delicately picked up a spoon. She took a spoonful of the soup and brought it not to the girl's mouth, but to her own.

It was simple; she was tasting for poison. Any noble of significance would have someone on hand to check their food.

The girl was used to this; she hardly reacted as the woman sampled the dish, checking the flavor and confirming it was safe for consumption. Virtually all the young woman's food was screened in this way, which ultimately meant she hardly ever got to eat freshly made dishes while they were still hot. She understood, of course, that it was a necessary precaution.

"How wearisome..." The words formed on her lips but barely left them; no one knew she had spoken but her.

Not heeding the girl's whispering, the food taster finished her job. When *her* turn finally came to have some of the now-cold soup, the girl looked at the dish with an exasperated expression that crossed her beautiful face.

"___"

She took a spoonful of soup and brought to her mouth. The way she immediately went back for another mouthful was, perhaps, an expression of her desire to get this dreary meal out of the way as quickly as possible. Well, so long as she observed proper dining etiquette, no one here could or would object no matter how fast she ate.

And in any case, neither speed nor manners were an issue any longer.

"——Hrk..."

A strangled noise escaped the girl's lips, and the spoon fell from her hand. Instead of her eating utensil, she grabbed at the tablecloth, pulling it toward herself and sending the dishes and silverware everywhere.

"Kah— Ghhh—"

With her other hand, she clutched at her throat, gasping. Her red eyes shot open, their natural crimson color now made even more brilliant by the tears of blood that rolled down her cheeks. Blood likewise flowed from her nose and mouth.

The servants around her were aghast at the unimaginable scene, yet all they could do was watch. Only one of their number stood in silent stupefaction: the food taster, who was bleeding from her head just like the young woman. "I d...did it," she rasped, managing to smile despite what must have been supreme agony. Then she collapsed, knees first, and the fact that she didn't even bother to throw out her hands as she tumbled to the floor was proof that she was already dead. She'd ingested the same poison as the young lady yet had managed to fight the effects long enough to convince her the food was safe. She'd held on to make sure her plan worked—truly, she had done everything an assassin could do.

Her tenacity had come at the cost of her life, but it had paid off.

"M—th—"

The girl's chair toppled over, and she fell hard. To the bitter end, her arms and legs spasmed as if clinging to life, but eventually, even her twitching stopped, and silence descended upon the dining hall.

"___"

Two bodies, the assassin and her target, lay next to each other on the floor. It was as if time had stopped; the corpses weren't going anywhere, of course, but the remaining servants were terrified of making even a single wrong move. If any of them made a sound, time might start moving again, and then this might all be their fault. Such was the strange but overwhelming certainty that gripped the servants and kept them from acting.

At that moment...

"What, what? Is the assassin dead, too?"

"___"

The girl who appeared in the doorway of the dining hall regarded the two bodies with something close to boredom.

At her appearance and her question, the faces in the room became masks of astonishment. And who could blame them? For the girl was identical to their mistress, the one who was now dead of poison. No—not quite identical.

"——" The girl crossed her arms and looked down at her collapsed doppelgänger. She certainly bore a striking resemblance to the dead child, but when they were side by side, it was possible to detect certain differences in the finer details of their faces. If the dead girl was the masterwork of an accomplished artist, then the one looking down at her was the very essence of that same beauty the artist had aimed for but could never achieve within the confines of this mortal realm.

As they stood there, mouths agape, the servants began to understand. This was the terrible nature of true beauty.

"Lady Prisca," said one of the nearby servants. Two simple words. Hearing them, the girl—Prisca—turned and cocked her head. Her hair blazed orange like the sun, and her eyes were almond-shaped and as red as set rubies. Confronted with the real thing, it suddenly seemed impossible that anyone could confuse her with a lesser. She was simply *made* differently.

"Th-thank goodness you're safe..."

"Hmph. Your sentiment doesn't even qualify as trite. Do you imagine I could ever have been laid low by such insipid means? It's not cheap, though, to find such a capable body double." She glared at the servant, who kept her head bowed, and then walked over to the double.

A body double—someone who looked sufficiently like a person of importance to stand in their place and do dangerous things for them. Wherever plots and plans were afoot, body doubles were standard tools of the trade, and they knew very well that they performed their duties with their lives on the line.

Even so, Prisca didn't specifically wish for her double to die in agony. Considering that they had, of course, chosen a young woman who looked very much like her, it was difficult to not find the scene disquieting.

"So there is someone who wished to make me wear a death mask like this," she mused.

"——"

As the girl, just eleven or twelve, contemplated the still bodies, the servants stood and quaked. Who could mock them for it, call it cowardice? Certainly no one who had seen the girl—so young and so fair, with a profile so cruel and eyes so very red.

"Chief Attendant. Come."

"Y-yes, ma'am!"

Prisca beckoned to a woman who stepped forward on behalf of all the attendants. Fear was written on her face and in the trembling of her shoulders, fear of a child at least twenty years her junior. This earned her a "Hmph" and a look from Prisca.

Prisca motioned the woman to listen: "You are the one who decided who would serve in the household today, are you not?"

"That's…correct, milady. Therefore, please let all responsibility for this oversight fall on me."

"Fool. To what purpose do you think I entrusted you with that job?"

"What purpose, milady?" The attendant's eyes widened at the question; she had clearly been expecting a dressing down at the very least.

Prisca smirked at the woman's confusion. A hideously cruel smile, a terrible sight to behold on the lips of one so young. And yet it could almost have been called alluring. Still smiling, Prisca continued, "If I appoint someone incompetent to look after my safety, certain people even stupider than you will regard it as the perfect opportunity to make me a corpse, bringing them out of the woodwork. A perfect chance to get rid of them all at once."

"____"

And indeed, no sooner had Prisca spoken than the bewildered chief attendant caught her breath as every other servant pulled out a knife, a dagger, or some other weapon from the folds of their clothes.

Regarding them with her crimson eyes, Prisca made her choice almost instantaneously. She grabbed the chief attendant by the lapels and shoved her against the nearest dagger. The woman cried out as the blade tore into her flesh, but she stopped shouting almost immediately, her eyes rolling back in her head—an obvious sign the blade had been coated in some sort of quick-acting poison.

While the chief attendant was in the process of dying, Prisca leaped backward, landing on top of the table, which was still set with food. She pulled the white cloth from under her own feet and flung it over the heads of the encroaching servants—or rather, assassins.

"——" Wordlessly, the assassins sliced through the cloth; it had only delayed them but for an instant. But that brief moment of blindness was precisely what Prisca had sought.

"Ghhh—!" A table knife had lodged itself in the throat of the closest killer, propelled by Prisca's delicate foot. It tore through skin, and the next kick plunged it deeper. Even with his throat pierced, even with a fatal wound, the man raised his dagger in a shaking hand. But Prisca leaped again, closing the distance to grab his arm and drive his knife into the chest of another assassin. Even getting grazed by a weapon bearing such a potent toxin would be enough to induce unconsciousness. Having it plunged directly into one's heart meant certain and immediate death.

"She's just one girl!" cried one of the assassins, infuriated at their dismal attempts on her life.

"And yet I'm clearly too much for you to handle. Trash like you were never going to be worth more effort than this." Prisca chuckled mockingly. Then she spun the nearest chair around, using it to strip the dagger from her opponent. It clattered across the floor, and the assassin watched it go—until Prisca drove her fingers into his eyes and stole his sight. Blinded, he fell to the floor, only for Prisca's foot to find his neck.

She'd managed to set this group of adults on their heels with the sheer tenacity of her assault, but although it wasn't a large group, they still handily outnumbered her, and they were regaining their composure and beginning to close on her again.

Prisca had another disadvantage: All she had to work with was a tablecloth and some silverware—nothing resembling a real weapon. Except...

"I'm getting rather tired of having to sully my own hands with such bothersome work," Prisca said. She looked at her enemies with actual boredom, as if this dire situation meant nothing to her. The look in her red eyes was enough to make the assassins stop in their tracks.

If they all attacked at once, many of them might die, but someone's dagger would reach her eventually. Just a scratch with one of the poisoned blades could be enough to take a life—even Prisca's. In turn, the assassins gave no thought to their own lives as long as they could achieve their goal. But there was one thing they hadn't counted on.

After one collective breath, they charged her.

"You must all be complete fools. Do you truly believe after seeing through your little ambush that I would come here alone?"

Her words seeped into them like a poison. Was there any possibility they had enough time to realize what was happening to them? The truth would remain a mystery, for they were each enveloped in flames, burned to a crisp before they had a chance to cry out.

"____"

The assassins who had come for Prisca's life, fourteen of them, were all simultaneously incinerated. That included those who had died in Prisca's counterattack. The flames burned green, and Prisca clapped her hands at what truly seemed like a phantasmal spectacle of lives being consumed in fire.

"Ha, quite a fine display. The beauty of fire never wavers. Not even when the fuel is the lives of stooges like these. I grant you my praise," Prisca said as she gazed at the still-smoldering assassins.

"It's an honor. The highest honor." The voice that answered came from a small figure who had interposed herself between Prisca and her aggressors.

"____"

Outwardly, she looked to be about Prisca's age, perhaps in her early teens. On her head were the large ears characteristic of the dog-people, and in her hand, she held what appeared to be a twig—and a rather unimpressive one at that, considering it looked like something she'd simply picked off the ground somewhere. Her young

body was slender, her pale skin covered with a minimum of clothing in a way that seemed oddly provocative. Her short hair was silver, except for one distinctive lock of her bangs where there was a shock of red.

She looked at the burning assassins, then turned to Prisca with eyes that showed scant emotion and said, "Disposal complete. I'm glad you're sa— *Burp.*"

"Hold on. Did you just burp at me?"

"Excuse me?" She shook her head. "No. I did not— *Burp.*"

"Fool. You did—that's what it's called." Prisca lightly smacked the other girl with an open palm.

"Ow," the girl said flatly. Then she touched her own ears and said, "Lady Prisca. How did I do?"

"A pointless question, but as I said, I praise you. There's not a scratch on me. And the way you took care of that lot was a sight to see."

"It is all thanks to the spirits." The girl took her hand off her ears, looking somewhat shy. A pale light began to float in her open palm— a spirit. It had no corporeal form of its own, but enough mana could give it a temporary one. This was a lesser spirit, an entity with minimal strength and will.

There were some spirits that could communicate with living beings, form contracts with them to offer their powers and assistance. This girl likewise relied on spirits for her abilities. But she did not make contracts with them.

"*Gulp.*"

Without hesitation, she tossed the lesser spirit in her hand into her mouth and chewed.

Prisca began to smile. "A unique sight, no matter how many times I see it: a spirit eater having a meal."

"*Burp.*"

Prisca crossed her arms but shrugged at the burping girl.

This girl's special ability was not making contracts with spirits, but gaining their powers by consuming them. A unique ability to usurp the capacities of others.

Obviously, not just anyone could obtain the power of spirits by eating them. It was a sign of very, very unusual qualities, and that was why Prisca valued this girl so highly.

"Arakiya, you've done well to heed my orders."

"...Because you spoke them, Lady Prisca."

Having said the name of the girl, Arakiya, Prisca walked over the ashes of the incinerated assassins, approaching the one body that had not been burned. Her double, whose face looked so much like her own—except the way it was currently contorted in a mask of agony. Prisca crouched beside the corpse, closed its eyes, and endeavored to shift the expression to something more peaceful. "Your face was mistaken for mine at least this one time," she said. "You deserve not to be seen like this."

"That girl... Who was she?" Arakiya asked.

"Someone who was of use to me. Her life held that much value, I suppose. I'll have her returned to her family, who will be suitably compensated. A reward befitting one who successfully took my place."

As Prisca stood up, it was plain to see from her expression that her interest in the body double was already fading. She looked now around the room, then up to the ceiling, and then she muttered, "Perhaps I'll let my brother deal with the cleanup."

3

"And just as you were supposed to be entertaining guests, *this* happens. I see my little sister remains as indefatigable as ever." The visitor indicated the awful scene in the dining room and flashed a smile that was equal parts amusement and sadism.

The one who was smiling was a young man with black hair. His almond-shaped eyes were both beautiful and seemed to shine with intelligence, as if he could peer into the dark heart of this world. He was only about twenty years old, but his bearing had not the slightest whiff of callow youth about it. In his slim build, he possessed all that was required to make others bow before him as a ruler.

The young man's name was Vincent Abelks—a member of the royal family of the Holy Volakian Empire, and half brother on his father's side to Prisca Benedict. He and about ten of his servants had come to call on Prisca at her mansion. They had been greeted by Prisca, who had killed all her own servants except Arakiya less than an hour before. Vincent's first reaction upon hearing the news was words of exasperation.

It was hardly the sort of thing anyone would ordinarily say to a little sister whose life had been in danger just moments before, but Prisca simply replied, "Indefatigable, indeed. When there are too many flies flitting around, you brush them away, crush them, or burn them. I only did what anyone would do. No one can nor should criticize me for it. And besides..."

"And besides, what makes me so conceited as to think I have the right—is that it?"

"*And besides*, my elder brother is no exception." Prisca appeared unruffled that Vincent had guessed what she was going to say. Vincent, meanwhile, winked at his little sister as he recrossed his long legs and looked at the girl beside her.

She was expressionless, emotionless, and—if put quite bluntly—not very well disciplined, considering the way she stood there like a stick. Given how particular Prisca was about her accessories, this one seemed oddly ill-maintained. Nonetheless, Vincent placed great stock in his little sister's judgment; she did nothing without reason. The green fire that had consumed the assassins proved that the girl beside her had some worth.

"Very well. I don't intend to pry, but have you any idea where the killers originated from this time?"

"None. Sloppy as their methods were, someone took great care to ensure that the source of this spark would not be found. As much as I hate to admit it, I don't believe I can follow the trail any further. Why, Brother—do *you* have any ideas?"

As his question turned back on him, Vincent offered a cruel smile in response. "Sadly, I can only say that there's any number of reasons why either of us might be targeted by assassins."

Prisca wasn't disappointed by his answer; she hadn't held out much hope in the first place. She simply replied, "Of course."

They were in the parlor of Prisca's mansion, one room that hadn't sustained any damage. Prisca had chosen this place to receive her brother and his entourage, leaving the dining room in its disheveled state. Vincent hadn't so much as flinched upon learning that a substantial number of people had just died in his sister's home; he, like Prisca, was more than used to this sort of thing. They had each been the target of such attempts on their lives since their youngest days. Among her many stepsiblings, Prisca judged that only Vincent could be as bold as she when it came to these happenings. That said, Vincent wasn't particularly interested to know that a sister seven years younger than him thought highly of him. In any case...

"As for the mansion, let me handle things. If I lost a little sister who'd survived so much for some silly, asinine reason, it would be...a lonely thing."

"Lonely! Very admirable, I'm sure. But I admit, I'm willing to be grateful to receive the largesse of a beloved older brother's fondness."

"You know how some little girls are lovable? You're not."

"And here I felt *beloved* was the greatest expression of affection that I could muster." Prisca held up a cup of black tea that she'd steeped herself—her one gesture in the direction of genuine hospitality—and lied as easily as she breathed.

Vincent sneered a bit, knowing perfectly well that the claim of love went no further than Prisca's lips; he took the proffered cup of tea, sipped, and let out a breath.

Brother and sister were here doing what they always did: baiting each other and probing at the same time. Despite what seemed on the surface like a rather prickly exchange, Prisca and Vincent were actually quite fond of each other. Indeed, the very fact that Vincent took a sip of the tea without hesitation was, in its own way, proof of that.

The quiet moment was interrupted by a shouting voice: "Excellency! Your Excellency! I've completed a quick patrol of the area." The parlor door burst open to reveal a distinctly diminutive but unmistakably self-possessed young man. Slim of build and about the same age as Prisca and Arakiya, his blue hair was tied behind his head. His features were notably androgynous; indeed, he was so pretty that he could almost be mistaken for a young woman, but his behavior and body language was distinctly boyish, making it difficult for anyone to confuse him for a girl.

The boy bounded toward them, finally resting against the backrest of the sofa where Vincent had taken a seat. Then he leaned over Vincent's shoulder and said, "Goodness gracious, Excellency, you do know how to run people into the ground. And for a job that's so boring. It's a boring job! It's not that I mind being worked like a dog, but don't you think I could be better used doing other things?"

"If so, jabbering is not one of them. An animal does not lecture his master. You don't merely work like a dog; you *are* my dog, and I think you'd best remember it."

"But every dog is supposed to have his day, right, Excellency? Likewise, everyone has a place to best display their performance—a stage! I must stand upon a stage that suits me, a place packed full of what makes me *me*! Life is too short."

Vincent sighed at the young man, who seemed to have a comeback for every remark.

As for the young man, he pursed his lips, but when he noticed Prisca right in front of him, he exclaimed, "Oh! Well, look at this lovely young lady. What beautiful eyes you have. Seeing myself reflected in those rubies, I can't help thinking I look rather manly—wouldn't you say?"

"Keeping your jester at your side is your prerogative, Brother, but I can't abide his yammering. It's not to my taste." Prisca leaned her arm on an armrest and rested her chin on her hand.

"Jester? Is there one here...?" Her comments seemed to be lost on the young man, who immediately began scanning the room. "Jester, jester, jester—I don't see any. Wait—perhaps you meant to say *puppy*? There's certainly one of those dozing right by your side."

"Puppy? Me?" Arakiya tilted her head and pointed at herself, apparently feeling ambushed by the change of topic.

"Of course—do you see any other? Your floppy ears are adorable, little puppy. But don't you think you're a mite...exposed? Even for one who likes to draw some attention? You're going to attract the wrong type of person going around dressed like that."

"Exposed... Too exposed... Puppy..." Arakiya looked at Prisca for her cue on how to deal with the boy and his oh-so-quick banter.

Prisca, immediately understanding, tugged on her chin. "Brother."

"Hmm?"

"I suggest you find yourself a new clown."

No sooner had she spoken than Arakiya disappeared. In less than the space of an eyeblink, she was on the ceiling of the parlor. She kicked off, flinging herself down at the heads of Vincent and the young man.

"Arf, arf," she said. Her outstretched hand began to glow blue, a flame forming to consume the boy.

"My my, how short-tempered. But I must say I don't disapprove of your reaction. Indeed, I like it very much." The boy had his sword in his hand—when had he drawn it?—and with it, he met Arakiya's palm, completely deflecting the surprise attack.

He wielded a unique weapon called a katana, which was found in Kararagi, the capital city of the great nation to the west. He wielded it nimbly, expertly avoiding Arakiya's killing blow. What's more, he'd drawn a second sword that he now held up to Arakiya's neck.

"___"

So much as a twitch of the boy's blade, and Arakiya's head would be on the floor; the young man's sword skill was honed and clean. The fact that his spirit as a warrior hadn't been perceptible before, hidden like a blade in a sheath, was a clear indication of his ability.

"I found him on a battlefield," Vincent said. "Scavenging abandoned weapons."

"Just couldn't seem to find what I wanted. I'd hoped to make my name fighting, then buy a nice sword with the money I earned, but His Excellency took a shine to me." The young man took his blade away from Arakiya's neck with a deft move and sheathed both his swords in a pair of scabbards at his hip. "Oh, feel free to come at me again. Shall we see if I can dodge you without physically stopping the attack this time? It might make me look even more amazing than I already do, and— Eeeyowowow!"

"Enough. Don't let it go to your head. I don't intend to make an enemy of Prisca. Not yet." Vincent pulled forcefully on the young man's ear before he had a chance to get even more carried away. Then he dragged the young man forward by his ear, saying, "Introduce yourself. It couldn't hurt if she remembers you."

"Most pleased to make your acquaintance, ma'am. My name is Cecils Segmund, confidant of Master Vincent Abelks here, destined to one day make my name known as the strongest in the empire—as the shining star of this very world!"

"——" At this exceedingly assured self-introduction, Prisca's eyes widened slightly for the first time. Then she parted her pink lips, and said, "Ha! Listen, you smug braggart. The worst thing about you is that there isn't one solitary lie in all you've said!"

"Well, I don't suppose there's any special reason for me to lie. Ahem, Mistress…Prisca, was it? Your puppy is no slouch, either. Even if she *isn't* a match for me."

"This man… I hate him," said Arakiya, drawn in by the guffawing Cecils. She puffed out her cheeks indignantly, but Prisca beckoned her over; Arakiya came and rested against her knees as Prisca patted her head.

Still stroking Arakiya's head, Prisca said, "So, Brother, you won't 'yet' make an enemy of me?"

"Ah, my sharp-eared sister. Yes, that's exactly what I said."

"I know that you, like me, use your words precisely. It's obvious enough why you would deliberately say something like that. You're referring to…"

"You always were a quick one, Sister." Vincent let his face relax into a smile that could almost have passed for pleasant.

Arakiya and Cecils, neither quite sure what the siblings were talking about, could only watch in befuddlement. Unlike the retiring Arakiya, however, Cecils showed no hesitation in asking, "Referring to what? The both of you seem to know what that means—does it have something to do with today's visit?"

In answer to Cecils's question, Vincent stood. "So you've figured it out...or I suppose, in your case, merely guessed. Yes, of course it bears upon this visit. You know we do not have the liberty to simply drop in on each other for a friendly chat." Taller than the younger women in the room, Vincent gazed down at his little sister. Her crimson eyes met his black ones.

"It will begin?" she asked.

"Yes, it shall. The Rite of Imperial Selection. Prisca, you must make preparations to go to the capital city." Vincent stopped for a moment, but then resumed speaking. He said, "Our father... The emperor, honor be upon his name, is going to die."

4

The Holy Volakian Empire was a vast state that dominated the southern half of most maps. Its territory was greater than that of any other country in the world, far larger than the three other great nations. Blessed with a temperate climate and rich land, the Volakian Empire might also be said to be the most livable of those nations. Speaking purely in terms of its natural environment anyway.

For the people who lived and thrived in this fertile place naturally wanted to grow stronger and stronger. It became a tradition in the empire that the powerful were venerated and the weak suffered. Through long ages of history, this value system had not changed—indeed, the weight of ages had turned it into an immutable law that bound the nation hand and foot.

And the foremost representatives of the nation's way of life, those who most fully embodied its ethos of strength, were the Volakian emperor and the royal family.

"I must admit, it's quite an impressive sight to see all us siblings gathered in one place," remarked Prisca as she looked around, checking who was present.

"True," replied Vincent.

Half brothers and half sisters sat side by side, tipping back glasses of alcohol. Prisca and Vincent between them could hardly have counted the number of their siblings on their fingers. Prisca's brothers and sisters numbered no fewer than sixty-six—although, if only counting those who were still alive, the number immediately dropped to thirty-one.

"——"

She had eighteen brothers and thirteen sisters, and all of them (all thirty-two, including Prisca) were the blood children of Dreizen Volakia.

The Volakian Empire was a melting pot of many peoples, and the emperor chose the strongest from each part of the empire, without regard to what group they belonged to, and took them as his brides, producing many offspring. Dreizen had only sixty-seven possible heirs—hence why he was frequently derided as a seedless boy-emperor. Such mockery was only natural when his forebears regularly sired a hundred or two hundred children as a matter of course.

"Not that it makes things any easier for those of us he *did* father," remarked Prisca, who was one of them. "With more than sixty brothers and sisters, it's hard to remember which name goes with which face. If only a sage king always gave birth to sages."

The situation was so bad that there were some siblings Prisca had never even met, people with whom she shared no bond other than a nominal connection of blood. Why should she ever love such people? And perhaps more to the point, why should she ever hold back against them?

Vincent's talk of mutual advantage—now, that was a bond that couldn't be denied.

"Ohhh, look who it is. Prisca, and not looking very impressed."

"——" Prisca said nothing.

"My word! No greeting when it's been so long? You're going to make your dear older sister cry."

The young woman who identified herself as Prisca's older sibling spoke in a voice that practically dripped with honey; Prisca regarded her coldly. They shared the same orange hair, but this young woman had drooping, come-hither eyes. She was four or five years older than Prisca, and her substantially more feminine figure showed it. She was indeed one of Prisca's sisters, and her name was...

"Begone, Lamia. Listening to that drawl of yours makes me sick to my stomach. I find the sound of your voice far more dangerous than a poisoned dagger," Prisca said.

"Cold, cruel, *and* sharp-tongued. What our dear Vincent sees in you, I'll never know. Care to enlighten me, Brother?"

"I like the saucy ones."

Prisca's words went beyond cold—they were barbed, practically deadly—but Lamia showed no sign of backing down. In fact, she smiled graciously, though making no effort to hide the venom in her voice. She had established herself as a presence in Prisca's life since long before. It might have been sweet had she been inspired by a desire to get her little sister to notice her, but Lamia was acting out of pure and simple hostility.

As if to underline the point, she said, "Oh, yes," and smiled very carefully. "I hear you were attacked by your servants—and in your manor to boot? How positively awful. I pity to think that you can't relax in your own home."

"So the bitch feels compelled to howl."

Under other circumstances, Lamia would never have let such information slip—it was a sign of her confidence that the attack would never be traced back to her. Prisca glared, knowing just how sly Lamia could be.

Lamia looked downright pleased with Prisca's reaction. "I love the face you're making right now, Prisca. The face of a sorry little child who doesn't know anything." She reached out and yanked Prisca's lips upward into a false smile. Then as if she had instantaneously lost all interest in her little sister, she sidled up to Vincent instead. "I can't help wondering, why call us all to this annex today? Why not the Crystal Palace? Don't you think it's rather odd—and with all the flitting rumors of Father's failing health?"

"There's a significance to it, I have no doubt. The Crystal Palace is the symbol of the capital city—he cannot afford for it to be destroyed. Instead, he chose this annex, a separate building that he does not care about."

"——Are you suggesting...?" A smile threatened to cross Lamia's face as she made to ask Vincent what he really thought. But before she could get the question out, it started.

"____"

The door opened with a hush, and every gaze in the great hall turned toward it. Slowly, someone came through the door—a white-haired man on the verge of old age. His arms and his neck were thin, and his skin was pale like that of a sick man. His crimson eyes, though, still glowed; it was not life but conquest that animated this body.

"It's the emperor...Dreizen Volakia," Prisca murmured when he appeared.

Yes—this was he, present ruler of the Holy Volakian Empire, father of the thirty-two children gathered in this hall, Dreizen Volakia.

"——" The assembled children knelt at Dreizen's approach, showing their respect. The chatter that filled the hall moments ago had disappeared completely, and in the silent room, Dreizen's slow footsteps echoed loudly. At last, he reached the throne-like chair at the far end of the vast space. He let out a long sigh and cast his eyes over the hall.

"I wish I could say it's good to see you've all come."

"____"

Nobody spoke.

"But I notice a few who have chosen not to kneel to me."

Those who had knelt looked up in surprise, discovering a number who were still standing—Prisca not least among them. Vincent and Lamia, too, stood. Not quite ten siblings in all...

"Might I ask what you think you're doing?" one of their older brothers demanded. "Our father—His Excellency the Emperor—is present. You insolent—!"

"Insolent? Don't make me laugh. If you and I are both true members of the royal family of Volakia, it should be self-evident which of us is right. And it isn't the brainless idiot who only knows how to stand on ceremony," Prisca replied, merciless.

"Wha—?!" the older brother exclaimed. When there were more than sixty siblings, the difference between the oldest and the youngest could be like that between parent and child themselves. This man was red in the face and quaking at the tongue-lashing he had just gotten from Prisca, who was twenty years his junior. "Prisca, you foulmouthed... How dare you speak to your older brother that way!"

"Older brother? Oh, yes, of course. I'm sorry—there's so many of you, and I've been blessed with so few siblings whose names and faces are worth remembering. I'd completely forgotten that you were one of my brothers."

"——!" Unable to bear the humiliation, the older brother in question jumped to his feet, his face flushing furiously. He looked ready to lunge at his much younger sister right then and there.

But they were interrupted by Dreizen, who simply said, "Stop."

"Hngh... But, Father..."

"Disrespect to me, you say? If she's doing it for show, it doesn't even rise to the level of stupidity. But I do not reprove her for failing to kneel before me. In fact, I prefer this."

With these words, the emperor halted a fight between his children—but not in favor of the elder brother. Rather, he permitted Prisca's behavior. As proof, Dreizen brought his bony hands together, looked at Prisca, and said, "Prisca. Why is it that you do not kneel to me?"

"Surely, you don't need me to spell it out. It's because I saw nothing worth kneeling to. You've grown old, Father. You hardly look like someone who belongs at the apogee of an empire whose first teaching to its subjects is: *Be strong.*"

"Bwa-ha!" Thus castigated by a girl of scarcely more than ten years, the emperor didn't become enraged, but rather, he laughed aloud. With his crimson eyes, he briefly scanned the others who had joined Prisca in not kneeling.

"——" None of them denied the truth of what Prisca had said. To a greater or lesser extent, all of them agreed with her. In their eyes, the current emperor was not worth kneeling to.

"And *that* is what makes you members of the Volakian Royal Family. That is what makes you my children!"

"Father...!"

"Rommel, a moment ago, you spoke of insolence. Insolence! What value is there in such trappings?" Dreizen paused, then said, "Rommel... Would you like to try yourself?"

"Try myself...?" The man called Rommel knit his brow at the emperor's words. Thereupon, the emperor reached out his hand into the air and gave a great, powerful wave of his arm. The space directly in front of Rommel warped and twisted, the hilt of a sword abruptly appearing from the rift.

"——" Rommel stared at it, wide-eyed. The others in the room inhaled sharply. The hilt that had appeared was just that beautiful. The scabbard and sword it held were decorated with such loveliness that some exclaimed without meaning to.

"The Bright Sword, Volakia," said Dreizen.

"The blade handed down from generation to generation through the Volakian Royal Family...," Rommel mumbled, looking as if he was flushed with heat. He took his father at his word; his face as stiff with excitement as it was with fear, Rommel swallowed and stepped forward. "S-such a tremendous responsibility is also a great honor, Your Majesty..."

Rommel was practically shaking with joy, but Dreizen didn't answer him. With every eye in the room watching him expectantly, Rommel steeled himself, then reached out for the scabbard that floated in midair.

The Bright Sword, which bore the name of its empire, had existed since the founding of the nation. As its name suggested, only the Volakian emperors were permitted to wield it—even Prisca had never seen it with her own eyes before.

Nor had she seen firsthand what it meant that *only* the emperor could wield the blade.

"Huh?" Rommel said stupidly as he grasped the hilt of the sword and attempted to draw it out. And well he might, for the moment he did so, the hand that touched the sword burst into flame, which quickly became a conflagration that consumed him in the space of an instant.

"——!" Rommel couldn't even cry out as the flames engulfed him. He could not even speak, for his throat and lungs were the first things to be burned away. He perished without so much as a death rattle.

In Rommel's place, those who had bowed to the emperor began to shout, desperate voices rising. But scant good it did. Rommel fell upon the carpet, seared, dead before he even had a chance to writhe in agony. He was so badly blackened, it was impossible to tell whether his corpse had fallen on its back or its front.

It had only taken a matter of seconds for Rommel, a member of the royal family, to be burned to death.

Several siblings looked like they might be sick as the stomach-turning stench of roasted human flesh began to rise, but Lamia, her brow furrowed, summed it up succinctly: "Ugh. He stinks." As for Prisca, who had recently witnessed her entire entourage burned to ashes, the scene was surprising but not repulsive.

Even then, her surprise wasn't directed toward Rommel's death, but rather at its source: the Bright Sword.

"Only the emperor is permitted to touch it. That much is clear." Among the startled siblings, maybe ten of them had quietly accepted the truth of Rommel's death. Naturally, Vincent—who offered this murmured assessment—was one of them, as was Prisca, who had come to the same conclusion.

"F-Father! What is the meaning of—?"

"Silence," Dreizen said, cutting off the expression of astonishment at Rommel's death. The aged emperor looked around the great hall, turning a penetrating gaze on each of his children. As his red eyes pinned each of them in turn with their cruel light, Prisca noticed something.

"Wh-what's going on?" asked one of the others in a timorous voice, having noticed the same thing.

Namely, the space in front of each of them was warping and twisting, and a red sword hilt had emerged before them. It happened in front of Prisca, and it happened in front of Vincent and Lamia as well. Was this some sort of joke? From thin air had appeared thirty-one Bright Swords, exactly as many as the number of siblings in the room (now that Rommel was dead).

"We will now begin the Rite of Imperial Selection," Dreizen announced. He made no acknowledgment of the staggering scene and spoke with only his own unamplified voice. Suddenly, he was no longer the withered tree, the elderly ruler, the guttering flame not worth kneeling to. His eyes open wide now, Dreizen looked like a raging fire.

"The Bright Sword chooses its own master. Being chosen by the sword is the first requirement for any who hope to assume the imperial throne."

"____"

No one made a sound.

"Your destiny stands before you in the form of the sword. Now! Draw it forth. It is the fate from which there is no escape."

As he spoke, the emperor—or rather, the former emperor—Dreizen Volakia stood, and the hilt of a sword appeared above him as well. He reached up and grasped it firmly—and in that instant, his body was wreathed in flames.

"____"

It was the sign that the sword itself was finished with the previous emperor and now sought a new owner. With the end of Dreizen Volakia, the throne now sat open. This, the destruction of the old ruler, was the sign that the contest had begun. The Rite of Imperial Selection, by which the emperors of Volakia had been chosen for generations.

While everyone else stood transfixed by the sight of their father's incineration, Vincent said, "Prisca." He had predicted the demise of the former emperor—but had he known this was what would happen?

It didn't matter. Prisca turned at his call, his black eyes meeting her crimson ones. An understanding was established between brother and sister.

And then without hesitation, Prisca reached out for the sword in front of her...

"This world bends itself to suit me."

The sword allowed itself to be drawn into her hand.

The Rite of Imperial Selection, which would determine the next ruler of the Volakian Empire, had begun.

The relentless, remorseless shedding of blood among the imperial siblings had started.

5

The Volakian emperor, Dreizen Volakia, was dead.

That fact, and the beginning of the Rite of Imperial Selection, filtered into the empire surprisingly quietly.

It was hard to argue that in his twilight years, Dreizen had been a very fitting ruler for the Volakian Empire, but at least, his final moments—consumed by a howling flame in front of all his children—had been suitably proud.

The emperor's death meant that there would be a span of time during which the throne sat empty, but the citizenry were used to these lacunae in leadership while the succession was determined, and neither the sovereign's demise nor the vacancy of the throne particularly upset them. After offering up a silent prayer in mourning for the deceased ruler, the interest of the empire's people turned toward who would be victorious in the Rite, the dispute for the succession. They went through the names of the emperor's various children, chatting and laughing as they discussed who would be the next sovereign.

Those participating in the Rite were the very ones who had witnessed the emperor's immolation and who had then passed the first hurdle to becoming the next emperor: grasping the Bright Sword to see if they were worthy.

Speaking of which—

"So eleven people survived drawing the Bright Sword. I'm not sure whether to consider that a great many or a great few, however." Prisca leaned on the armrest of her seat and sighed.

The Rite of Imperial Selection had begun, and the battle to determine the next emperor was already underway. Naturally, Prisca was among those who had drawn the sword and survived. Upon the annihilation of the emperor—which was to say, after the crisping of Prisca's foolish older brother Rommel—thirty of Prisca's siblings had remained. Not all of them had chosen to attempt to draw the Bright Sword, however, and ultimately, the number of people who could potentially claim the imperial throne had dropped to eleven. Meaning Prisca had ten enemies, ten rivals for the imperial seat.

"Enemies—it's almost funny, suddenly finding myself in a death match with brothers and sisters whose existence I was hardly aware of until yesterday." Prisca perched her shapely chin on one finger, her posture rather extreme.

Eleven candidates for the throne. All the others had either refused to draw the sword, fearing their own fiery destruction, or were fools who had met that same blazing fate when they overestimated themselves and mindlessly tried their hand at something they were not qualified for. Neither cowards nor the dead warranted Prisca's concern.

Thus, her only real enemies were the other ten contenders for the succession—and of course, Vincent Abelks was among their number. All the siblings could at least agree that at present, he was both the greatest threat and the biggest obstacle to the succession of any of the others.

And so...

"An alliance?"

"Good heavens, does it sound so strange to you? I should think that in a situation like this, joining forces would be the first thing you would think of. Well... Maybe not *you*, Prisca. You've never exactly been the cooperative type." Lamia Godwin, her lips rouged scarlet, smiled, but it only made her look like a venomous flower.

Prisca's half sister was another of the children who had survived the drawing of the Bright Sword—and she was also among those Prisca despised most in the world. Lamia must have felt a similar hatred for Prisca. They had spent every day until this moment hating each other so intensely that it had seemed one might well kill the other long before the Rite gave them an excuse. Hence, Prisca could only smirk when Lamia visited her mansion—and came bearing a suggestion like this—immediately upon the beginning of the succession dispute.

While Prisca considered the proposal, Lamia, sitting on the sofa, let her eyes wander around the empty parlor. "This house does feel a little lonely, doesn't it? Not nearly enough servants... I know how much you like showing off. It's a little pathetic somehow to think you live your private life in such meager circumstances."

"I'm afraid you've caught me just after I uprooted each and every useless servant I had. Some she-devil planted a whole troop of fools in my home, and I'm afraid good replacements have proven hard to find."

"A she-devil? Oh my. That must have been terrible for you." Lamia smiled innocently and checked her fingernails as she offered a banal bit of sympathy. Given how Lamia had behaved on the day when they saw the emperor die, it was abundantly clear that she had been somehow involved with the treacherous help—but Prisca didn't pursue the matter at this moment. She had no proof, whereas she was sure Lamia was more than prepared to talk her way out of the matter. Prisca's victory this day would have to consist of making sure those preparations went to waste. Anyway, she had more important matters at hand.

"___"

"—? Yes, Prisca? Whatever's the matter?"

"Nothing. I simply never imagined that, servants or no, I would ever be entertaining *you* in my house."

"Goodness, I'd almost think you don't like me. Well, I *know* you don't like me. Neither of us likes the other."

The obligations of hospitality held no meaning. After all, Lamia didn't so much as take a sip of the tea Prisca had offered her. This went double when the person you were entertaining was a blood relation—such was the way of the Volakian Royal Family. To do otherwise was to evince a great deal of trust in one's host—or else to demonstrate that one had absolutely no enmity toward that person. Otherwise, it would be unimaginable.

Ultimately, neither of these conditions could be hoped for between Prisca and Lamia. But it was precisely because of their relationship, in which only blood could wash away blood, that Lamia's suggestion was worth considering.

"What do you say? Will you think about your *dear* older sister's idea?"

"Fair enough. At the very least, I offer you this much praise: It is an unexpected move. I never thought the first person to approach me for an alliance would be you. I was sure—"

"That I would immediately take advantage of the excuse I finally had to kill you? Ooh, you do know how to push a person's buttons, Prisca. *Surely*, you don't think I would do something so reckless, do you?"

Lamia perched her chin on her hands in imitation of Prisca and smiled cruelly. Mimicking the other person's behavior was one way of establishing a rapport in conversation. Lamia understood that not through logic but by instinct.

It wouldn't work on Prisca, naturally, but Lamia didn't shift positions as she went on to say, "Of course, I'd be lying if I said it hadn't occurred to me to crush you first. But even I know how to use my head, you know. My lovely, perfectly coiffed head."

"___"

Prisca didn't respond.

"Say I impulsively destroyed you—what then? What happens after that? Only an idiot acts without thinking about the consequences. Like our brothers and sisters who didn't take up the challenge of the Bright Sword. Although, of course, the ones who *did*, and failed, were even stupider."

To mock the dead, and dead relatives at that—Prisca winced. It wasn't due to anger at Lamia's remark. She was just irritated that, for once, she completely agreed with her sister.

Indeed, thus far, Prisca was in total agreement with Lamia. She shared her disdain for their more cowardly siblings, as well as those who had been incinerated when they tried to take up the sword. And she, too, had briefly considered immediately making her first move of the Rite against her most hated sister.

Most hated, of course, not so much because the two didn't get along, but because Prisca had judged Lamia to be one of her most dangerous enemies. She had no doubt that Lamia was among those whom she would want to eliminate most swiftly.

There was, however, another, even more deadly foe. Namely...

"Our beloved brother, Vincent Abelks," Lamia said.

"You never cease to be the most unpleasant woman..."

"I think I'll take that as a compliment." Lamia smiled triumphantly, having all but read Prisca's mind. Prisca felt the bile rise in her throat when she saw the barely concealed viciousness that rested deep in Lamia's eyes. At least it appeared that she was not the only one struggling to endure the humiliation of talking to the sister she hated most without letting it turn into an outright duel to the death.

"The only way to stand a chance against our brother Vincent is to work together. And as long as I have to work with someone, I see no point in choosing chaff and trash. If you're going to take poison, who would pick anything but the strongest poison? And besides, I somehow suspect you agree with my assessment."

"And that's why you come to me with talk of alliances? Exactly the sort of underhanded scheme you would come up with."

"Underhanded? I'm hurt. I wish you would say *sly*."

"*Sly*—indeed. The perfect word for a vixen like you. I don't object."

Lamia laughed, emitting a sound like a tinkling bell; it was the laughter of someone who was sure that even here, her back was not against the wall. Sure, because her Pruning Force would ensure that Prisca could do no violence to her. It was her private army, recognized as the strongest among all the retinues in Volakia.

It wasn't as if the Pruning Force was surrounding Prisca's mansion at that moment, of course—but its very existence posed a threat to her. She and Lamia might be speaking in solitude, just the two of them, and this might be Prisca's home—but the sisters were certainly not on equal footing. Lamia might look defenseless, but she was anything but, and she knew it.

"——"

What did Prisca have to contest Lamia's army? Only the modest forces of the Benedict household—not something she could count on—and Arakiya.

Any alliance between them would not be one of equals. For Lamia, there were virtually no advantages to joining forces with Prisca—other, perhaps, than the perverse satisfaction of forcing Prisca to bend the knee.

"Prisca, I think highly of you. I haven't the *slightest* interest in House Benedict. Only you personally."

"——" Prisca said nothing.

"So I decided to make you my friend before you became my enemy. Sure, we might have to kill each other before this is over, but that's all the more reason to play nice now..."

"You're suggesting you'll protect me so that I won't snap like a delicate branch? Awfully conceited of you, I'd say."

"I'm sorry to hear it bothers you so much. But do you even have the option of saying no?" As she spoke, Lamia spread her arms, making her chest—far more generous than one would have expected for her sixteen years—bounce. Then she looked Prisca straight in the eye and said, "I've been preparing for a long time. Getting ready for this very day. Judging by the age of our now-dearly-departed emperor, I knew it would have to come soon. A few years sooner than I expected, perhaps, but within tolerances. I don't expect any trouble from anyone else, unprepared and thoughtless as they are. Except…"

"Except what?"

"Except *who*. You and Vincent are different. Everyone knows Vincent is a threat. But you, Prisca—you're a threat, even if you don't look like one."

"——"

"I know you're dangerous. The question is, how dangerous? In what way? If you don't know an animal is venomous until the moment you reach out and it bites you, it's too late. And so…"

"So you mean to keep me close and observe me?"

"Surely, one sister is allowed to bounce another on her knee?" Lamia uncrossed and recrossed her legs, which were hidden by her skirt, before stroking her own thigh invitingly. She gave a thin smile, the look of a woman who understood that her beauty was one more weapon she could use to bewilder those around her. Many a man would not hesitate to do the unthinkable for a chance to lay a hand on that body. And Lamia Godwin had the allure and the wiles to make them think they could.

Her tricks didn't work on Prisca, a sibling who hated her, but there was enough value in Lamia's suggestion that Prisca couldn't turn her down out of hand. So she didn't.

Lamia looked at her and nodded in satisfaction. "I never thought I'd have a chance to say this to you—but you don't need to decide right away. Take as long as you need to reach a *favorable* answer and then tell me." Smirking in the knowledge that Prisca couldn't reject her proposal immediately, Lamia stood up slowly. Then almost languorously, she turned her back on Prisca, as if inviting her to cut her down then and there— No, it was more like she was emphasizing the fact that Prisca wouldn't, couldn't rise to the bait. "Ah yes, I'll be back for my answer… I'm sure you know when."

"When you're done *pruning*, no doubt."

"Heh-heh. That's right!" Lamia turned only her head to glance back at Prisca, and then her beautiful, malevolent visage exited the parlor, letting the door close noisily.

"Damned vixen," Prisca muttered as she watched Lamia leave, not bothering to escort her even out of the room. Lamia knew Prisca's mansion well enough anyway; she didn't need a guide. And with the Pruning Force waiting for her outside, there was nothing in the empire that could have stopped her.

With Lamia gone, Prisca was alone in the room—until a new voice spoke. "Princess. Is this all right?" The voice belonged to a silver-haired girl who slipped out from Prisca's shadow—Arakiya. As Prisca's attendant and the sole person she could count on in battle, Arakiya alone had been present at the meeting, watching from the shadows. It had been overkill; there had never been any real chance that Lamia would attack Prisca under those circumstances.

In fact, Lamia had probably known she was there.

"There's no *all right* about it whatsoever. I have nothing to gain by striking now. Much as it nettles me to say it."

"You could have had her head."

"Yes, but think: What would we have lost in exchange? I'm sure you *would* have taken off her head, had I not insisted that you refrain from doing so."

"—I hate her. She makes fun of you, Lady Prisca." Arakiya stubbornly held on, like a child; Prisca put her hand on her chin, pleased with the way Arakiya's eyes glinted with hostility. The way she wore her heart on her sleeve and the devotion she showed Prisca made her seem like a pet. That adorable side of hers was one of the reasons Prisca kept her around. Unfortunately, the trade-off seemed to be that she wasn't always the quickest thinker…

"And comparing myself and our older brother—what a bit of cruelty. In any case, I know you will obey the strictures I've given you. So long as you do, then you should grow strong and healthy."

"——? Yes. I will. I understand."

She didn't sound like she really understood, but Prisca knew she would try her hardest. That was enough.

"As for that scheming woman, let her think I'm dancing to her tune for a while. Don't do anything rash, Arakiya."

"——" Arakiya didn't say anything.

"Arakiya, answer me." Uneasy that there was no response, Prisca knit her brow.

Finally, Arakiya touched the lock of red hair at her forehead and said, "I wasn't helpful. Are you mad?"

"What do you mean?"

"I lost. To Master Vincent's blue-hair."

"Oh, that." Prisca remembered: The source of Arakiya's insecurity was her defeat by the young blue-haired swordsman Vincent had brought along to the mansion the other day. Arakiya rarely fixated on anything other than Prisca, an attitude she justified with her special qualities as a spirit eater and her fighting prowess. To have that self-confidence shaken by a boy her own age must have been quite unsettling for her. To her, it must have seemed that she had failed Prisca. However…

"Fool."

"Ow!"

…Prisca flicked Arakiya on her drooping forehead, causing tears to brim in her eyes. Prisca found the sight rather endearing, but she repeated "Fool" once again. "I am neither stupid nor mad enough to hold on to tools that are of no use to me. Remember that, Arakiya: It is not your place to denigrate my tools."

"Even…myself?"

"Do you believe that you are your own?"

"——"

That drew a wide-eyed look from Arakiya, who quickly shook her head. Her ears flopped with the motion, almost as if she was wagging her tail. And indeed, the tail on her behind was wagging energetically, so perhaps she was feeling better.

"Then, Lady Prisca, what is…*pruning*?"

"Pruning means to allow plants or trees to grow by cutting away unnecessary leaves and branches. In a word, it's a chore that will have to be done to seize control of the Rite of Imperial Selection. I have no intention of involving myself in such trifles, but..."

"Yes, Lady? What is it?"

"I think it's the first thing Lamia will do. That's just how vulgar she is."

6

The Rite of Imperial Selection was how the new emperor of Volakia was chosen; it was an inviolable ritual, and it consisted of precisely one thing: blood relatives brutally slaughtering one another.

The Volakian emperor picked his wives from among the strongest of his subjects, and they gave birth to many, many children, as had been made amply evident. And one among them would become the next sovereign. The Rite of Imperial Selection, beginning with the death of the prior emperor, would continue until only one of those with a claim to the throne remained—meaning whoever became ruler, they would by definition have killed their older brothers, their younger brothers, their older sisters and younger sisters. They would kill them, or the throne would never be theirs.

O citizens of the empire, be strong.

Such was the most basic teaching inculcated among all those who called themselves citizens of Volakia, and it was their fundamental way of life. This also served as the ironclad rule that the Volakian Royal Family, and the emperor themselves, had to embody. And it was at the heart of why the Rite of Imperial Selection could not be conducted without copious bloodshed.

"However, to mindlessly continue a tradition simply because it's existed for centuries lacks a certain refinement. Perspectives change with the ages, and we must respond appropriately to all things." Bartroi Fitz swirled the wine in his glass as he spoke.

At twenty-seven, Bartroi was right in the middle of the former emperor's children; the oldest of his more than sixty siblings was forty, while the youngest was just ten years old. But just because they were related didn't mean they got along. Every child born to the Volakian Royal Family had the Rite in the back of their minds. True camaraderie among these siblings was rare. Getting too close to any of them ran the risk of developing attachments—and that could hamper their ability to coldly go about the business of murdering them when the time came. Thus, the children tended to keep their distance or otherwise hate one another openly.

"But even that is groupthink. Don't you agree, Lamia?" Bartroi turned toward his visitor—his younger sister Lamia, with her beautiful red eyes.

"Oh, yes," she said with a thin smile. "Bartroi, my dear brother, I do so admire how you think. Whenever did you start having these ideas?"

"During the time I've had to think—naturally, there's been enough of it. This accursed ritual has been around for ages. And when you grab a rusted chain with your bare hand, you risk cutting yourself."

In other words, careful preparation was crucial.

Bartroi clenched his fist demonstratively; Lamia nodded, acting deeply impressed. Bartroi's hand, however, had not grasped the Bright Sword, as hers had, on the day Dreizen had died. Bartroi had declined to participate in the Rite of Imperial Selection.

Nine others had joined in him in electing not to reach for the sword—everyone else accepted the test, and ten of them had burned to death, leaving only eleven to contest the succession. Including Rommel, who had died before any of them, eleven siblings had lost their lives that day. And quite frankly, Bartroi wished to keep further sacrifices to a minimum.

"That, Lamia, is why I made my agreement with you."

"That when I ascend the throne, you and the others who chose not to participate in the Rite will be under my protection. I know."

"Yes, exactly." Bartroi nodded. "And that's why I convinced the other nine to come around."

Ten of the siblings, including Bartroi—the dropouts—had surrendered their right to participate in the Rite of Imperial Selection before it had even begun. Ultimately, those Bartroi hadn't persuaded had challenged the sword and lost their lives to the flames. That said, his work was not in vain. Ten people who would otherwise have burned had been saved from being annihilated by the sword.

Once again, as a rule, the siblings of the Volakian Royal Family were not close to one another. Bartroi, however, endeavored to be an exception. He engaged proactively with his brothers and sisters, creating relationships that made them feel safe coming to him with their problems or asking for advice.

It was all in anticipation of the Rite of Imperial Selection.

"But if I may ask, why choose me? I'm just a little girl among all our siblings, if I may say so myself."

"That should be obvious. Because you were the one who inspired these thoughts in me, Lamia."

"I was?"

"Indeed. I believed you of all people would understand me. You asked when you were little—you wondered if there wasn't some way that this could end without siblings having to harm one another."

At the time, Bartroi, still young, had been seeking something that might possibly be done—and these words, spoken by his little sister like a passing dream, had hit him like a revelation. He had contemplated them ever after, followed them to where he stood today.

"The Rite began as you predicted, but you don't seem to be getting any closer to victory. I and our other nine siblings will work with you. Then maybe…"

"Then maybe we can overcome our brother Vincent? Is that what you're thinking?"

"That's right." Bartroi nodded, although his throat went dry at the mention of Vincent's name.

Vincent Abelks was one of Bartroi's half brothers. But his greatness, his strength of personality was tremendous, and for better or worse, it didn't feel much like they were related. The young man stood at the top in every realm of knowledge and strategy. Fearsomely clear-eyed, Vincent had restored the fortunes of House Abelks, once fallen to among the least of the noble families of Volakia, raising himself to the rank of high count entirely through his own talent and skill.

By all rights, Vincent appeared closest to the imperial throne. Thus, it would have made sense for Bartroi to approach him with his offer of cooperation.

"Except that I highly doubt I can expect any familial sympathy from Vincent."

"And it's so much harder, isn't it? Negotiating with someone who can get what he wants without your help."

"You truly are insightful, Lamia."

"Hee-hee. Don't worry, I'm not angry. After all, this just means that when you couldn't go to Vincent, the next person you thought of was me. That's not such a bad feeling."

Bartroi smiled slightly at the way Lamia's pride and self-regard slipped through in her remark. And she was absolutely right, of course. After Vincent, Lamia seemed most likely to emerge victorious. That wasn't to say that the other ten candidates weren't all perfectly qualified, but in Bartroi's opinion, it was Lamia who had the best chance of besting Vincent.

Her, and another of my little sisters—but she's no more sympathetic than Vincent is.

"She may be young, but she has everything she needs to be ruler of Volakia..."

If the Rite had begun perhaps five years later, that young woman might very well have been a prime contender in the imperial succession. But it was simply not to be. And so Bartroi had approached Lamia with his proposition.

"All right, my dear brother, let's talk about what comes next."

"Mm, yes, pardon me. I was lost in thought. What comes next. Yes, that's important." Bartroi would have to communicate to the other nine refusers what they were going to do after this. At the moment, none of them had any idea whom he was working with. The plan he and Lamia were hatching could shatter the Rite of

Imperial Selection, the most important ritual in all Volakia—there was no telling where information might leak from. He couldn't be too careful.

The day was near at hand, though, when all his travails would be rewarded. *She will keep her promise*, he told himself.

"I know it was to save our siblings, but I do regret obliging you to challenge yourself with the Bright Sword. That day, if—"

"If I'd burned, too, it would have been quite the problem, wouldn't it?"

"There are no truer words! Ahem, not that this is any laughing matter." Bartroi shook his head, chastising himself for the sardonic smile that had crossed his face. Trying to relieve the persistent dryness in his throat, he refilled his empty cup with more wine. Maybe it was the sense of accomplishment at having fulfilled his great mission that made the drink seem to go to his head so quickly. Or maybe he just wanted to try to blind himself to the fact that even as they spoke, people to whom they were connected by blood were openly killing one another.

He drank some more, swallowing noisily.

"By the way, Bartroi. There's something I've been thinking about, just in passing."

"Oh? What's that?"

"You know how they say that humans can perform tremendous displays of strength when gripped by rage or desperation?"

"Rage…or desperation?" Bartroi looked at Lamia from his place on the sofa, not sure what had brought on this subject. His sister sat stone-still, except that she held up two fingers and nodded.

"Yes, exactly. These nine siblings that you've brought me, Bartroi… Well, they know the situation they're in. I'm sure they'll all cooperate with me out of desperation. But do you think some of them might be frightened as well?"

"Well, it's true that they're hardly a group of born fighters."

"And yet we must band together if we're going to achieve our objective. They need anger. Fury powerful enough to overcome their terror. Such as…"

"Such...such as what...?" Lamia's honeyed voice sounded oddly distant to Bartroi. His head felt so heavy, and the world around him seemed...insubstantial. His head bobbed forward. His throat was so *dry*. He needed another drink. That had to be it. He poured more wine, more and more, until the glass overflowed. Finally, it fell over, and the drink began to dye the carpet scarlet...

"Well, for example, what if the dear, sweet elder brother all of them were counting on lost his life to a cruel trap?"

He couldn't even hear Lamia's voice anymore.

So dry. His throat was so dry. He wanted more wine. Yes... The wine Lamia had given him as a gift.

"___"

The wine...

7

Lamia looked down at Bartroi, who had followed his glass in toppling to the wine-stained carpet. Her older brother had already stopped breathing; he didn't so much as twitch.

On a whim, she flexed her fingers and took her own glass, from which she had not drunk a drop, and poured the contents over Bartroi's head.

Her brother still didn't move.

"Gracious, I must say I'm surprised. To think, he hadn't taken a single measure to protect himself." Until that very last instant, Lamia hadn't abandoned the possibility that Bartroi was feigning death, but her caution turned out to be astoundingly misplaced. He had died for one very simple reason: He was not careful.

Lamia flung the empty glass on the ground and then smirked at her brother's corpse, her red eyes narrowing. "All these years you spent preparing...only to die a dog's death. You truly were a stooge, Brother."

Lamia had never understood Bartroi's thinking, what delusion he was laboring under. He spoke of some revelation he felt she had given him, but as far as Lamia was concerned, she'd only played the simpleminded younger sister, giving him a little push—a push in a direction that would be advantageous to her. And even she had never dreamed that it would result in no fewer than ten potential adversaries never even entering the competition.

"Although to be fair, all ten of them would probably have been burned alive had they dared to grasp the Bright Sword."

She just didn't know what Bartroi was thinking; he seemed to believe that he could invoke a blood relation as the one and only reason she should protect him and his cohort. The hubris of believing one could save others was an amusement permitted only to those who wielded power. The moment Bartroi had decided to cozy up to someone stronger than him, the very instant he had elected to use his wits in an attempt to cultivate their sympathy, he threw away his own best hope of making his wish come true.

"And that's why you're dead now, dear Brother," Lamia said.

O citizens of the empire, be strong. The unwritten rule of the Empire of Volakia, the custom of might, which held that the strong had the right to torment the weak. By this custom, the stronger would feed upon the weaker—even be they a member of the royal family. And the strong were free to capitalize on the deaths of the weak as they saw fit.

"Your Excellency, we've safely overpowered them," a man said in a rasp as Lamia continued to stare down at her dead brother. They were in Bartroi's mansion, where Lamia had been invited as a guest, but the man who appeared in the reception room didn't belong to the household staff; he was one of Lamia's agents. He was elderly, with a luxurious head full of white hair, and intelligent eyes tucked among the deep wrinkles of his face. He addressed Lamia as "Excellency," the term of highest honor in the Volakian empire: he was Lamia Godwin's master strategist...

"Beautiful work, Belstetz. I presume you didn't have any problems?"

"None at all. As Your Excellency indicated, Master Bartroi kept the bare minimum of personnel here at his mansion."

"Hmm. Interesting. Imagine, we were blood relatives, yet it never occurred to him to protect himself."

"——" The man she called Belstetz bowed respectfully and was silent. Useful people did not speak out of turn. Lamia hated the elderly, but that was because so many of them were so thoroughly incapable. As long as they knew how to handle themselves, she didn't mind their existence. Still, she felt the elderly were too eager to speak in general, and the best way to handle them was to shut them up.

"That, at least, is something I admire about my dearly departed father's dedication. He knew that expiring pathetically on his death-bed would cast a pall over all his achievements. And we wouldn't want that."

No matter how strong and virile in youth, age made fools of everyone. It was Lamia's opinion that the system of imperial succession, which replaced the ruler before that could happen, was supremely logical. She, too, hoped the curtain would come down on her life before she grew old and her intelligence and beauty withered.

"Although, I do plan to make it last as long as I can," she commented.

Belstetz paused, then said, "—Very well, Your Excellency. If you have no objections, shall I continue with the plan?"

"Yes, please do."

The strategist wasn't interested in entertaining Lamia's stray remarks, but in continuing his work. She didn't blame him for that nor reproach him—she only nodded and winked.

Bartroi was dead, and the moronic siblings he'd rallied to his cause had lost their standard-bearer. Already unqualified to take part in the Rite, bent as helplessly as branches in the wind, they had only one choice: to seek someone new to guide them. They would find Lamia.

"We're dealing with a cabal brought together by my brother Bartroi. I can only assume their heads are empty, every one. When they hear our brother is dead, it will be a simple matter to wrap them around my little finger."

He was just as foolish as the siblings who, misjudging their own ability, had attempted to grasp the Bright Sword and been destroyed;

that was Lamia's true opinion of Bartroi. However, in that his fool-ishness had ultimately resulted in at least some advantage to her, there was admittedly a measure of value in his life.

As she made to leave the room, Lamia stopped and turned back toward her brother's corpse, his face still buried in the floor. "Say, Bartroi... Dear Brother. I want you to know, I didn't hate you—not really."

There was no answer—of course there wasn't. But Lamia wasn't looking for one. She wasn't trying to apologize or somehow salve her conscience. She was simply offering a report.

"You were just the easiest to manipulate. The most susceptible to the innocent blathering of a sweet little girl."

She was letting him know that it had all been nothing more than an opening gambit, a strategic move made when she was still very young. It was her last gift to the dead man, and then she sinuously glided out of the room, leaving the rest to her strategist, who stood with his head bowed. By the time she emerged from the door of the mansion and started boarding the waiting dragon carriage, she'd already forgotten her brother's face.

Then she smiled sweetly. Her attention was already on her next objective. "Now, the pruning is done. I can't wait for what comes next, Prisca."

8

Looked at another way, the Rite of Imperial Selection was a domes-tic conflict within the empire—a civil war.

The battle for the throne was a contest of wits, ingenuity, and combat prowess among the members of the royal family, one that turned the entire country into a battlefield; any place within its bor-ders could become the stage for a decisive conflict at any moment. And, of course, civil wars were also times of heightened tension with neighboring countries. It was only natural that some diminishment of national military power was unavoidable given that domestic affairs were in disarray.

It was much like how, decades before, the Kingdom of Lugunica had had to be extremely vigilant against incursions—not least from Volakia—when a major domestic conflict had broken out within its borders. And although that was hardly the only reason, it was one explanation for why the Rite tended to come to a conclusion quickly. The imperial throne couldn't be allowed to sit empty for years on end. Perhaps that was the practical reason why the Rite generally lasted no more than a year.

The point being...

"I think this will be the outermost extremity of the Rite of Imperial Selection," Prisca murmured, tapping a red folding fan to her lips as she observed the completed cordon. She was encamped atop a small mountain, protected by the Benedict family's personal army. They were all dressed in red armor—Prisca's personal preference—but they were something less than elite troops, lacking in training and untried in battle. But morale, at least, they had in spades.

"I don't need them to be gifted, I just need them to do what I tell them. Arakiya, you're there?"

"Mm... Beside you," Arakiya said, appearing from among the Redmongers at Prisca's call. She startled the soldiers, who hadn't noticed her presence at all.

Prisca held up a hand to still the murmuring, then turned and looked at Arakiya. As ever, Arakiya was dressed in minimal clothing, her arms like twigs, but battle-ready. She looked so frail compared with the soldiers in their full armor—but there was a reason she was dressed the way she was. Vincent's boy swordsman might have ridiculed her for it, but leaving her skin exposed was a way of maximizing her abilities as a spirit eater. According to Arakiya's own account, lesser spirits prized harmony with nature and thus shunned anything worked by human hands. Hence, her minimal state of dress was a way of attracting those spirits—her food.

It was all so that Arakiya could use her powers to the fullest. If she needed to expose herself to that end, Prisca thought, then let her go naked for all she cared.

"Maybe I'd feel differently if she were ugly..."

"—? What do you mean, Princess?"

"I only mean that you are beautiful. Lovely enough to withstand even my scrutiny."

"Thank you...I think?" Arakiya tilted her head, somewhat perplexed that her appearance was suddenly the topic of conversation. But Prisca didn't intend to pursue it further than that. At any rate, this was no time for idle chitchat.

"Reporting, Your Excellency!" said a messenger who rushed up to Prisca. He pushed through the army, his red armor rattling, and knelt before her, offering up a scroll. Arakiya took it, broke the seal, and handed it to Prisca.

Prisca looked it over and grunted, "Hmph. Who gave this to you?"

"Count Belstetz Fondalphon, the strategist of House Godwin!"

"Belstetz... That old fossil." Prisca considered, recalling the face that went with the name, then closed one eye in contemplation. She didn't make a habit of remembering the dirt under her feet—which meant the fact that she remembered Belstetz indicated he had some value that made him worth remembering.

Lamia favored venomous strategies. She had a cruel streak and intelligence of her own, but there were more than a few people who had nourished those innate gifts. Belstetz was one of them. If Lamia was a poisonous flower, Belsetz was one of the gardeners who had dutifully watered her and helped her bloom.

"Princess. The letter... What does it say?"

"Nothing important. We're to act as the rear guard when the assault on the castle begins."

"Rear guard..."

"In other words, we're to watch from behind while everyone else does the fighting."

Arakiya's face went through a series of expressions as she learned the content of the message. First, her brow was knit in incomprehension; then her eyes went wide; and finally, she puffed out her cheeks in displeasure. "Princess… I think, maybe, they are making fun of us."

"I'm sure she seeks to humiliate us, yes. That vixen is never above inflicting her little cruelties. But she would never be reckless enough to endanger the victory."

"What, then?"

"I think she believes she can win without seeking our help. Although, with *that* army at her command, I can't say I entirely blame her." Prisca, seeking to placate the annoyed Arakiya, gestured around them with a thrust of her chin. Arakiya looked in the direction she indicated and spotted a series of banners; several other private armies were encamped around them, just like Prisca's. A combined force of six of the selection candidates, summoned to the field by Lamia Godwin.

It was not clear whether Lamia had offered the others the same terms she'd offered Prisca or not, but in any case, she had spoken to four of their other siblings and concocted the plan they were now enacting. Namely…

"The encirclement of Vincent Abelks."

In the distance, ensconced in the forest, was the castle that belonged to the Abelks family. The collective army looked down on it from a ragged cliffside—and Prisca, who was now just one part of the threat to the brother who was most likely the greatest threat to her, smiled.

It was a very logical plan. Vincent was the closest to the throne; if they could get him out of the way promptly, it would be worth joining forces with brothers and sisters they would later have to destroy. Even Prisca found herself obliged to approve of the idea.

Historically, it'd been said that the attacking force in a siege must outnumber the defenders three to one for any hope of prevailing— well, by numbers alone, they had five times Vincent's forces. No wonder Prisca's troops were in such high spirits despite their lack of honing. There was no reason for them to feel otherwise; they could see that they held an overwhelming advantage.

As much as Prisca loathed to admit it, Lamia had planned the perfect encirclement. All that was left…

"…is to see just how hard my brother plans to fight now that he's trapped in the vixen's hunting ground."

9

Lamia Godwin was an unparalleled masterpiece.

Such was the conviction among the soldiers of the Pruning Force of House Godwin. Their fearsomeness, clad in matching armor from head to toe and carrying their great shears, was known all over Volakia.

Their military renown had exploded seven years before, when Lamia had been nine years old. That was when the Godwin family had faced a rebellion by one of its counts that had cost it nearly half its fiefdom. In Volakia, with its veneration of the strong, rebellion against a wolf was valued more highly than loyalty to a pig, and thus, no outsider offered any aid to the embattled Godwin family estate as they sought to quell the rebellion.

What *had* subdued the rebels and turned the family's fortunes around in a single stroke was none other than Lamia Godwin. She induced the head of the family to seclude himself on the grounds that he was sick and might soon die—and instead, she herself seized power over the family, using the ploy as an opportunity to overwhelm the count's army. She even discovered and unveiled the instigator who had tempted the count into rebellion, in a display of political acumen that would be spoken of in the empire for years to come.

The Pruning Force was the unit she had created to accomplish all this, and they would later be the Godwins' trump card. They all wore masks that hid their faces, and with the huge shears they carried, they would mercilessly cut through any enemy. Word of their cruel disregard for human dignity or warrior pride, and the brutal retaliation they enacted on their enemies, soon spread to every corner of the empire, and with it, the name of Lamia Godwin.

To mold ordinary, feeling humans into these cold-blooded soldiers who shed no blood and cried no tears required a domination that verged on the religious—one had to make them embrace a certain brand of faith. That was what this girl had done. And it was why the Poison Princess, Lamia Godwin, was a masterpiece.

The true mission of the Pruning Force was to bring the princess's plans to fruition.

"____"

It was a sort of fatalism, almost an abandonment of rational thought—but ultimately, this was the only way for the members of the unit to save their own hearts and minds. The Pruning Force could not have been built on any concept that was totally sane. Instead, they surrendered their sanity in exchange for the belief that their every act was just or embodied justice itself—and thus, they carried out their orders. This was the quality, and the gift, of she who stood above them. And so...

"Destroy Vincent Abelks! For Lady Lamia!"

"For Lady Lamia!"

With a collective roar, the Pruning Force launched its attack against the enemy fortifications. In concert, the rest of the combined army began advancing quickly on the Abelks castle. Even as their combined footsteps became a rumble and then seemed to shake the very earth, the Abelks forces did not move.

The defenders of a castle siege were known to have the advantage, but against such vastly superior numbers, their odds did not look good. Perhaps they didn't intend to fight at all but had simply given in to resignation and despair. If that was so, then the appearance of the Pruning Force would only confirm that choice.

"Brace yourselves!" someone shouted, and the first wave broke upon them.

"Ahh! Good spirit I'm seeing here. I don't disapprove—in fact, I like it!"

*   *   *

At that instant, the men in the vanguard had the impression that a breeze had blown past them. The thing that had swept by them from ahead was just that overwhelmingly fast—too fast to see with the naked eye.

It was not a breeze; that was a simple misapprehension. But there was no mistaking its consequences.

"Oh…"

Struck by a sudden unsteadiness in their vision, many members of the Pruning Force stopped in their tracks and put their hands to their heads. They dropped their shears, trying to hold up heads that were suddenly heavy. But it was no use. For the necks that should have borne those heads had been sliced clean through.

"——" Unable to support their heads, they tried to cry out in vain. But before they could even fall to the ground, the rest of the unit, still charging from behind, slammed into them and trampled their bodies before finally, their erstwhile bodies parted ways with everything above the neck.

Only then did the others realize that the vanguard had been cut down—but it was too late.

"You need all kinds of speed on the battlefield. Quick intuition, quick judgment, a quick sword arm. I think that makes me something pretty special—but even so, aren't you all a bit too slow?"

Astonishment spread through the ranks as quickly as a silver flash spread destruction. Soldiers were dying almost before they knew they had been killed; by the time people realized a terrible swordsman was among them, there were too many heads on the ground to count.

"Ah, His Excellency truly is incredible! It's like he knew that if he gave me the sword I wanted, I would become twice as effective on the battlefield!" These words came from a blue-haired boy who shook the blood off his blade and laughed merrily. He was an attractive youth wearing a pink kimono and zori sandals, with two swords at his hip—and it was obvious at a glance that a deadly aura cloaked this reaper who had taken a great many lives.

A collective shudder ran through the Pruning Force, and they all turned their shears toward the young man. "Keep your guard up! Surround him and cut him down!" someone shouted.

"Ooh! I do like how quickly you collect yourselves. Very good. I was just thinking that it wouldn't be very impressive if the enemies I was chopping up during my big moment were just a bunch of straw men. If a man doesn't know how to die dramatically, how's the main character supposed to look good?"

"The kid's crazy...! Are you Vincent Abelks's—?"

"Crazy? Now, that's not very nice. But to answer your question, yes. Absolutely. Very much so. You couldn't be more right!" The boy turned his head, scanning the Pruning Force before raising his sword with a flair. It wasn't a practical battle stance; it very much seemed like he was just trying to look cool.

He deliberately slid his sandals across the ground and announced, "My name is Cecils Segmund! Confidant of His Excellency Vincent Abelks, and destined to one day be known as the greatest swordsman in Volakia! I am the flower and main character of this world—and I will cut you all down to clear a path to the imperial throne for His Excellency!"

"___"

The Pruning Force didn't respond.

"What's this? That's where you're supposed to cheer and applaud... Come on, don't be shy." The boy cocked his head, his tied-up hair bobbing from the motion. But Cecils's hoped-for applause didn't materialize—instead, anger erupted among the Pruning Force's ranks at the perceived mockery. They charged at him, shears clacking menacingly. Cecils scratched his head. "Maybe it *was* a mistake to offer my name before I got yours?"

And then still working under that misimpression, he set to work greeting the great shears with his sword.

10

"The Godwins' elite forces have made contact with the Abelks troops!"

And so battle had been joined. War cries shook the air down below. Beginning with Lamia's private army, the Pruning Force (was there ever an armed band of grimmer repute?), the net began to close around Vincent. The front line was steadily approaching Abelks castle.

However…

"The first line of defense should have crumbled almost immediately. The fact that it hasn't—I suppose it's because that accursed swordsman is so skilled." Prisca snapped her folding fan shut and gazed at the line of battle with her crimson eyes. At this distance, the troops looked no bigger than beans, but she could see him at work, the overwhelmingly powerful swordsman keeping Lamia's forces at bay. A secret weapon that Vincent had deliberately revealed to her before the Rite of Imperial Selection had begun. She'd known he was even better than Arakiya, and yet… "It is still stunning to see him like this."

He was literally a one-man army, holding fast against their entire force. It was difficult to believe.

Lamia had brought more than five times Vincent's forces to bear on the siege of this castle—and yet that calculation was based on the assumption that one of her soldiers was worth the same as one of his. A single fighter who could hold off a thousand troops naturally upset that calculation.

"I feel antsy…"

"Does he bother you so much, Arakiya?"

Arakiya, who was waiting as Prisca had bidden her, watched the battle unfold as well, letting her lips curl in displeasure. "Yes. Yes, he does," she replied. "Is it okay? If I go?"

"As much as I would like to indulge you, I can't permit it. Stay here by my side. You might not get your chance at him on *this* battlefield, but…"

"But…?"

"…your strength will be needed in due time."

That was all Prisca had to say for Arakiya's expression to change. She blinked, and her look of annoyance became the mask of a warrior. Prisca nodded approvingly, then ordered a nearby soldier to prepare a detachment. The numbers of the clashing armies were within tolerances—just.

Prisca was preparing to sally with the detachment when she heard a voice. *"Prisca. Where are you going?"*

"___"

She winced at the unexpected question. Nobody nearby noticed her reaction, nor did they respond to the voice—for they didn't hear it. It spoke directly into Prisca's mind. A one-way mode of communication, essentially telepathy. She knew only one person who could do that—someone who, like her, was here on this field as a participant in the Rite of Imperial Selection.

"Mind your manners, Paladio. Who said you could speak to me?"

"——I didn't realize I needed special permission to talk to my own sister."

Telepathy took a certain knack, but Prisca was able to respond immediately—something that seemed to surprise him, even if only slightly. The entire point was to be able to capitalize on the way telepathy set someone back on their heels.

"What a petty little ploy. Booby traps and parlor tricks—is that all the Demon Eye Clan is good for?"

There was a beat before Paladio said, *"Lamia told you to stay in the back. I advise you to refrain from acting on your own."*

"A doll that does whatever you tell it. How cute. I'll be happy to dress you, too, if you like. But as for me, I never had any intention of dancing to that vixen's tune."

"So...treachery? At a moment like this?"

"Ha! There, you finally made me laugh. I'm going to plug the hole in the line."

Paladio's concern was evident even through the telepathic connection. This mode of speaking utilized the voice of the heart, which made it difficult to conceal emotions—a clear drawback. And the more pitiful emotion the user felt, the more obvious their thoughts when using telepathy. Paladio was no exception. Meanwhile, Prisca's contempt and mockery would be perfectly evident to him.

"I'm not going to waste time explaining myself to the ignorant at this moment," she said. "Tell Lamia whatever you want."

"You're so profoundly crude that no one would believe I'm your older brother. I've always hated you, Prisca."

"Well, then I've got good news for you. To pay you back for that little remark, I've decided to take off your head with my own hands." She smiled sadistically and cut off the telepathic communication with a feeling of annoyance. Entering directly into the mind of another was Paladio's own uncanny skill, but he seemed to have no comeback. *Coward*, Prisca silently grumbled.

He was of the Demon Eye Clan; he possessed a Demon Eye somewhere on his body that granted him unusual abilities. It was a very rare gift, but it was wasted on someone so timid.

"Princess...?"

"It's nothing. Just a man who fancies himself my minder trying to put me in my place. Thinks he's going to tell on me. Is everything ready?"

Arakiya nodded in confirmation. Prisca smiled, her crimson eyes narrowing, and opened her folding fan. The sound as it whipped through the air seemed inordinately loud, drawing the attention of the small detachment.

The main force was fighting on the front lines, but Prisca, standing importantly before her troops, led them in a completely different direction.

"We're going to kill Vincent Abelks," she said. "You lot need only follow me."

11

"Please watch your step, Your Excellency. It's muddy."

A slim, black-haired man named Chisha Gold emerged from among the trees, leading another handsome young man and urging him to tread carefully.

The area had been secured by handpicked troops, the strongest of the strong, but Chisha felt he'd drawn the short straw. This was the closest he could be to his master, and he hated every moment of it.

Chisha had not been born to this station; his status shouldn't have been high enough to entitle him to serve a noble household like the Abelks family. He was simply a common subject of the empire. It had been sheer coincidence that he had helped a dragon carriage that turned out to belong to a prince—and that this prince, Vincent, would summon Chisha to stand by his side. The Volakian Royal Family was known to be a little odd—and when Vincent saw the power of calculation Chisha displayed in getting the carriage moving again after its wheel had snapped off in a gutter, he'd plucked him from the street then and there.

From that moment, Chisha began to serve Vincent personally, although he was always intensely aware of how unsuited he was for the position. And he was most unsuited for a battlefield like this— for the war of succession they called the Rite of Imperial Selection. How many nights had he spent asking himself why he was here?

And yet no other person could have been entrusted with such a major role—which left only him. He hated to give detailed instructions, and anyway, there was the pressing issue of whom his master would trust. On that point, Cecils was technically an option, at least, but Chisha was of the opinion that the idiot mutt couldn't be expected to stick to a given strategy. And so after much deliberation, Chisha had concluded that if he wanted this job done right, he was going to have to do it himself.

"You don't look pleased, Chisha. Your pallor is even worse than normal."

"I suppose so, sire... I was just lamenting my own position."

"Lamenting? Why so?"

"First, because I'm not fond of plans that involve risking my life. And second, because I not only suggested the plan but agreed to take part in it myself—quite strange, coming from me." He ran a hand through his neatly coiffed hair and sighed dramatically, as if to indicate how much trouble it all was.

His voice almost sounded like a quiet cough, and yet oddly, no one had ever complained that he was hard to hear or understand. At this moment, too, he spoke softly, but his master, listening to him, simply chuckled.

How exhilarating would it be to interject that this was hardly the time for laughter? Of course, Chisha was too rational to do such a thing, and his master too important to reproach.

In the distance, they could hear shouting punctuating the cacophony of battle. An explosion of lives being stolen and defended, each pitting their own values against the other. And at the center of it all stood the man who was now here with Chisha: Vincent Abelks.

Vincent, the man well understood to be the closest to the throne at the beginning of the Rite. It was only natural that he would become the target of the other claimants, but this encirclement was even more vicious than expected. The attacking force they currently faced sat on the high end of the scale of danger they'd anticipated. However…

"It *is* still within my expectations. Which means the progress of events is still within my con—"

"I see, I see. You've found yourself some decent pawns, Brother. You have my compliments."

"——" Chisha's quiet murmur was interrupted by a fiery voice that almost seemed to burn his eardrums. For a brief instant, it felt like his thoughts had been lit on fire. The voice, strong and overpowering, belonged to a girl who brimmed with the confidence that her flame could consume all.

Chisha felt compelled to swallow hard, his face stiffening. He watched as a group emerged from the shadows: a princess cloaked in crimson, flanked by Redmonger soldiers and a silver-haired girl at her side.

"Prisca Benedict." Standing across from the unflappable young woman, Chisha was suddenly aware that his throat was strangely dry. He forgot to include any honorific when he whispered her name, but Prisca herself chose not to remark on it. Indeed, it—*he*—was beneath her notice.

She cast her gaze past the stunned Chisha to look at Vincent standing beside him.

"I'm glad you made it, Prisca. I hope you're well."

"Of course I am, Brother. And just imagine how much better I would be if your head were to fall from your shoulders right here and now."

They stared at each other, a brother and sister with an unbridgeable gulf between them, their reunion reeking of blood. But they were both smiling.

12

In the three months since the Rite of Imperial Selection had begun, the empire's civil war had swiftly reached its climax.

A number of the would-be rulers of Volakia had surrounded the most likely successor to the throne, Vincent Abelks, and were tightening the noose. Each had brought a formidable and accomplished personal army, which were currently busy staining High Count Abelks's land with blood, spreading the stench of death and destruction across the battlefield. The shouts of anger and cries of hatred that flew from both sides made it inescapably clear just how cruel, how brutal this bloody civil war was. Any sane person would want to look away, would be scarred by the tragedy. Except, that is, for a very specific few.

The members of the Volakian Royal Family who sought to be the next emperor of Volakia; the loyal retainers who served as their shields and spears—and the dropouts, the ones who had suppressed their destructive egocentrism and now worked only to achieve their own ends.

These people could be considered chosen in a way; they and they alone watched the tragedy unfold around them, unmoved by the brilliant shining and abrupt fading of the lives on the field. This was a place one could not come to without the uncommon spirit that these people possessed.

In a sense, they were *Übermenschen*, those who were rulers by nature—or might one day be so.

Deep in the forest, a man and a woman confronted each other, each backed by a small cadre of supporters. Siblings by blood were no exception to the rule here—in fact, that was exactly what made these two its grandest exemplars. For each of them, at this moment, only the other existed. Their very existence would influence the fate of a great many lives and could drastically change the future of the empire. They both knew this and acted accordingly.

They each saw that the path they walked led to the future of their nation…

"Heh!"

The reunion shared by the brother and sister facing each other, Vincent and Prisca, was as violent as a thunderclap. Standing there amid the greenery, they exchanged what amounted to brief pleasantries, and then as if on cue, they both stretched out a hand. Instantly, each of them was grasping a beautiful sword that glowed red.

This world was said to be home to ten magical swords of unparalleled power. The Bright Sword was one of them, and if anyone unworthy touched it, they were burned to a crisp instantaneously. The sword had been passed down in the Volakian royal household for generations, and for the span of the Rite of Imperial Selection, there were as many Bright Swords as there were candidates for the throne. Nobody knew why.

But did the existence of multiple Bright Swords dilute their luster? Absolutely not.

"——"

The twin blades cut through the gloom of the forest like lancing sunlight. Prisca and Vincent advanced toward each other easily, swords in hand, and offered an exchange of blows as elegant as if they were dancing, bathing the forest in a shower of red-and-white light.

The two opposing flames intertwined, each heightening the heat of their opposite; the scene was beautiful. Fire consumed fire and threatened to consume anyone else who dared touch it or even get close. By all rights, several of these swords should not have existed at the same time; to see them pitted against each other was a vision beyond the wildest of fantasies.

The siblings' entourages were slow to react; they felt their skin singed by the wave of heat—and it was only then that they comprehended what was happening. Only then did they realize that their masters were already engaged in a life-and-death duel.

"What a grave miscalculation! It turns out I had no time to be staring and wondering!" The hot wind against his skin brought Chisha back to himself and made him lament his mistake. He searched in the folds of his clothes and produced a folding fan—made of iron, turning it into a proper instrument of war. He readied himself to assist his master.

Before he could reach the fighting, however, he was thrown to the side, cast away from the very spot he had been about to use as a springboard to leap into the fray. The blow was as vicious as the bite of a wild animal. Chisha glared at the one who had dealt it to him, and then he smiled with his almond-shaped eyes.

"The princess is busy. I won't let you interfere." Arakiya stood with her back to the heated confrontation between Vincent and Prisca. She was a young member of the dogfolk with brown skin, a good deal of it exposed. In her hand was a perfectly ordinary tree branch; she almost seemed to stand at total ease, appearing highly vulnerable. And yet Chisha found himself swallowing hard, his cheeks stiff.

He realized that she was a wild animal, just like Cecils.

"I'm not the kind to do physical labor myself," he said. "You must be Lady Prisca's secret sword."

"——? I'm Arakiya. For the princess's sake, I fight."

Her answer was utterly brief—but that itself spoke to her deeply rooted, immovable loyalty. Chisha sighed deeply. In that case, they weren't going to get anywhere by talking. He settled into a fighting posture with his iron fan, while behind him, Vincent's soldiers likewise readied their weapons.

"I myself and these soldiers behind me fight for another, but with the same dedication. I'm afraid I don't plan on participating in any-thing so inefficient as a duel. You must forgive me."

"Um...?"

"To put it succinctly, I intend to overwhelm you with sheer num-bers," Chisha announced, and the soldiers took this as their order to charge, which they did with gusto, screaming and shouting.

Arakiya's eyes went wide. She glanced behind her at the bat-tling siblings—Prisca wielding the Bright Sword gleefully, Vincent receiving her every blow and responding in kind. Arakiya stepped forward, intent on preventing any interference. "Difficult things, I don't understand. But this is for the princess. For the princess, I would die."

13

Every soldier who pressed in against her was charged with the fer-vor of battle.

"___"

Sword and spear were the only means they had of expressing their lust for war; they would drive them into Arakiya's skin, tear her flesh, shatter her bones, and end her life. Battle was merely a ritual to achieve such ends. Life pitted against life to the finish.

Well, Arakiya could enact that ritual, too.

"*Nom.*" Almost lazily, she popped a spirit into her mouth. It was good timing; lesser fire spirits, touched off by the battle between Prisca and Vincent, had begun to gather around. Arakiya simply took one into her body and turned its strength into hers. That was the natural course of action for a spirit eater.

"Bowwow." Arakiya crouched low, her entire body surrounded by a faint-blue glowing fire. They were too beautiful to be described with ordinary terms like *the flames of hell*, but regardless, it was impossible to avoid the impression that she was wreathed in fire. As a momentary shock passed through the attacking troops at the sacred vestments, Arakiya poured her strength into her legs and leaped at them.

Her body floated as easily as the wind, passing by the first line of soldiers. She simply dodged their attacks, and the men, as they turned to pursue Arakiya back into the formation, noticed something: Their own bodies were now engulfed in blue flames.

"Nggghhhaaaa!!"

The soldiers howled in agony, consumed from head to toe by scorching heat. Unlike Arakiya, who wore the flames as if they were a cloak fit for the gods, the flames that took the soldiers were not lovely or pleasant. The men threw themselves on the ground or tried to scoop dirt on themselves, but the flames wouldn't go out. The fires burned down into their very being, taking their lives and scorching away everything until the soldiers were nothing but piles of ash.

"Hold fast!" someone shouted. These were Vincent's personal soldiers, and having determined that they could do nothing to save their obliterated comrades, they immediately refocused on attacking Arakiya.

But how sad—even the calculated violence of numbers could not withstand an even greater violence. Numbers often decided the outcome of a battle. All other things being equal, two people were stronger than one, and a hundred were stronger than ten. That much was clear. Indeed, the measure of a strategist was his ability to come up with a plan to overcome such differences in fighting strength.

"Well, this is downright annoying..." Chisha, the one who had commanded the soldiers, placed his free hand over the hand that held the iron war fan. He indeed knew strategy was his mission; to bury the enemy was his role. That was the talent Vincent sought when he had plucked him from obscurity; that was why he was with Vincent in this situation now.

To concoct a plan, to control circumstances, to annihilate the opposition, and to do all this with strategy—that was his duty. He had performed it on many battlefields—and that was why he knew. In this world, there were some superlative beings who upset every strategic calculation, because they transcended numbers.

The boy whom Vincent had taken into his fold just a few months ago was one of them. And this Arakiya, whom Chisha watched tear through his troops like a wild animal, was another.

"Gah!"

"Gghh?!"

"Gyaaahhhh!"

A series of screams came from large, powerful men as they were flung upon the ground. Some were immolated in their entirety; others found their faces maimed or their arms or legs broken, while others still were torn open and collapsed on the ground, never to rise again.

Arakiya was down on all fours like an animal; her only weapon was a simple branch, but it was enough to break soldiers' swords, to rob them of their pride and their lives. To rob them of everything.

"No more of this..." Chisha, making the difficult choice to end this pointless hemorrhaging of troops, stepped forward. To spend so many common soldiers against someone who was beyond numbers was simply a waste of life. As the person entrusted with those lives, Chisha couldn't allow it to continue.

"Soldiers, fall back, please," Chisha said. "I will deal with that... thing."

The moment he had the unit retire, Arakiya stopped moving. She remained crouched on the ground like a dog, but she looked up at the tall young man, tilting her head and staring at him intently.

The young man sighed at the almost animalistic gesture. "I am Vincent Abelks's strategist, Chisha Gold."

"I am Princess Prisca's dog, Arakiya."

Introductions complete, the two bosom companions of the participants in the Rite of Imperial Selection launched themselves at each other. But it was only a single clash, the contest decided in a blink.

Arakiya approached Chisha, with his iron war fan, from the ground. Recognizing the low attack, Chisha brought the fan down, slamming it into the girl's head. Her silver hair, with its single lock of red, was stained with dark blood—at least, such was what Chisha had expected to happen. But the instant before his blow connected,

Arakiya opened her mouth wide and swallowed a pinprick of light. Suddenly, she was gone; he couldn't see her.

As Chisha stood there with his eyes wide, Arakiya, still on the ground, kicked out at him. His slim frame lifted into the air with the impact, which almost seemed to pierce him. It ran through him from his back to his belly, Arakiya's branch tearing through his torso and pinning him to the earth.

"Gah—hhh—" He wheezed. He coughed up a spectacular amount of blood, but with the branch holding him in place, Chisha couldn't even collapse to the ground.

Arakiya backed quickly away from him, looking toward him only to say, "There," her fingers steepled. She turned to report to her mistress that she had vanquished the powerful foe. "Prin—"

But a second later, a red light from above swallowed up Arakiya, along with the entire forest.

14

Lamia Godwin would never forget that garden party.

The party was held each year on the occasion of the birth of her father, the emperor, Dreizen Volakia. It lasted seven days, and all the royal siblings were obliged to be present—and thus forced to come together—whether they wanted to or not. Of course, with the Rite of Imperial Selection hanging over their heads, they usually arranged their schedules so as to see as little of the others as possible. Still, with more than sixty brothers and sisters in one place, it was impossible to avoid everyone all the time.

"_____"

That year, Lamia—nine years old at the time—was looking for her brother Vincent, whom she knew had come to greet their father on the same day she had.

Many of the Volakian royal children were mature for their age. This was an environment in which an egg that didn't hatch quickly would simply be broken—you either grew up fast, or you died. Hence, Lamia had none of the sweetness of the average nine-year-old girl; she was already a sharp, perceptive young woman. By this time, she was learning how to evaluate those around her, and she liked capable people. That was why she was looking for Vincent; talking to her intelligent, handsome brother made her heart race.

She'd worked her way around the vast Crystal Palace, where the party was being held, looking for Vincent and meanwhile working on her brother Bartroi, who always seemed a little too unwary of his younger siblings. Just as she finally found the brother she was looking for—

"Prisca Benedict. That's my name."

"____"

—next to Vincent, she discovered a young girl in a bright-crimson dress.

Three scant months later, Lamia Godwin took stern measures to depose the feckless family head and punish a rebellious count.

"Magic-stone cannon strike confirmed. When the smoke clears, I will inform you of the results," Belstetz reported.

"I don't care if you use up every magic stone we have; just make sure you get me what I want. You're to keep me updated as and when the situation develops," Lamia said.

"Milady," Belstetz replied with a respectful bow. Lamia rested her chin on her hands and looked out at the forest, which was now a blazing field of light. She smiled. She'd brought so many of her brothers and sisters together to enact this encirclement of Vincent. That she had included even her mortal enemy, Prisca, in this number was not in fact a sign of how much she wished to be sure she had the strength to defeat their brother.

It was because she knew that Prisca's presence was itself the poison that would finish Vincent.

"Didn't I tell you, Prisca? I think quite highly of you. You're the next most dangerous sibling after our dear brother... You think more like him than any of us. That's why I knew you could find him. I was sure."

Vincent would have known that he would be everyone's favorite target when the Rite began. Most likely, he'd even predicted that a coalition of his siblings would attempt to encircle him—and because the battle would be fought on Abelks territory, he'd no doubt prepared plenty of escape routes. Much as she hated to admit it, Lamia found it difficult to predict how exactly Vincent might try to slip her net. But she had a simple rule: If she couldn't do something, she would just rely on someone who could.

And so she did.

"Vincent and Prisca were in the same place. I'm sure they were both caught in the blast." The telepathic report from Lamia's coconspirator, Paladio, assured her that her plan had worked. Paladio kept it a secret from their other siblings that he carried the blood of the Demon Eye Clan and that his abilities allowed him to track a given target with incredible accuracy. He required some part of the target's body in order to do this, and while Lamia hadn't been able to obtain any such thing from Vincent ...

"Surely, you didn't really think I came all the way to your house just to corral you," Lamia said. She'd had this plan to use Paladio's special abilities brewing ever since the Rite had begun. Vincent, her real target, was a very careful man. But she didn't have to track him directly—she just had to track someone she knew would be with him.

Prisca was perfect for that role. That was why Lamia had gone herself to propose an alliance and why she'd made certain to involve Prisca in the encirclement.

It was why Lamia had resisted the urge to kill Prisca for more than seven years.

"My heart finally feels lighter, Prisca," Lamia said, placing her hand to her generous chest as she pictured the repulsive face of her half sister. Once she was sure Vincent and Prisca were dead, all that would remain would be to use the Pruning Force to massacre Vincent's troops and then checkmate her other siblings. The biggest threat and the unknown quantity would be eliminated; the rest of her brothers and sisters were no match for Lamia Godwin.

"Lamia, when this is over..."

"Yes, yes, I know. I'll give you a fingernail or a lock of my hair or whatever you want. You'll be able to come after me anytime, day or night."

Her alliance with Paladio would last only until Vincent was dead. After that, the agreement was that Lamia would hand over some piece of her body to him—but even the Demon Eye, which held an incomparable advantage in the war of information that was key to every victory, was worthless if its user was a witless fool. Sadly for him, Paladio simply couldn't beat Lamia. He could try to rally the other siblings against her as she had done against Vincent, but it wouldn't get him anywhere. She already knew the vulnerabilities, weaknesses, and dark secrets of most of the more powerful candidates; they wouldn't join Paladio.

Vincent and Prisca—they were the only ones with any hope of besting Lamia. And Paladio was helping head off that possibility himself. The absurdity was that he didn't even notice it—he was little different from Bartroi, who had died a dog's death by the maneuvering of his own little sister.

"For that matter, the fact that he actually still thinks he can beat me makes him even stupider than dear Bartroi."

"Your Excellency, the smoke is clearing."

The use of magic-stone cannons had been banned for sheer destructive force, and as the haze began to drift away from over the forest, everyone could see why. The devastation caused by ten cannons acting in concert was self-evident.

The power of a magic-stone cannon depended on the size and purity of the magic stone used with it, but regardless, the devastation wreaked on one corner of the battlefield was a testament to how sincerely Lamia wanted her targets dead.

She'd obtained magic crystals, which were magic stones of the utmost purity. The firepower they could generate must have been second in the empire only to the stones used in the construction of the Crystal Palace in the capital city of Lupghana. The stones were so powerful that the cannons had proven unable to cope with the resulting force, tearing themselves apart in the process of firing. Not even a member of the Volakian Royal Family could have escaped unscathed under such an assault. Not even if there were two of them.

This was the masterstroke that would secure Lamia's victory. And now…

One of the scouts, peering through a spyglass, could be heard muttering, "That's impossible!" With his telescope, he must have been able to see the outcome of the assault, which could not be discerned with the naked eye.

Even if she couldn't make out exactly what was going on, however, Lamia herself could tell that something wasn't right. The forest, which should have been reduced to splinters by the barrage, was still intact in one place, the trees still standing. And what had caused this inconceivable state of affairs?

"There's someone at the point of impact!" the scout shouted, trembling. "A silver-haired dog girl… It's Prisca Benedict's right hand!"

Lamia's eyes widened. Prisca's right hand—Lamia remembered the taciturn, inexpressive mongrel…

"I've got to hand it to you, Prisca…," she growled. She stood and marched over to the scout, snatching his spyglass. Through it, she could see ground zero, where Prisca's little friend lay prone on the ground, breathing out smoke. Somehow or other, that mutt had completely foiled Lamia's cannonade.

The dogfolk girl didn't so much as twitch; Lamia couldn't tell whether she was dead or alive. But she didn't care. What mattered was the scale of the destruction in that patch of forest—or rather, the lack of it. There was no way Prisca and Vincent were dead.

Meaning the first phase of her plan had failed. But Lamia had another arrow in her quiver—and another after that. "I never imagined I would actually have to use Bartroi's little insurance policy…"

She was recalling a suggestion left to her by her brother, the one who had voluntarily thrown away his right to the throne. The other nine siblings who had likewise declined candidacy were cards in her hand, and she would play them to finish off the wounded Vincent and Prisca both at a stroke.

Lamia lowered the spyglass and started to give her next instructions: "Begin the ambush. Their hearts might not be in it, but they'll slow them down at least..."

"Your Excellency!" a sharp voice interrupted.

No sooner had the voice sounded than a shadow came slicing across Lamia's vision. She reflexively raised her arm, and the Bright Sword she grasped in her hand singed the air it passed through, incinerating the arrow that had come flying at her.

She might have blocked the first attack, but the arrows came relentlessly; her soldiers, slow to react, surrounded her to shield her with their own bodies.

"But how did they figure out where I was camped?" she asked. "Wait... It can't be!" Sensing the answer to her own question, Lamia peered out at her attackers from behind her soldiers. Looking directly into the oncoming barrage, she saw that her guess had been correct; it was the dropout brothers and sisters, the ones she'd stolen from Bartroi, the ones she'd tried to use to complete the encirclement of Vincent. The cowards who should never have been able to turn on her were all rebelling at once.

What? Had the sight of battle suddenly inspired the lot of them to desire the throne at the same time? No, they were incapable of such decisive action. That left only one explanation.

"Vincent Abelks..."

Fight an encirclement with an encirclement. Lamia ground her teeth after realizing her opponent had been wily enough to pull off this maneuver. The handsome face of Vincent, the man who had put her in this situation, floated into her mind, and she thought about how much she hated him.

It was a classic double cross. Lamia, the Poison Princess, had allowed the poison directly into her own inner circle. When had it started? Lamia was perceptive enough that the moment she had the thought, a possibility occurred to her.

"Don't tell me... He was working with my dear brother Bartroi all along?"

Bartroi, who had died a dog's death, who should have been the ultimate loser. The brothers and sisters he had gathered to his cause became the very spear tip of Vincent's counterattack. Lamia shuddered at the possibility that she had been outplotted by Bartroi and at the realization that Vincent had dug in his heels even more than she had. Perhaps even allowing her to attack with the magic-stone cannons had been part of his plan. That neatly took them out of the equation, leaving an opening he could exploit to trap her.

But that plan involved one thing that should have been impossible. To protect himself against Lamia's cannonade, Vincent needed Prisca's dog-girl. And that meant Prisca's trust and aid were indispensable if he was to succeed. It all led to just one conclusion: "You've been working with him this whole time, haven't you, Prisca?"

A secret alliance between Prisca and Vincent—that precondition was necessary for successfully encircling Lamia. And with that condition achieved, the attack against the now-outmaneuvered Lamia intensified.

"Your Excellency! Leave this to us. You must find your way to the Pruning Force and retreat." Her commander, Belstetz, seeing that the enemy had the upper hand, was advising Lamia to flee. For a second, she almost spat on the suggestion out of sheer spite, but Belstetz was right. Cold, rational judgment quickly prevailed; if she stayed here, she could only die.

"Belstetz, you have the line. Hold them here, even if it costs you your lives," she instructed.

"Yes, Excellency. Be safe."

With that brief farewell, Lamia left her camp, which had become a battlefield. She took with her only the elite troops of her personal guard. Meanwhile, Belstetz was launching a vigorous attack against the traitorous siblings, but he no longer occupied her thoughts. She was already thinking about how to get out of this situation and planning what she would do once she was free.

It seemed like the same thing always happened to her plans.

"If you control them with emotion, they can be taken from you by someone who wields a greater emotion. There's something cheaper and simpler than jealousy or greed. It's fear."

"——" Lamia could almost hear the plans crumbling in her

mind—and the one who had brought them down, had destroyed everything she had worked for, was none other than the person who stood easily in front of her. Vincent's man, the true manslayer.

"Hey there. Real sorry I was late getting here. I tried to hurry, I really did, but it's tough work being the first sword on the stage. I think I've caught the mood here, though. Maybe I can finish this up without *too* pathetic a performance." He smiled—a young man holding a sword and drenched in blood.

How many crowds of people had he slain? He was almost entirely red with splattered gore, his unusual kimono so badly stained that it was impossible to tell what color it had once been. What made the young man so aberrant, however, wasn't that he was covered from head to toe in blood but the fact that he paid this no mind; it was the way he moved and spoke with total nonchalance, and the overwhelming, almost demonic presence he exuded that made it clear beyond any doubt that he only dealt in death. That was the strangest and most awful thing about him.

"Excellency..." The soldiers wearing the armor of the Pruning Force stepped forward, putting themselves between Lamia and the young man, choosing to make themselves a shield so that he could not approach her. Every one of them knew that this choice meant their deaths.

"Hmm, yes! You shine with a brilliant resolve to protect your mistress. That's a beautiful attitude! Truly stupendous. I don't disapprove of such tragedy—in fact, I like it."

"We'll never let a monster like you get near Her Excellency!"

The young man struck like lightning; the soldiers met him with their giant shears. At the instant of collision, what could be heard was not the terrible sound of blades cutting flesh, but the echo of a great crashing of weapon against weapon.

Lamia knew her soldiers were dying; still, she stepped over the bodies of the Pruning Force, escaping to where the boy and his sword could not reach her, fleeing to where he could not follow, running, running, running.

And when Lamia Godwin finally reached the place she was running to...

*   *   *

"Don't worry, Lamia. He won't get you here…because I'm going to bury you with my own hands."

…Prisca Benedict was waiting for her, grasping the Bright Sword.

15

"Prisca Benedict—that is my name."

So she'd said arrogantly back when they had first met at that garden party. Prisca had been five years old at the time; it had been her first garden party. Vincent, whom Lamia had been searching for so intently, had introduced them, and Lamia had been so shocked that she hardly heard anything her brother had said after that.

Lamia Godwin had understood instinctively—this girl was destined to be her lifelong archenemy.

"Oh? I'm Lamia Godwin, your oh-so-sweet elder sister." She'd forced herself to smile, but Prisca had the same instinct. She sensed Lamia's true feelings at a glance. From their very first meeting, the sisters had considered each other enemies.

"___"

The only reason Lamia hadn't strangled Prisca to death then and there was because Vincent was watching like a hawk. He was an intelligent young man; the tension between the two hadn't escaped him.

Lamia had sent assassins after Prisca on a fairly regular basis after that, but she'd always known it would be little more than a nuisance to her sister. She'd also recognized that as long as Prisca existed, it would be impossible to bring Vincent into her fold. That meant the two of them were nothing more than obstacles on Lamia's path.

The freedom to maneuver she'd thought she'd had was gone. Best get to work, then.

"Say, Bartroi, my dear brother… Why can't all us siblings just celebrate our father's birthday together in peace?"

"Oh, Lamia… The same question pains me, too. But it's simply not possible for us."

"Not possible for us to get along? That's… That's so sad…"

"——" Bartroi said nothing.

Lamia, her mind made up, had already begun to play the game.

She planted seeds, watered them as they began to grow, and cultivated possibilities. As the profusion of flowers began to bloom, she tested them to see which were poisonous.

"Yes… You're right. It's just like you say, Lamia. If only we siblings could go without hurting one another…"

She played the part of the innocent little sister to the hilt, and Bartroi swallowed it hook, line and sinker. He appeared to be deeply moved. In this way, Lamia packed the earth beneath her feet, forming the path she would walk in the future.

And eventually…

"To think I spent seven long years trying to carefully position you, trying to make you a poisoned blossom to destroy our brother Vincent." There was no emotion in Lamia's voice as she came to a sharp stop at the end of her flight.

Prisca stood in front of her without a single soldier at her side. The same was true of Lamia, who had assigned her body double to go with her guards, telling her to flee as conspicuously as possible.

Here, Lamia and Prisca were alone.

Lamia was by no means so stupid as to imagine this meant Prisca took her lightly.

"Truly, you are the most unlovable little sister…" Lamia straightened her hair with one hand as she watched Prisca, who stood with arms folded. Prisca's crimson eyes were far from cold; indeed, they burned intensely, the same way they had that day at the garden party. Prisca looked at Lamia, and Lamia looked at Prisca, a perfect mirror image of that day when they had each realized the other would be their mortal foe.

"How did that little puppy of yours save you from my cannonade? If it hadn't been for her, I could've wiped out you *and* Vincent with a single stroke."

"I know how good your hearing is. I'm sure you know Arakiya is what they call a spirit eater. Her power depends on the spirits she consumes—and that should make your answer obvious."

"—You're suggesting she ate a spirit strong enough to repel that assault? I doubt such a thing—" She was about to conclude *exists*, but then she stopped. She looked at the ground and nodded as if it made sense now. "I've been assuming that Vincent, knowing he would find himself surrounded, picked this place because the castle was sturdy enough to repel attackers. My entire premise was wrong, wasn't it?"

"Abandoning the castle was part of our brother's plan from the beginning. He chose this place not for its fortifications, but for the land itself."

"I assume you mean, more precisely, the spirit sleeping in the land, yes?"

Prisca didn't deny it. Observing her little sister's reactions, Lamia grasped the reason she'd been led here and why her cannon barrage had failed.

"The Boulder. Muspel."

Prisca nodded. "We are currently standing in a corner of what is reputed to be its sacred territory."

Muspel, the Boulder—this was the name of one of the four most renowned spirits in the world. The so-called Four Great Spirits were said to wander Volakia at will. If one was able to consume one of these powerful beings, it might indeed be possible to protect one's master from Lamia's artillery assault.

"And your little puppy dog survived taking the power of one of the Four Great Spirits within her?"

"She consumed only a small portion—and even that would have annihilated a lesser vessel. But victory doesn't simply fall into one's lap. There are always sacrifices."

"—I suppose you did this knowing what would happen if the great spirit went berserk after it was eaten," Lamia said.

Prisca had determined that her strategy required risking the life of one of her closest confidants. Lamia understood now that the plan had involved leveraging the power of one of the great spirits. But the Boulder was a transcendent being, impossible to communicate with, let alone control or command. Perhaps Arakiya had consumed only a portion of it, but it was always possible that her own being would be consumed in turn and she would go on a rampage.

"I have another question," Lamia cooed. "How ever did Vincent manage to trap the Boulder in this location? It seems humans aren't the only ones our dear brother can manipulate with his plans."

"There's no doubt that plans and manipulation are our brother's specialty. But the means are immaterial. All that matters is that I have my results."

"Yes... Yes, you're right."

Prisca, who had decided she wasn't interested in a lengthy chat, held out the Bright Sword. In response, Lamia drew her own sword out of the air and took up a fighting stance. Neither tried to stop the other from drawing, but it was not a sign of trust. To abide by what you knew to be a fact could not be called trust. The sisters simply knew it was what they would do. As they knew that the matter would shortly be settled by their own hands...

"I've always hated you, Prisca, since the day we met."

"Don't worry. Of all those whose names I've bothered to remember, I despise you the most."

Elder sister faced younger, their hostility and animus on full display. They would have done nothing differently, said nothing differently, even if this had been the last time they were to see each other in their lives.

"___"

They each stepped forward, their swords crossing, the world enveloped in a flash of white and red and heat. Lamia saw nothing around her; she was in a world in which only she and Prisca existed, and she laughed, more certain than ever before that she should have murdered this girl when they first met at that party.

The sisters hated each other to the end, reviled each other until the very conclusion of their relationship.

16

"Prisca and Lamia should be about done settling things by now," Vincent said, looking down at the half dead Arakiya. She was completely exhausted, leaned up against a large tree with her legs kicked out, limp.

It wasn't exactly surprising; she'd single-handedly repelled a magic-stone cannon barrage with the power to annihilate an entire army, and to do so, she'd taken one of the Four Great Spirits into her small body. The consequences were dire; Arakiya had done it knowing full well that it might cost her very soul.

Thus, Vincent's plan succeeded, and Arakiya had been instrumental.

"It can't have been easy. Prisca is blessed with good help—I'll admit that much."

"I did it…for the princess…"

"Yes, I'm sure. I don't doubt you." It was rare for Vincent to praise such loyalty. Nearly everyone who served the royal family was at least as loyal as Arakiya—some even more so. That included Vincent's personal soldiers, who had been used as bait for the enemy, never knowing that Vincent himself had made a secret agreement with Prisca. "I suppose Chisha is going to give me a piece of his mind, though," Vincent muttered.

He was looking at Chisha, who, after being skewered by Arakiya, had been right in the middle of the meeting of the cannonade with the power of one of the Four Great Spirits. He was being given heroic treatment but was badly wounded both inside and out. His odds of surviving were no better than a coin flip. He was a clever strategist, a devoted servant whom Vincent would be able to entrust with important positions in the future—and yet even he had been part of the plan, a way of selling the ploy to ensure that it would avoid detection and succeed.

Nonetheless, Vincent was confident that it had been worth it. "I have much the same opinion of Lamia as she did of me and Prisca. The Rite has only just begun, but with this, I've eliminated my greatest rivals for the throne."

From the perspectives of ambition and aptitude, and from the perspective of whether they had any likelihood of actually obtaining the throne, only Lamia and Prisca had been worth worrying about in Vincent's opinion. Sadly for all the other siblings, not one of them was a match for Vincent. Although, there was one who—though still no threat for the throne—had taken Vincent by surprise in another way.

"Imagine—apparently, I also misjudged my older brother Bartroi."

Bartroi Fitz, who had departed this world shortly after the beginning of the Rite of Imperial Selection, pruned away by Lamia. He'd hated the idea of brothers and sisters killing one another and had sought to keep the death wrought by the Rite to an absolute minimum with a plan that surprised even Vincent.

"Declining to participate in the Rite himself, he promised the submission of several other siblings in exchange for my guarantee of their territories and persons. A bold move, if nothing else."

If it worked, the number of heads Vincent would have had to sever in order to achieve the throne would have been ten less. And if each of them had raised personal armies in contesting the succession, the loss of life would have been that much greater. The proposal was predicated on a worldview that ran counter to Vincent's own avowedly more correct reading of the situation—that none of his brothers or sisters could be allowed to live.

Broadly speaking, there had been two keys to his escape from Lamia's encirclement. One had been Arakiya, capable of using the great spirit to neutralize the cannonade; the other was the double cross that Lamia had never anticipated—in other words, the siblings and their armies, whom Bartroi had secretly entrusted to Vincent. True, if they succeeded, he would essentially be honoring a contract with a dead man, but Vincent didn't have it in him to simply consider the matter null and void. Reward must be no more forgone than punishment—that was one thing Vincent always bore in mind as a member of the Volakian Royal Family.

Those siblings Bartroi had persuaded to abandon their right to the succession were no doubt fighting desperately for Vincent's triumph, for what they saw as their own survival. Never knowing the true nature of the deal. Bartroi had buried the truth. He had always been so convincingly sweet and friendly in order to get what he wanted. Vincent was particularly impressed that Bartroi had even been prepared to incorporate his own death into his plans if it would achieve his goal. Bartroi Fitz had, in truth, been a worthy member of the royal family of Volakia.

"——" Arakiya, breathing shallowly, had no response to Vincent's reminiscences. Ultimately, she'd never been anything more than a loyal dog, following Prisca's orders. She held no opinions of her own, had never needed a mind to think for herself. She was a very useful girl, someone who had never been touched by ambition or traitorous impulse. And yet Vincent doubted it was only her usefulness that made Prisca treasure her so much.

There was something more between Prisca and Arakiya than simply a relationship of master and servant. There was a genuine bond. Arakiya would not hesitate to throw away everything for Prisca—although both she and Prisca lacked enough imagination to fully grasp what that meant.

"You said your name was Arakiya, yes?"

"——? Yes… That's right." Arakiya looked at Vincent suspiciously. He came and stood before her, where she looked at him like a skittish small animal—and then he winked at her.

"I'd like to make you an offer. From me—" There, Vincent stopped and gave a small shake of his head. The emotion in his dark eyes never shifting, he corrected himself: "From your emperor."

17

Two months had gone by since the attempted encirclement of Vincent Abelks.

"Damn you, Prisca…!"

"Silence, varlet. I have nothing to gain by speaking to you."

The face of the man with long hair was a mask of rage as he pulled the Bright Sword from thin air. However, the half-circle slash of crimson was met and beaten back by a strike from above, forcing the magical blade out of the man's hand.

Disarmed, the man's eyes shot open as he witnessed a flash, a sword stroke far more beautiful and cruel than his own.

And it was the last thing he ever saw.

The slash easily separated the man's head from his body, ensuring his death. The now-disconnected head and torso simultaneously went up in flames, great red tongues of fire that reduced the corpse to ashes.

These were the last moments of Paladio Manesk, son of the Volakian Royal Family.

"In the end, you were never more than ordinary. That was your limit." Prisca's judgment on the fate of this foolish older brother, who had holed himself up in his castle to await his destruction, was harsh.

The little turncoat had worked so hard to team up with Lamia and steer the Rite of Imperial Selection. As she had promised, Prisca had taken his head with her own hands. The honor was presumably lost on the now-dead man, but Prisca herself didn't give a second thought to Paladio's predicament. All she knew was that she had removed another obstacle between her and the throne. That was the only fact worth noting.

"Princess..."

"Arakiya? I've cleaned up here. How goes the rest?"

"No problems. It's over."

Sheathing the Bright Sword in thin air, Prisca turned as Arakiya emerged. She'd been around and about taking care of the soldiers who peppered Paladio's base of operations, but nowhere on her exposed skin was there so much as a scratch.

Paladio's Demon Eye abilities were the standout feature of his faction, but he lacked either the wits or the supporters to make the most of it. And so Arakiya had handily taken care of his arms and legs elsewhere while Prisca had hacked off his head.

"Lamia was at least more entertaining. I never imagined I would *miss* that spiteful villain."

"——" Arakiya didn't respond.

"What's the matter, Arakiya? It's not like you to look so serious." Prisca made a show of seating herself on her deceased brother's throne, then turned a questioning gaze on the silent girl.

"Oh...," Arakiya replied finally, then blinked. After a moment, she said, "Will you soon fight? With Master Vincent?"

"My brother? Yes… Yes, I suppose I will. Whether it will be soon, I can't say, but we will eventually have to settle matters."

Prisca, realizing that Arakiya's demeanor had to do with Vincent's continued existence, allowed herself to relax into a smile. Vincent Abelks was her greatest opponent in the Rite of Imperial Selection, her true test. Ever since the day she'd helped him escape Lamia's encirclement, she'd watched as his army had grown ever larger and as he eliminated their other siblings—the other claimants to the throne—one by one.

Lamia had known this would happen; it was exactly why she'd sought to strike at Vincent early on, even if it meant working with the others. If those others had been smart, they would have continued to work together after the encirclement failed, when Vincent had been at least nominally on the back foot. But they had missed their chance, and Vincent had licked his wounds and taken the opportunity to recover.

"For such idiocy, they deserved no better than destruction," Prisca said. After all, when one emerged victorious from the Rite of Imperial Selection, what awaited them was the throne of the Volakian Empire and all the responsibilities that went with it. Those siblings had shown that they would never have been able to bear the burden. Now with Lamia gone and Paladio dispatched, all that remained was…

"Ah, Mistress Prisca, your perspicacity never ceases to amaze." The conversation between master and servant was interrupted by the tapping of shoes on the floor as a new figure emerged. "I must express my profound admiration."

Prisca rested her chin on her hands and turned her crimson eyes on the newcomer, who bowed with elaborate politeness. It was a young man with white hair. Just for a second, Prisca closed one eye, searching her memory, but she soon recalled who the man was. Except that he didn't quite look the way she remembered.

As Prisca recalled, the last time they'd met, he'd had black hair.

"Did I surprise you, milady? My apologies. My near-death experience on the occasion of our last encounter seems to have robbed me of my color."

"So I see. Strange things do happen. But I was going to refrain from asking about this appearance of yours that I briefly found so confusing. You're Chisha Gold, are you not?"

"I'm most honored that you remember me." Chisha bowed again; he was indeed the young man Prisca had seen at her battle with Vincent. Prisca, who had been busy playing at sword fighting with Vincent and had then turned her attention to Lamia, didn't know the details, but from what she had heard, Chisha had had a close encounter with Arakiya that day and sustained near-mortal wounds.

"I've brought a little token of His Excellency's esteem to mark this occasion. It might seem a touch precipitous, but we do hope you'll accept it."

"I only took my enemy's head a few minutes ago, and already, my brother has managed to send a messenger into this camp. How very like him. And what is this congratulatory token?"

"Fine wine, if it please you." Chisha produced a bottle of what was known to be some of the finest wine around.

Even at the tender age of twelve, Prisca was already acquainted with the taste of alcohol. And even for someone who prided herself on having the very best of everything, as she never failed to do, that wine was not easy to obtain.

Nonetheless, she said, "Arakiya, destroy it."

At those words, the bottle in Chisha's hand shattered, the sound ringing around the room as the wine cascaded onto the carpet.

Chisha's smile was almost reptilian. "Some nobles would have sold themselves out of house and home for a bottle like that."

"I'm well aware. If we hadn't been in the midst of the Rite of Imperial Selection, I might even have accepted it. But my brother will have known perfectly well that I would destroy any gift he might send me at this moment."

"And so he did," Chisha said, nodding, betraying no sign that he found any of this upsetting in the slightest.

Gifts were always assumed to have some ulterior motive in the Volakian Royal Family. With assassination by poisoning being so popular, it would have been unthinkable to simply drink something another member of the family had sent without further inspection.

The reaction had no doubt been completely expected, yet even so, Vincent's young friend watched Prisca as calmly as if the emotion had been drained from his body along with his hair color.

"Go back and tell my brother that the most obvious obstacles are gone and that it will soon be time for he and I to settle things. We can no longer act toward each other as we once did, nor should we wish to."

"If you'll forgive my asking, Lady Prisca, do you honestly believe you can win against my master?"

"Certainly. For this world bends itself to suit me."

Chisha responded to this expression of Prisca's philosophy with an admiring bow. Prisca looked away from him, waving a hand as if to say the conversation was over. She expected him to go back to Vincent and tell him that it was time to prepare for the final battle. However...

"And if the world turns for your benefit, how does the future look to you?"

"What?" Prisca's gaze returned to Chisha, probing, seeking the meaning of the pregnant question. Then her eyes widened—for someone was kneeling on the floor before her.

"——" It was Arakiya, her knees in the pool of wine; she was leaning down toward the alcohol that stained the ground. As the liquid slowly spread, she reached out with her quavering tongue and lapped at it audibly.

"Arakiya, what are you doing? No attendant of mine should so demean herself as to—"

"Princess. I'm...sorry..." Arakiya's eyes were full of tears as she looked up at Prisca, who watched her in amazement. It was the first time she'd ever seen such sadness from her milk sister, and even Prisca could not help but be stopped in her tracks. Nor was it the end of her amazement, for then the strength left Arakiya's body, and she collapsed to the floor.

Arakiya uttered only a few inarticulate groans: "Ah...hh... Hkk!" Her limbs began to spasm, her eyes rolled back in her head, and it was obvious that she was suffering in her final moments.

"——" Prisca had only been watching for an instant before her eyes revealed that she had begun a series of cold calculations. Now that

Arakiya was on the cusp of death, countless possible choices presented themselves to Prisca's mind, rising up and then disappearing.

The average person would have taken too long to sort through them; Arakiya would have died while they were making their decision. But Prisca was not an average person. Nor was Vincent, who had foreseen what she would do.

That was why this brother and sister, closer to each other than to anyone else, had no choice but to engage in a mortal contest.

"Goddamned fool," Prisca muttered, coming to the side of the fallen, twitching Arakiya. She sat Arakiya up in her arms and, in almost the same motion, pressed her lips to Arakiya's mouth, then began to suck out the poisoned wine. She spat it aside, mouthful by mouthful, as if sucking poison out of a wound. This toxin, though, had been powerful enough to overcome even Arakiya; merely coming into contact with it would be enough to affect most people.

"Grr..." Prisca, too, felt the effects, but even as the poison ate away at her body, she continued to draw it out of Arakiya and spit it away.

"A most terrible pair," Chisha remarked, observing them with true praise on his tongue. Both for Prisca, who managed to endure the poison—even if only just—as she drew it from Arakiya; and for Vincent, who had seen that this was the only possible way to poison his ever-vigilant sister. In Chisha's eyes, both siblings were masterpieces, plotters of unrivaled ingenuity.

Arakiya had stopped spasming, and although she was unconscious, the moment of greatest danger had passed. Prisca, who had brought her to this point, wiped her lips, and she couldn't hide the tremble in her voice as she asked Chisha, "How did my brother convince Arakiya to work with him?"

"Do you not know?" Chisha asked, tilting his head in some confusion even as he remained impressed with her boldness. "I should think you, Lady Prisca, are better placed to understand His Excellency's thinking than I am."

"Hmph... And yet he gave you a starring role in his little play."

"I can only regret being unable to repay his kindness."

Prisca stood slowly and returned to the throne. Chisha was

privately astonished to see that she still walked steadily. But he was also, just as privately, relieved to see how she leaned against the backrest, betraying what a steep toll the poison had taken on her.

There was no need to say what Chisha said next, but he couldn't help himself. "Lady Prisca."

"Yes, what?"

"Had I not served His Excellency Vincent, I would have whole-heartedly served you, milady. It's only a shame that I didn't have the chance." He shook his head.

"Ha." Prisca laughed as if she was letting out a sharp breath. Then she looked down at Arakiya, where she lay on the floor, and wore a small smile with her lips that were now the color of blood. "I have no need for a charmless clown like you. If you wish to serve me, then at least make yourself presentable. Pretty. What a ridiculous commoner."

She let out a long sigh, but to the bitter end, she wanted to be herself; she insisted on that final snipe.

And then she stopped breathing. That was the end of Prisca Benedict.

18

"And so the poor, sweet princess was caught in her enemy's trap and lost her life. The princess's elder brother claimed ultimate victory and became the nation's emperor, and they say he still rules and prospers to this day."

"Wh-what a very thrilling story! And what happened after that?"

"There is no *after that*. I told you, did I not? The princess, the main character of the story, dies at the end. The story can't continue."

"What?! But…but nothing says that!" The young boy's eyebrows were raised adorably in his distress. It was a most unusual state for him.

The beautiful princess who had been reading him the story—er, rather, we should say Priscilla—cocked her head. Her orange hair cascaded down her shoulders, flashing as it went. She crossed her arms in front of her ample chest. And then she chided the frantic boy: "Come, now, Schult. Have you grown so high-and-mighty that you can critique the story I choose to tell you? What about the tale has so upset you? Tell me, if you can."

"Yes, milady! The princess in that story was just too, too tragic! She worked so hard and tried her very best, but her brother tricked her, and her pet dog tricked her, too… Oh, I simply don't know what to do!" Schult puffed out his bright-red cheeks.

Priscilla felt herself smile a little. She'd massaged a few of the details, but her story largely followed the facts. As such, Schult's reaction was touching, given that he himself knew the "tragic princess." However…

"However you may discover you feel about it, the princess is already dead, and the story is over. It can't be changed. That's the nature of the tales that we tell."

"Aww… But that's so sad. It hurts so much."

"What are you going to do about it, then? Waste time complaining and being upset?"

If that was how he planned to conduct himself, Priscilla's evaluation of Schult would change dramatically. Schult's future, in fact, hung in the balance of how he responded to a story she'd told him on a whim.

Schult was totally unaware of this as he crossed his stubby arms and nodded distractedly. Priscilla didn't rush him but waited to find out what his answer would be. At length, Schult unfolded his arms, looked at Priscilla, and said, "In that case… In that case, I'll write the rest of the story myself!"

"What?" She raised an eyebrow. This answer, she had never imagined.

Schult met her response by clenching his small fist with determination. "Lady Priscilla, you said that the story was over. But I'm going to think of what happens next, so that the princess doesn't have to meet a tragic end!"

"——" Priscilla didn't say anything right away. So Schult, with his modest command of language, was going to weave the continuation of a story that was supposed to be done. Priscilla took in a small breath—and then she closed an eye pensively. "Continuing what's finished, eh? Well, how will it go on? What future will you give to a dead princess, Schult?"

"Well, uh… Well, first, the princess drank the poison, but she didn't die from it! She went into a deep, deep sleep, and then later, she wakes up again!"

"Hoh. She wakes up, does she? And why is that? The poison was very deadly. Strong enough to kill a person easily."

"But the princess and her dog both took half of it! That's why!" Yes, there had been enough to kill a person between them, but by taking just half and half, neither the young princess nor her pet dog died. The simple logic of it, the blind application of basic arithmetic, was deeply childish—but that was how Schult sought to tie it together, and Priscilla didn't argue with him. Instead, she simply mussed his pink hair and smiled. "Lady Priscilla?" he said.

"You think of the strangest things, Schult. Rewriting a finished story to suit your own druthers—haughty behavior, don't you think? Spitting in the face of the one who gave birth to the story in the first place?"

"Er… Um, was I wrong to do that?"

"Why would you be wrong? There's nothing wrong about taking a story you can't accept and bending it into a shape that suits you. Nothing wrong at all. In fact, I'm impressed."

If Schult had simply cried himself to sleep from sheer frustration, Priscilla would almost certainly have cast him aside as nothing more than a spoiled child, without remorse and without a second thought. But Schult had risen to her expectations.

"I hope you'll tell me the rest of the story of the poor princess. Tell me the tale that suits you."

"—! Y-yes, milady! Well, first, the princess didn't die from the poison! And then someone very kind helped her…"

Schult, his eyes shining now that he had Priscilla's permission, began weaving the rest of the story. Priscilla rested her chin on one hand and watched the ecstatic boy go on at length, her free hand gently brushing the cover of the book. The book had inspired her to tell this tale. She couldn't say how valuable it was to be given that inspiration. To some, it might not seem of any value at all. To those who didn't know better, the book might simply look like a meaning-less profusion of letters. But to her...

"Lady Priscilla? Are you listening?"

"But of course I am. Who do you take me for?" Priscilla patted Schult's head again and smiled. She was remembering another head she used to pat, smiling then, too...

19

Prisca cannot triumph over me. She has more weaknesses than I do. Therefore, if we fight each other, Prisca will die—it is inevitable.

However, even I do not wish to kill the little sister I love the most. And that's why, suitably impressed with your actions here today, I grant you an opportunity. A chance to save Prisca.

As for how...

"____"

"Finally up, are you?" Someone, just a face in profile, spoke to her as her eyes fluttered open on the bed. She found herself looking up at an unfamiliar ceiling, but a quick glance to the side revealed a man in most unusual raiment, pure white from head to toe. The man's name... It was...

"You're all white..."

"It's Chisha Gold. I wish that you would at least take the effort to remember my name. Merely my own opinion, of course." Chisha, as he called himself, showed no change of expression despite his com-plaint. The girl on the bed—Arakiya—paid no heed to his objection. She felt something was wrong; she brought a hand to her left eye. Sometimes, the world looked fuzzy when you first woke up, but the hazy quality it had at that moment was different somehow. Almost as if she had no vision in her left eye.

When he saw Arakiya's fingers brush her eyelid, Chisha explained calmly, "Consider it the price you paid in exchange for being left with your life. Much like how I've turned white as snow. But the important thing is that, indeed, both of us *are* alive."

Arakiya wasn't particularly shocked to learn she'd lost her eye. She'd done what she did knowing full well that it might cost her very life. The fact that she was still there at all was the more surprising thing.

Moreover, her being alive was as much as to say that Vincent's plan had succeeded. Otherwise, the poison would certainly have killed her.

"The princess. Where?"

"You mean Lady Prisca? I'm afraid she's quite dead."

"——!" Arakiya drew a sharp breath. Chisha sounded every bit as calm as he had explaining about her eye, but she couldn't ignore what he had said. Her right eye, the one remaining to her, opened wide, and she reached violently toward Chisha, seeking to wring his pale neck.

"Oops! Not now—you're still convalescing. Calm down, sweet little puppy."

"Gah!"

No sooner had he spoken—almost bantering—than something hard hit her in the forehead and she felt herself go limp. She blinked, trying to understand what had happened. At the edge of her vision, she saw a blurry but smiling face. The figure bent over her, peering down at her where she'd collapsed—it was the blue-haired boy.

The instant she realized who it was, Arakiya, who hardly ever betrayed emotion, felt as if her heart was in a million pieces.

"Smiling jester…"

"Ha-ha-ha! I know you must be happy to see me, but there's no need to call yourself that. After all, there's not a person alive who can help grinning when they see my face!"

"——" With her remaining eye, Arakiya glared at the boy who'd jabbed her in the forehead, revealing a very obvious desire to kill him. Chisha shook his head slowly. "Allow me to apologize for his blathering. And also for my all-too-easily misunderstood answer to you. I reiterate that Lady Prisca *is* dead. However, your princess remains with us in this world."

"But…that…"

"His Excellency will be true to his word. You became the poison that felled Lady Prisca, and for that reason, he will not perjure himself. However..."

"I can't ever...see the princess..."

"——That's correct," Chisha said softly and nodded. Arakiya all but ignored him; she pressed a hand to her left eye and held her breath.

Vincent will keep his word. If what Chisha had said was true, then Prisca was dead but had survived. The Rite of Imperial Selection had ended for her with Arakiya's betrayal.

"Princess..." Arakiya called to mind the beautiful face she had spent so long studying. Did she hate Arakiya now? Did she hate Arakiya, who had given in to Vincent's plan and become poison to her? Arakiya, who had been unable to have faith in Prisca's ultimate triumph and had instead acted on her own initiative to save her princess from death?

It was not that Arakiya had been enraptured by the magic of Vincent's words. If Prisca truly could not hope to best Vincent, then it was not because of a matter of strength or wits. It was a matter of the heart. Prisca was so deeply compassionate, so kind. That was why she couldn't hope to defeat the cold and cruel Vincent.

"Oh... Ohh..."

"Oh my, she's started to cry. Chisha, what do we do with the puppy? His Excellency says she's a stray now."

"I'm told her course of action is to be left to her discretion. Anyway, what about you? The brutality with which you annihilated the Pruning Force is getting around."

Chisha and the boy chatted by Arakiya's feet; Arakiya herself covered her face with her hands and wailed. She completely ignored the other two; instead, she cried, and as she cried, she prayed. Though she was a spirit eater, a barbarian with nothing to pray to, she cried out to Heaven. She begged that what the princess of her heart had always said would be true.

That the world—

20

"—bends itself to suit me," the girl murmured, holding down her orange hair as the wind tried to pick it up and flutter it behind her.

The beautiful young woman stood in a grassy field, studying a grave site built in the shadow of some trees. The marker bore the name *Prisca Benedict*. The name of a member of the Volakian Royal Family who had died in battle. The girl gazed at it, her crimson eyes creasing into a smile.

"Princess, you'll catch your death if you stand out here in the wind," someone said from behind her. It was an old woman, dressed in noble garments that she wore as easily as if she had been born in them. Several servants stood behind her, their appearance signaling that the woman was everything she looked to be. It was equally obvious that the young lady to whom the old one showed such respect was in a more august position than hers. "Princess," the old woman repeated, "please listen to me…"

"Enough with your 'princess.' It's foolishness. Prisca Benedict is dead and in the ground. And that being so, it cannot be right to call me princess. I'm supposed to be your precious granddaughter."

"——" The old woman bowed her head. The girl's attitude was awfully self-important for a granddaughter.

The girl could sense the gesture of submission behind her. "Hmph," she said and looked back at the grave. Those who had died in the Rite of Imperial Selection were not usually commemorated with such things. There was no mercy for the defeated; such was the way of the Rite that the losers were typically reduced to ash, leaving not even corpses. So this grave marker for one Prisca Benedict was out of the ordinary. So was the fact that a girl's body lay interred beneath it.

"She looked so much like me… To think that she would serve me twice."

She thought of the body double who'd sacrificed herself against the assassins sent just before the Rite had begun. A girl with the same orange hair as the princess whom she had successfully protected. Her body had been treated respectfully, sent back to her family along with suitable compensation. But even in the grave, she was not left in peace; she had been given a new role. She would play the part of Prisca Benedict, in death as she had in life.

"A valuable thing," was all the young woman said, and then she opened the scarlet folding fan in her hand with a *crack*. She'd taken it from her repulsive older sister—and now she fanned herself with it as she turned toward the old woman and the servants waiting behind her. And finally...

"Princess..."

"How many times must I tell you not to call me that? The princess who bore that title died pathetically. Tragically, perhaps, but it was only what she deserved for her inability to leaven the anxieties of her followers. The one before you now is... Hmph. What was it again?" The girl tilted her head in curiosity.

The old woman closed her eyes, and after a beat, she answered, "Priscilla."

"Yes, that's it." The girl nodded slowly and closed the fan with a *snap*. Her older sister always used to tuck it away amid her cleavage— and the girl couldn't do that, but perhaps in the near future, she might become able to. For she was alive. And as long as one was alive, there was a future. In which case...

"That means we can continue. After all..."

She looked up at the sky. Hovering in the almost disgustingly blue heavens, the sun burned so bright, it nearly seemed scarlet. She reached out a hand as if to grasp it, and she could still feel the warmth of the Bright Sword against her palm.

Comforted by the heat, the girl—Priscilla—smiled and said:

"...the world bends itself to suit me."

THE SCARLET SWORDWOLF

1

Everyone finds a death match entertaining when it isn't their life on the line.

That might sound like an extreme statement, but from where *he* was standing, it had a distinct ring of truth. It wasn't something to be laughed off as a silly exaggeration.

He heard wild cheering from overhead as he rolled back across the hard ground. The cheering turned to jeering at his cack-handed escape, but he didn't give a shit.

"After all, I'm the one risking my goddamn life here!" he spat—along with some phlegm—before he brought the huge sword in his right hand up in front of him. It was enough to check his opponent, who had been about to follow up with a bare-handed blow. The pale, bald man coming at him adopted a lazy posture, both arms dangling as he sneered.

The bald man held no weapons, an unusual choice around these parts. But in one sense, something much worse than any sword or spear resided in the man's swaying arms.

There was a technique called the Poison Hand. A means of murder that involved soaking one's hand in poison, storing it up until just before the point of death. Eventually, the impregnated toxin gathered in the fingernails, meaning the slightest scratch could kill an enemy. The bald man's purplish-red fingers and nails were the evidence that he possessed this technique.

"Looks like we've got a shinobi who screwed up some important murder." The hands, and the man's unflinching readiness to kill, were enough to guess at his background.

Shinobi were killers who had undergone the most rigorous possible training and submitted to unimaginable augmentation of their bodies. Some people doubted they really existed—said they were just an urban legend—but if so, they were an urban legend worth believing in. They were hired by the great and powerful as elite troops in the game of kill-or-be-killed that such people lived in. No telling how this one had ended up here, but now he was trapped, just like the rest of them.

For this was…

"A disgusting little hole called Ginonhive, the sword-slave island, where its captives are forced to fight each other."

The sword slaves were literally enslaved—and this was the status of the two men fighting at the moment. The words represented the lowest of the low; every day, much of their blood was spilled, many of their bones broken, and many of their lives lost. And this, the so-called sword-slave island, where these fights to the death passed for entertainment, was the perfect place for the awful crowds of imperial subjects to slake their bloodlust. It was the kind of place one would naturally expect to find in a land as thoroughly brutal as the Volakian Empire.

"Not that it makes it any better to have them pulling our strings!" the man growled, standing slowly, the heavy sword in one hand. The weight of the weapon meant it didn't lend itself to being swung around one-handed for very long—but sadly, the man had no choice save to rely on his right hand to do the fighting.

For his left, which might otherwise have helped it, was gone.

"——" His long, wild hair was tied back behind his head, so that he could glare at his opponent with eyes that some called evil. It was all he could do to keep the enemy at bay. The one-armed man let out a sigh. It wasn't as if the arm was a recent loss. It had happened in the distant past, and he'd long since adapted to how it impacted his balance. Even so, when he fought opponents whom he had to be careful around, like this one, it still sometimes felt like a heavy burden to him.

"Which means I can't be draggin' this out," he said. "How about it, Mr. Might-Be-a-Shinobi? What say we work together to forfeit this game?"

"Forfeit…?"

"Hoh, interested, are ya?"

The man with the Poison Hand warily raised an eyebrow. Sensing his chance, the one-armed man plowed ahead. "It's easy: I keep runnin' from you, and you keep attacking me, but you don't hit me. That goes on for a while, the spectators and the owner are gonna start getting restless. Chances are, they've got a demon beast or something on hand that they'll send in to get things going. And then we don't have to fight each other, just the creature."

"And if we defeat it together, we survive today—is that what you're saying?"

"Yeah, that's the idea! Aw, it's great to find a guy I can talk to for onc— Hgggh?!" Just as the one-armed man was grinning and thinking what an easy conversation this was turning out to be, Poison Hand lashed out with his sharp nails. The one-armed man just managed to dodge, rolling backward to gain himself some distance from his foe.

The bald man sneered at him. "Don't be stupid," he said. "Work with you to fight a demon beast? And maybe getting myself killed in the process? Anyone with a choice between a one-armed man and a demon beast would pick the cripple. I'm no different."

"Hey, look, I know how you feel, all right? But as a fellow human being…"

"Besides, this is my chance to show off the skills I've honed. And I can't stand when someone stops me from having my fun."

"Oh! Sorry. I didn't realize you were one of those natural-born killers. Guess we just look at things too differently to see eye to eye, then." He would have liked to scratch his head with sheer embarrassment, but the moment he lowered his arm, his only guard, a finishing blow would have come his way. He settled for a sigh—and then his opponent's Poison Hand twitched.

He felt it coming—or rather, he knew it was coming. It would start with the venomous right hand, and if he dodged that, the man would strike with the left— No, he would only appear to. It would be a feint. He would come up with his leg—his trump card wasn't a Poison Hand, but a Poison Foot. All very complicated.

But a trick couldn't surprise you anymore if you knew how it was done.

"—!" With a sharp breath, the one-armed man dodged his attacker's right hook, but even as he saw the left arm move at the edge of his vision, he was bringing his sword up to meet the man's spinning leg. The blade bit into the leg just at the knee, severing it and spraying dark blood everywhere. A few drops spattered on the one-armed man, who had to hope that at least his enemy's blood wasn't toxic.

"Just bad luck...or should I say, a bad star," the one-armed man said, and then the loser's head went arcing high up through the air, still wearing an expression of disbelief.

2

"Another close shave today, huh?"

"Hey, I'd love some easier wins. But these old bones have seen more than thirty years, and with just one arm, these clumsy little victories are the best I can manage."

The one-armed man retreated from the arena, which was still echoing with cheers, through a passageway reserved for the sword slaves. He was met by one of the guards—jailers, really—who were stationed around the colosseum. They were in charge of overseeing the slaves who provided the entertainment, and the fighters sometimes affectionately referred to them as slavers.

Many of the guards treated the slaves with contempt, but this one, Orlan, was unusual in that he was almost friendly with the fighters. What with his genial attitude, it was seriously questionable whether he was fit for guard duty, but he was evidently good enough at it that he'd remained at his post for the last several years, and he and the one-armed man had something of an acquaintance going. In fact, they were almost less like guard and sword slave than they were like friends.

"Here ya go," the one-armed man said, tossing his blood-soaked weapon to Orlan. The sword slaves were not allowed to carry weapons except in the arena proper, and everywhere outside the fighting grounds, they were required to wear handcuffs. Even if such restraints were purely decorative on a one-armed person.

"Okay, cuffs are on," Orlan said. Then he added, "You know, I'm glad you survived today. Maybe it's not my place to mention, but there were some ugly rumors about that guy you were fighting. He grabbed a couple of guards by the arm, and they both died. Everyone claimed it was an accident, but..."

"But a Poison Hand user having an 'accident' is pretty much like saying he cut off their heads with his own weapon, isn't it?"

"You said it. But we don't get many of his kind through here. He was too big a draw to ask any questions. Gah, guards' lives are as cheap as sword slaves' here. Don't tell anyone I said any of that, hey?" Orlan smiled thinly; he really wasn't cut out for guard work. Or maybe it wasn't guard work that didn't suit him—maybe it was Ginonhive. Maybe the whole Volakian Empire.

The empire prized tangible virtues: unshakable conviction and the willingness to put one's life on the line in a fight. Bleeding hearts and bountiful compassion earned no respect here. It could be hard to live with people who possessed such a rigid view of the world. But that was the Holy Volakian Empire.

"Well, still gotta be better than being a sword slave like me!"

"That's not funny... Oh, hey, I'm not trying to say the only reason I'm glad you won is because the other guy was a jerk. It's also because you're pretty decent yourself."

"Hey, watch it. You get too mushy, you're gonna end up going down *my* route!"

"What do you mean, 'route'?"

"Ah, never mind. Let's just get out of here." The one-armed man smacked Orlan, still confused by the unfamiliar vocabulary, clapping a hand on his shoulder as he tried to get them moving. For one thing, he wasn't that interested in standing around shooting the breeze, but for another, this passageway led to the arena. Which meant that eventually, the fighters for the next match would be coming through it…

"Ohhh my. I was just wondering who could be flitting about here—if it isn't my sweet little Al."

"Ugh…"

This was exactly what he'd been hoping to avoid—a run-in with the next competitor. Al felt his mouth twist into a scowl.

"Oh my, oh my, oh my," the new fighter said when she saw it, her voice tinkling like a bell. She came up to him looking like she was having a grand old time, her long, tall body swaying as she walked. "'Ugh,' he says! How positively *mean*! And here I thought we were friends…"

"Gimme a break. I'd have no end of trouble on my hands if I went around claiming I was friends with you. The best thing you could call us is acquaintances who occasionally stand and chat."

"Hee-hee-hee! You do say the funniest things, my sweet." The woman with the rather beautiful smile and laugh was tall, with close-cropped dark hair. Indeed, she was uncommonly tall for this world at over six feet. She was blessed with a perfect figure, curves right where a woman would want them, and she displayed them proudly with an outfit that showed plenty of skin. Combined with her angular face, it all made her look like a sculpture escaped from an art museum.

But there was something about her that was far more memorable than even her striking appearance: her arms. So far from being as long as her tall body would suggest, neither of them extended below the elbow.

Thus, she faced an even greater disadvantage than Al with his one arm, yet she was the flower that had bloomed against this adversity. Spectators didn't shout and jeer at her from the front row; instead, she enraptured all of them. She herself was the main event here on the sword-slave island of Ginonhive.

"I'm grateful to ya, Hornet, I really am, but let's think about our respective positions here. If a little ant like me stood next to you, I'd get blown away."

"Oh, *please* don't say things like that. You'll make me sad. You're my very, veeery best friend, after all."

"Veeery best, huh? I guess that means all the others are dead."

"Tee-hee-hee!"

With turnover as high as it was on this island, one could rise through the ranks of sword-slave life with startling alacrity. The fact that the Hornet didn't contradict Al was somehow endearing.

Between her unforgettable appearance, the way she talked, and the way she behaved, the Hornet had a way of grabbing people's attention and never letting go. She was indeed like her namesake; two or three stings of her venom and your life might be over. Compared with a toxin like that, the Poison Hand that Al had fought a few minutes earlier was like child's play.

"Mistress Hornet, it's almost time…"

"Oh, I know. If you please?"

It was, believe it or not, one of the guards addressing her in this deferential tone. Orlan's colleague knelt in front of her and removed the foot shackles she wore in lieu of handcuffs. But the gesture was that of a man bowing before his queen.

This innate capacity to make others grovel before her was where she had earned her nickname, the Empress of the Sword Slaves.

"Well, I hope you have another of your lovely, elegant fights, eh?" Al ribbed her. That earned him a glare from the guard attending the Hornet. "Ooh, scary," he said. The guard had become the Hornet's man down to the bone—he probably wouldn't have hesitated to attack Al if she'd told him to. However, she stopped him instead.

"Don't be silly. Come, dear, my arms."

"Yes, ma'am." Still kneeling, the guard gave a nod, and from down the hallway appeared a low-ranking jailer, his face covered with a scarf, pulling a cart that bore two massive swords. Each was nearly as long as a grown adult was tall, but the hilts were very strangely shaped. That was only natural, as these weapons were exclusively for the Hornet's use.

"Aaaand here we go!" the Hornet said languorously, turning her foreshortened arms toward the swords. The stumps fit neatly into the empty hilts, settling in with an audible *click*. Then the woman's muscles tautened, and she hefted the huge blades easily, even though each appeared to weigh more than two hundred pounds. An ordinary person wouldn't even have been able to lift one, let alone handle two of them at the same time. That was what made her style absolutely unique—and what made her the strongest fighter on the sword-slave island.

"Won't you at least watch me fight before you go, Al, sweetie? Pretty please? You're already here. I want to dedicate my victory today to you and you alone."

"Thanks but no thanks!" He couldn't resist another snipe despite the continued glaring of the Hornet's guard. Even at that, though, the Hornet smiled again and walked past him into the arena. A moment later, there was a loud cheer; she had entered the ring, and the crowd was going wild.

"A'right. I'm going to head back underground and get some sleep."

"Wha…?! How dare you, ignoring Mistress Hornet like that!" the guard snapped.

"The hell are you talking about? I told her to her face I wasn't going to watch. She *smiled* about it. That's a good enough answer for me. Am I wrong?" Al gave the angry guard a good, hard glare of his own and watched as the man flinched back, overawed.

He was fresh from a fight—just finished risking his life. Apparently, it was enough to make even his blood hot. The guard had seen the Hornet grin and let Al's comment pass, so he hardly had grounds to press the matter. He could only stay silent, even if he didn't seem very happy about it.

"Holy hell, does she know how to keep you on your toes! She hardly acts like a sword slave, does she?" Al said. As he walked past the Hornet's silenced attendant, away from the arena, Orlan fell in beside him. He had practically made himself invisible from the moment the Hornet had appeared, and it had been the right choice.

For better or for worse, the best thing you could do for yourself was never to run into the Hornet. If she took an interest in you, it was a dangerous thing—and if she didn't, it wasn't particularly safer. That was an unspoken rule here on the island.

"Hey, at least she seems to like you all right, Aldeberan," Orlan said without malice.

"Give me a break, Orlan. And I thought I told you..." The one-armed man, Aldeberan, winked at the guard. "Call me Al. You know I hate my full name."

3

The sword-slave island, Ginonhive, lay in the western reaches of the Volakian Empire, so thoroughly surrounded by a lake that it could very well have been called the island of unrelenting water.

The only way to reach the island was a single bridge—specifically, a drawbridge that was usually kept raised and impassable. Admittance to the island—as well as departure from it—was strictly controlled, and the reason for this near-total isolation of those on the island was quite simple: The sword slaves could not be allowed to leave.

The sword slaves were exactly what the name implied: slaves who were allowed to have swords. However, such possession was permitted only during their death matches in the arena at the center of the island, matches staged for the amusement of spectators who came from outside. Put in the frankest of terms, the island was home to a twisted spectacle in which the slaves were put on display as they killed one another.

Most of the sword slaves were either criminals or people who had been left with no choice but to sell themselves into this life when they had been unable to repay a debt. Every once in a great while, though, some unlucky person with nowhere to go would be caught and brought here. Wherever they may have hailed from, once they had fallen to the station of sword slave, they each wanted one and the same thing: to survive one more day by killing their opponents. That was all.

"I've been thinking, Al. You really think we can go on like this?"

Underground beneath the island were living quarters where the sword slaves boarded. *"Living"* was a relative term, however; there were no conveniences or considerate touches that might make the place more welcoming. It was just a space in which the slaves could exist.

Each of them claimed a place to camp out down there, then passed the idle hours until they were led away to fight again. Al was no exception.

He had just been lying in his bed, grateful to have made it there another day...

"Hey, Al? Are you listening? Helloooo, Al!"

"——" He frowned at the man's syrupy sweet voice and rolled over on the hard floor. Putting his back to the other person was supposed to signal that he wasn't interested in talking, but the man didn't seem to take the hint.

"Hey, come on," he said, shaking Al's shoulder. "I'm telling you, you have to listen. I'm talking about something really important!"

"I'm not listening, and would it kill ya to sympathize with a guy? I just wrapped up a job, and I'm tired. I want to go to sleep. It's my only damn pleasure."

"This again? You know there are things to enjoy on this island besides sleeping. After all, you're very popular, Al." The man grinned and gestured with his chin at some figures who could just be seen in the distance. They were women in provocative clothing, and though they were officially sword slaves themselves, they served as the island's prostitutes. They were never—well, almost never—summoned to fight in the arena, but instead, they were expected to make themselves available as an outlet for the other sword slaves.

The idea of being "popular" with them was more credit than Al would ever give himself...

"Ugh," was all he said.

"Wah! Al, you can't— That's just too rude! These are beautiful women we're talking about! Neither of you has a better job than the other!"

"I'm not discriminating because of what they do. It's...like, a feelings sorta thing." Al scowled, fighting down the nauseous feeling that accompanied this flurry of criticism.

He could grab the women and play games with them, sure. They would wave to him, smile, each of them looking for her next trick. Some of them were broken by the tricks they found. These were women who were given no kindness. But even in this place, they were trying to live as best they could. Who was he to treat them as less than him?

"You're not very comfortable around women, yet you're always respectful toward them. No wonder they like you, Al."

"They just don't have a lot of choices. If they had more options, they wouldn't give a second look at a run-down old fart like me."

"Hoh-hoh, ain't mincing words! But that's one of the things I like about you, Al." The outrageously gorgeous man smiled at him. Al sighed, not sure what to do with the man's ingratiating attitude.

The pretty boy with the long gray hair—Ubirk was his name—had been brought to Ginonhive as a sword slave five years before. He was slim and pretty—but not exceptionally talented. In fact, he was about as unsuitable for fighting as they came; it was obvious that he would be trampled into the dust after no more than a few minutes in the arena. So how had he survived five years here? The same way as those women.

The Hornet might have been the most noted of the female sword slaves, but no small number of women proved capable fighters in the ring. Ubirk's job was to keep a number of them fulfilled, just as the female prostitutes did for many of the male sword slaves. His abilities in *that* regard were what had kept him alive this long.

"So, Al, to get back to what I was saying..."

"Didn't you hear me? I'm not in the mood for a chat."

"Oh, don't be like that. I have a special invitation direct from the Empress herself."

"Then I'm even *less* interested." Al gave an exaggerated frown; that was a face he didn't want to see and a name he didn't want to hear for a while.

Ubirk grinned at that. "Wow, you're talking about the Hornet like that! Nothing scares you, does it, Al?"

"Don't be ridiculous. You saw me a few minutes ago. I'm terrified of women. Which obviously includes the Hornet. QED."

"*Kyooo eee...* What? Another of those funny words from your homeland, Al? I never do understand what they mean!" Ubirk tilted his head, trying to grasp Al's unusual vocabulary.

Al had no intention of going out of his way to explain. Ubirk, perfectly accustomed to this behavior, didn't press the matter. Unfortunately for Al, that didn't mean he was done talking.

"Come on, just listen. Otherwise, the Hornet might crush me the next time she makes love to me. And wouldn't you feel really guilty about that?"

"Oh, for the love of... If I listen to you, do you promise not to bother me during my sleeping time? If you can manage that, I'll give you a few minutes to talk."

"Ha-ha! You're such a nice guy, Al. It's such a shame you can't handle women."

"Shaddap," Al growled, dismissing Ubirk's teasing and demanding he hurry up and talk in the same breath.

Finally, Ubirk got to his point. Namely: "Rumor has it there's going to be a major event happening here at the arena very soon. Bigwigs from all over the empire are going to be there."

"Really? They haven't done that in years. Why now?"

"It's 'cause... You know. The Volakian emperor died, and we've got a new one now. In other words, all the imperial candidates are dead."

"They're all dead, so we've got a new emperor? Oh, you mean the last surviving candidate becomes emperor. Yeah, I guess that would mean the others are gone."

Ubirk's explanation left something to be desired, but Al was wise enough to figure out what he meant. He winked silently.

Even here on this isolated island, they'd heard of the death of the Holy Volakian Emperor and the so-called Rite of Imperial Selection, which was conducted to choose his successor. Whatever this upcoming event was, it must be intended as a celebration of the new ruler.

"None of 'em probably like each other very much, but I guess even they throw a party at times like this. I'm betting it's not very good news for the likes of us, though."

"A ten-year sword slave just has a different level of experience, doesn't he? You have my respect!" Ubirk said, half earnestly and half sarcastically.

Al gave a click of his tongue. "Stop it. Thinking about all my 'experience' is only gonna make me depressed."

Reflecting on examples from his past, Al knew that the celebration of a new emperor was likely to involve death matches of some "special" variety. The usual one-on-one rules would be modified or done away with. In at least one case, ten slaves had been pitted against a massive demon beast caught especially for the spectacle.

"The fight against that mountain of a magic beast four years ago… That was the hardest. Without the Hornet, we would all have bought it right then and there. The horns from that thing are still decorating the hall."

"Truly, a battle to inspire legends. Too bad you and the Hornet were the only ones to survive it."

"Yeah, and it's what made the Hornet start paying attention to me."

Until that point, she'd regarded him as hopeless small fry, but his lucky survival of that hellish encounter had piqued her interest, much to Al's chagrin. Now she tried to involve herself with him every time they passed each other. She was truly the author of his worst nightmares.

And yet it wasn't as if he owed her nothing—she was the reason he *had* survived that brutal battle four years earlier.

"But sometimes, when ya can't cope, ya can't cope. So what is it? What does the Hornet want?"

"Nothing complicated, I promise. This is going to be a big, special event, so lots of people who don't normally come will be here. And *that* means..."

"——" Al didn't say anything.

Ubirk dropped his voice to a whisper. "We might just be able to take someone important hostage, maybe even a high count or better. Then we can demand our freedom!"

Al winced again. Audacious as that might sound, it was old hat to him. "You guys really don't know when to give up, do you? How many times have you kicked that idea around?"

This wasn't the first time Ubirk had brought this extraordinarily unlikely fantasy to him, and Al was starting to get tired of it.

Ubirk wasn't alone; many of the sword slaves on this island were secretly plotting their bids for freedom. As long as they were here, no sword slave was assured that the next day would come. It was the most natural thing in the world to wish for freedom. And yet...

"I guarantee you that hundreds, maybe thousands of people have dreamed that dream before you. And you know how many have escaped? Not a single one. It's a ridiculous, impossible idea, getting away from here."

"Believe me, I know. But that's because they didn't plan well enough, or they didn't pull it off right. Those plans were always going to fail, and they failed."

"I guess that's one way of looking at it." Al didn't disagree with Ubirk, but everyone thought in terms of ideals when they were planning. Ubirk's argument wasn't enough to overcome Al's inertia on the subject. "Anyway, I can't see the Hornet ever actually agreeing to that sort of bullshit. The Empress *likes* it here. She's a berserker. Lives for the fight."

The Hornet lived without impediment and wanted for nothing; she had found a place where she could fulfill her every whim. Al couldn't see why she would relinquish such exceptional treatment. Which, in turn, made the whole idea that this invitation came from the Hornet deeply suspicious.

"I'm on to you. You apologize right now, I might just forgive you," Al said.

"Ha-ha-ha-ha! No good, huh? The Hornet seems to like you, Al, so I thought maybe if you could talk her around… Ouch!"

"I only said I *might* forgive ya." Al rapped the guileless-looking Ubirk on the head with a knuckle, causing his eyes to brim with tears, then swept him out of the way.

Al was substantially worse off now than he had been before indulging Ubirk's little chat. Nonetheless, it was probably worth paying attention to the fact that there would be a major event here on the island, and soon. Especially considering how many such events he had suffered through in the past, how many times he had been sure he was going to die.

"That's exactly why we need to push through this difficult moment and—"

"Get out of here already! Next time, I'll hit ya for real!" Al brandished his fist at the ever-persistent Ubirk, intent on being rid of the little jinx for good.

Ubirk could talk, but there was no way he really believed his plans for escape would ever work. It was a dream no sword slave would ever realize, a wish that would never come true.

And Al had spent enough time on futile dreams.

He'd been a slave on this island for more than ten years now. It had become the only life he could imagine.

4

The tension in the room made the old servant's muscles so tense that they almost creaked. For the ancient butler, this life of service to others had been a gift. He had worked for the Pendleton family for more than fifty years, since the time of the parents of the current head of the household. And even if he hadn't owed his master such a great debt, there was still the sense of intimacy that came from having watched him grow up. All of which was to say that the butler wished nothing but happiness for his master.

And yet…

"Hmm…"

A hand picked up the cup that the butler had set out, a finely shaped nose taking a sniff of the contents. He was sure he'd gotten the basics right—how long to steep the leaves, the temperature of the water, and every other detail. The extent of his dedication might have seemed surprising, but the taste of the tea could change dramatically with the slightest variation in any number of factors.

An eye, bright with both beauty and knowledge of all these things, studied his work intently. Would he be able to please its owner? That was the challenge that possessed every member of the household now. Work better and work harder in order to show proper respect to their master. It didn't exactly bother the butler, but perhaps he took exception to the cup's beholder.

"May I ask how you find it, Mistress?" The butler didn't rise from his bow.

"I'm willing to accept the aroma. Which just leaves the flavor. Let's see, now…" The speaker was the second most important person in the household after the master: the spouse of Jorah Pendleton, whom the butler had served for so long.

"___"

Cherry-colored lips kissed the rim of the cup. The butler watched the woman's profile as she sipped the dark tea. He smiled at the sight. His master had gone so long without a decent prospect—now, at last, at his advanced age, he was blessed with his first marriage. It was a joyous occasion. Even if his wife was a scant twelve years old.

Age gaps were hardly unusual in marriages among nobles, and loveless unions were practically de rigueur as a way of solidifying connections between houses. But for a man of more than fifty to welcome a bride of twelve—even this long-serving butler found himself taken aback. Not least because this particular wife seemed to offer no advantages at all.

At the same time, Jorah's basic decency was beyond doubt. He possessed that rarest of things among the empire's elite—kindness—and it was more than enough to inspire unflinching loyalty in the butler. That loyalty moved him to try to help the young woman in every way he could, knowing she would be quite overwhelmed by her new environment. Yes, the butler welcomed his master's young spouse with his own firm resolve.

That resolve had quickly crumbled in the face of the woman herself.

Yes, the girl was twelve years old. Yes, she'd come to Jorah's mansion young and with no household of her own. But she was arrestingly beautiful, and her soul burned more intensely than any fire.

Priscilla. That was the name of the forceful young woman who had appeared in this home like a conqueror. Priscilla Pendleton.

"Not bad," the girl said, her voice emanating from her pale throat in a way that seemed to penetrate deep into the listener's brain. It took the butler a moment to realize this was her appraisal of the tea. The reason for his belated understanding was simple: the girl's face. Nothing in particular had happened or changed—she was simply so beautiful that he had been captivated; it had felt as if time had stopped.

And when time resumed flowing, and the butler realized she had spoken words of praise, he shivered. This girl, whose age didn't amount to one half of one half of his own years, made his blood seem to run faster with her compliment; a feeling of paralysis gripped his very soul.

Being a butler at all was like a gift from the heavens to these old bones. It was only natural, perhaps, that such a person should bow before a girl like this, someone who was obviously a born ruler. For to serve someone meant to be dominated by someone.

"Withdraw. I wish to speak with my husband."

"Yes, ma'am." Without a second thought, the butler bowed and backed out of the room. He wondered if she might not take just one more sip of the tea as he was leaving. He wondered if the youthful conqueror wouldn't mind putting that seal of approval on his work.

The hope almost physically burned in the old butler as he silently left the room.

When the butler had withdrawn and they were alone, a thin voice spoke: "It seems you have everyone quite under your thumb, Priscilla." The voice's owner was an old man who sat in the seat farthest from the door—the most important seat in the room, for what it was worth. He looked listless, and his hair was beginning to go white, but he was the master of this house—Jorah Pendleton.

As a count in the Holy Volakian Empire, one could say this man had been fortunate in status and family background. At the moment, Jorah's awkward gaze rested on a beautiful girl with eyes the color of blood and bright-orange hair held back by a hair clip worked with a jewel—Priscilla.

The way Jorah started the conversation suggested that the gap in ages wasn't the only thing that separated the couple.

Priscilla responded to her husband's hesitant approach with a "Bah" and a loud sniff. "Don't speak to me in that cringing, raspy way. I can barely tell the difference between your voice and a faint breeze. Or wait—*was* that a breeze I heard just now?"

"N-no, no, it wasn't. It was me talking... I simply meant that you seem to be getting along well with the servants."

"Hmph. If that's what you think, it only proves how blind you really are."

"What?" Jorah said, his eyes widening.

Priscilla met her husband's ridiculous reaction with a look of exasperation. "Listen. The relationship between me and them is not one of *getting along*. They simply obey me. They know of no other way to live except to bow and scrape and serve. All I need to do is give them some instructions, and they wag their tails happily."

"I—I see...I think..."

"If anything, I'm surprised you managed to hold on to such passable help for so long."

"Hold on to…? I'm sorry. I'm afraid I don't quite follow…"

Priscilla's one open eye grew even sharper at Jorah's continued gibbering, but even with the heat of her gaze concentrated upon him, he showed no sign of changing his behavior.

"—You are ever more inscrutable. What I'm saying is that you seem to lack the desires and the motivations that almost every person naturally has. I'm not saying I've never encountered such people before. But…"

"Y-yes?" Jorah stammered.

"…that being the case, I continue to fail to understand why you took me as your wife." Priscilla also continued to stare at him, hard.

The generous way to describe Jorah's disposition would have been to say that he was a good-hearted man. The less generous way was that he was a coward who lacked either backbone or any spirit of adventure. He was perfectly happy to walk well-trodden paths, never veering off into the untamed wilderness.

He might not be very interesting, but he was steadfast and reliable— difficult qualities to find here in the empire, which so prized lives of untrammeled intensity. Jorah was often mocked as weak-willed, and perhaps that was why he'd gone so long without a wife.

Jorah Pendleton lived by simple precepts: He sought no adventure, and he didn't gamble. Yet his marriage to Priscilla seemed to go against both those principles. It was, perhaps, the biggest gamble of all. For…

"I know you're aware of my true identity. I'm Prisca Benedict, a young woman who was supposed to have died during the Rite of Imperial Selection."

She uttered the name of a member of the royal family who had been defeated in the bloody contest to determine the next emperor of Volakia and had supposedly died as a result.

But Prisca had not died. After feigning her death, she still lived. Not under her real name, but with an assumed identity as a young woman named Priscilla Pendleton who was still learning how to navigate polite society. Many people had given everything to ensure that the girl survived—but when Priscilla wedded Jorah, she hadn't hidden any of this from him.

Of course, if he had refused her, knowing what he knew, it was highly unlikely Priscilla would have let him live. So in a way, her telling him the truth was an unspeakable disaster for Jorah. But that didn't change the fact that, despite knowing the circumstances, he had still agreed to marry Priscilla. Why was that? Even Priscilla, who'd had the old butler bowing and indulging her every whim practically within moments, couldn't seem to solve the riddle of Jorah's true motives.

"——" Jorah looked moderately surprised, but then his lips softened into a slight smile, a gentle expression such as one might give to a small child who couldn't figure out the answer to a question.

"You may be my husband, but that does not give you the right to humiliate me with a look like that," Priscilla said.

"P-pardon me. I just... Until now, you've carried yourself like a young sage, always seeing through everything. It surprised me to realize..."

"Realize what?"

"...that sometimes you do act your age." From Jorah's perspective, the remark was a substantial gamble in and of itself. He seemed to be privately considering the possibility that he would get his head knocked clean off. "You n-needn't worry. I don't intend to use you or expose you or any such thing. On that point, I am absolutely sincere."

"Very well," Priscilla said after a moment. "It wouldn't have mattered what you were planning anyway. For this world bends itself to suit me."

"——"

Jorah didn't answer. One might characterize Priscilla's philosophy as a belief in fate or perhaps destiny. As soon as the words had left her mouth, Jorah's expression softened once more. Before Priscilla could remark on it, however—

"Forgive me, Master," said the butler, reentering the room with a knock at the door. It was wrong of him to interrupt the master and mistress of the house when they were having a private conversation, and a man of such long service ought to have known better. The reason for his indiscretion was explained by the report he gave them: "We have visitors from High Countess Delacroix."

"The high countess? I haven't heard anything about that," Jorah said with a frown, but then he exclaimed, "Priscilla?!" For his wife was already up and striding out of the room. She didn't slow down despite her husband's shout, instead making straight for the mansion's entry hall.

When she appeared in the hallway, she was greeted by a drawl: "Well, now. That's one cute young lady who's found us." The words came from a slim young man Priscilla didn't recognize; she arched an eyebrow in response. The young man was still just perhaps seventeen or eighteen, and he clutched a thin package. He waved at Priscilla with a friendly smile on his face. "You Count Pendleton's little girl? Is your daddy home toda—?"

"Bal, ya blathering idiot! Count Pendleton doesn't *have* a daughter! Don't get ahead of yourself!" A smaller man standing beside the chatty newcomer gave him a sound smack on the back of the head.

"Yowch!" the young man yelped, the strike producing an audible *whack*. "Miles, Brother, what'd ya do that for?! I know my head's empty, but it'd still be bad news if you cracked it open!"

"Pipe down! If your head's empty, then go fill it up before you show your face around here again! And don't go dragging *me* into your stupid screwups!"

"Screwups?! Just what exactly are you referring to? What do you think I did wrong?"

"Count Pendleton only just married a young wife! So use that empty head of yours and try to think! We come to the manor of Count Pendleton, who *doesn't have a daughter*, and a young lady appears…"

"Oh! I get it." Finally connecting the dots, the young man nodded and ran a hand through his auburn hair.

"Took ya long enough," the little man grumbled, shrugging as if he was exhausted. "Two things you always were—slow, and a handful.

If I hadn't been stuck with you since you were a tot, Bal, I swear I'd have cut you loose ages ago…"

"Believe me, Brother, I owe you lots. But haven't you made a little mistake yourself?"

"Eh? What did I—? Oh!" At this moment in the conversation, the little man noticed the person who had inspired the entire argument and stiffened.

But all well and good. Priscilla—the topic at hand—had been listening to the exchange without a word. As the two visitors turned toward her, she shrugged with her slim shoulders and said, "What's the matter? Go on. Don't mind me. Watching two clowns argue is proving quite an amusing spectacle. Go on, go ahead."

"Grrr… Played like a goddamn instrument by a little girl…"

"Careful, Brother, your language is getting worse. How about we start by apologizing?"

"*Grrr…*"

The pair started shaking at Priscilla's words. She hadn't specifically been seeking to ridicule them, but she was disappointed to have to relinquish these entertaining jesters, who seemed likely to jump and squirm at anything she said.

"P-Priscilla, these are my guests. Please don't have too much fun at their expense…"

"Hrmph. Finally caught up, did you?" Priscilla said, interrupted in the act of deciding what to say next by Jorah's arrival.

"Ah," the count said, raising an eyebrow slightly at the pair facing his wife. "I was told messengers from High Countess Delacroix were here. I didn't realize that meant you, Miles."

"Count Pendleton! It's been too long, much too long," said the small man whose name was Miles, evidently an acquaintance of Priscilla's husband. He knelt before Jorah, and the young man beside him hurriedly followed suit.

"Who's this?" Jorah asked, observing the noticeably less experienced of the two messengers. "I don't recognize him. A newcomer?"

"Yes indeed. A friend of mine from way back. High Countess Delacroix was kind enough to give him a job to do. You see, he has

an all too rare ability as a sky-dragon tamer." He nudged the young man. "Introduce yourself!"

"Sure thing, Brother. Introducing myself!" The young man looked at Jorah, and Priscilla observed that her husband was nearly overwhelmed by the directness of his gaze. She smiled to see such forcefulness in a look. The young man might hide it behind his easygoing manner, but he might just be something special.

Completely unaware of Priscilla's evaluation of him, the young man placed a hand on his chest and said, "A pleasure to meet ya. My name is Balleroy Temeglyph. My big bro Miles here has been taking care of me since I was a kid—and he still does, as you can see."

"I do. Miles always was good at looking out for others. And this sky-dragon tamer business, you...?"

"Yessir. I have a real spirited one entrusted to my care." Balleroy's broad smile seemed to suggest he knew no fear—but with this final remark, the character of his expression changed. Inappropriate though it might have been, the smile became one of self-confidence.

"As I recall, the ability to tame sky dragons is a secret art passed down among certain families," Priscilla said. "A way of gaining the services of a sky dragon, creatures not otherwise known for being very fond of people."

"That's right, miss. You really know your stuff. You may be little, but you must have studied hard— Owowow!"

"You're the one who needs to study! About how to have some damn manners!" Incensed by how quickly Balleroy let any semblance of propriety fall away, Miles gave the tall man a solid pinch on the behind, his own language taking a step down the politeness scale in the process.

"Please, please," Jorah interjected. "You needn't let such minor matters upset you so. I should have introduced her sooner. This is Priscilla Pendleton... That is, ahem, my wife."

Priscilla snorted at the idea that this was the best Jorah could do by way of introduction. "Imagine, a man in his fifties getting tongue-tied introducing his wife. Stand up straight and speak with confidence! You're the luckiest man in the world. For you are blessed with *me* for your spouse!" Jorah could only smile awkwardly, while Balleroy and Miles looked on, their eyes slightly wide.

"Goodness gracious! Ya know, this struck me when we were chatting earlier, but that's a feisty wife you've got there, Count Pendleton."

"Yes, I'm afraid I'm quite at her mercy..."

"Fool. All the more reason to consider yourself honored, then. And you, you common cur, I won't be described with such trivial words as *feisty*." She paused. "Hmm. No, perhaps the word *common* doesn't quite fit you."

"Er, should I take that as a compliment?" Balleroy said, looking at Jorah questioningly, but the count only smiled fondly but awkwardly; he certainly didn't have the reins of his new wife.

It was Miles, having been silent for some time, who finally broke the impasse. "Right. Ahem, Count Pendleton, we come with a message from our mistress. May we deliver it to you?"

"Oh, of course, sorry to keep you waiting. Word from Serena? What does she say?"

"I think it's about the sword-slave island," Balleroy volunteered.

"The sword-slave island... Yes, I suppose that did come up," Jorah said, taking the sealed letter and scanning the contents. He let out a breath. He didn't seem very happy about the idea of the island.

"The sword-slave island...Ginonhive. You know, I don't believe I've ever been there," Priscilla said.

"Hoh! Interested, missus?" Balleroy asked. "Aw, y'know, I've always wanted to see the place myself, so this is great news!"

"Hmm. Am I to gather that your mistress intends to invite my no-account husband to the sword-slave island?"

"Mm-hmm, I'd say that's about the size of it," Balleroy confirmed. Priscilla was very quick on the uptake. Miles, though, looked annoyed by the exchange between his "younger brother" and Priscilla. "Say, Miles, what's the matter?" Balleroy asked.

"I'm wondering why we even bothered bringing a letter..."

He certainly seemed to have his hands full with this so-called younger brother. But maybe that was just the way it was. "If you pour in more water than your vessel can handle, of course it's going to overflow," Priscilla observed. "If you wish for it not to spill, you must constantly sip from it. And even then, it may run over."

"I'll remember that," Miles said. He seemed quick-witted enough. The fact that he didn't dismiss Priscilla's words as the jabbering of a little girl showed well why he had Balleroy's respect.

All that remained was the response to the message.

"I'm very pleased to receive High Countess Delacroix's invitation," Jorah said. "However, I'm afraid things are quite busy here, so I'm going to have to—"

"Just ignore him. We accept the invitation to the sword-slave island."

"P-Priscilla?!" Jorah had folded the invitation and had been just about to politely turn it down when Priscilla interrupted him. His face betrayed an uncharacteristic intensity of emotion as he leaned down and whispered in her ear, "Priscilla, the sword-slave island receives many visitors. What if someone were to recognize you?"

"Is that your reason for refusing the invitation? Then allow me to give you my reason for accepting it."

"Y-your reason? Whatever could possibly move you to...?"

"It's quite simple. I am interested in this island."

Jorah looked at her in pure astonishment. This was how Priscilla lived her life; it was almost the equivalent of a wife sweetly begging her husband for a favor. Even if the situation made it a little difficult to call the moment *sweet*. Regardless...

"——" Jorah could hardly speak.

"Count Pendleton, what would you like to do? Our master is in no hurry for a response, so if you'd like to take some time to consider...," Miles suggested.

Jorah, however, declined this kind offer with a "No, thank you," and a shake of his head. "There's no need for you to wait for my answer. Please tell High Countess Delacroix that we...we accept her invitation."

"Aw, that's great to hear. I'm sure the mistress'll be glad," Balleroy said, seeming as pleased by the answer as he was oblivious to how hard it had been for Jorah to give it.

Miles was giving Jorah a rather more conflicted look, but he didn't dare question the man's judgment. Instead, he bowed deeply and said, "Very well, sir. You'll find the details of the date and time in the letter. If you'd like us to carry a response back for you, we'll gladly do so."

"That won't be necessary. I doubt even your heads are empty enough to forget a one-word answer on the way home. So take it back to your mistress and deliver that," Priscilla said.

"Ha-ha-ha! She's got us there, Brother. Right on the money!"

"Pipe down!" Miles shouted, his voice ringing throughout the whole mansion. In the end, they had let their demeanor as formal messengers slip one last time.

5

With a great flapping of wings, two sky dragons soared away.

Even by dragon standards, sky dragons were particularly temperamental, a tempestuous race that were sometimes reputed to be almost as volatile as demon beasts. Unlike land dragons, which enjoyed human company, or water dragons, which were fearsome but manageable, sky dragons were inherently difficult to interact with. Those who had the knack for it were called sky-dragon tamers, and the secrets of this art had long belonged solely to Volakia, never revealed outside its borders. And it appeared that Balleroy and Miles were both among the vaunted ranks of sky-dragon tamers, of which there were said to be fewer than a hundred in the entire empire.

"You know, I don't seem to recall ever having ridden a winged dragon myself…"

"Priscilla, d-don't tell me you wish to ride a sky dragon…"

"Ha. You needn't fret so much. Even I recognize that it is something not easily done. I know that even refinement as cultivated as mine is lost on beasts that merely obey their natural instincts."

"I see. Yes… Yes, that is reassuring." Jorah put a hand to his chest with relief.

Priscilla turned from watching the messengers go, glancing at her husband instead. As ever, he gave the impression of a timid coward dressed in a grown man's clothing. However, he had committed to a dangerous decision: to go to the sword-slave island, with Priscilla at his side.

"Hmm?" Jorah asked. "Is something the matter?"

"—Your motivations continue to baffle me. Hmm. Or perhaps that's precisely the quality that allowed you to fulfill the minimum requirements to be my spouse," Priscilla murmured, contemplating the unfathomable nature of Jorah's inner life. Had he been consumed with Priscilla's beauty, seeking to use her only to fulfill his own animalistic desires, he wouldn't have lasted beyond the first night of their marriage. On the other hand, trying to take advantage of Priscilla's true identity was too dangerous for him. He was unsuited for such plots and ploys, and that made him something of a bomb that had yet to detonate.

Finally, recognizing that she was unlikely to resolve the riddle right away, Priscilla said, "I'm willing to set it aside for now. At the moment, I'm far less interested in my rather unremarkable husband than I am in this sword-slave island."

"U-unremarkable? That hurts…"

"If you do not wish to be hurt, then make yourself something of interest to me. At least as of this moment, you are certainly not more intriguing than an entertainment I've never witnessed before."

Jorah's shoulders slumped under his wife's merciless assault. That said, he was evidently able to withstand the punishment, because even though he didn't straighten his posture out, he nonetheless managed to say, "Just to be clear…you weren't simply taken by the moment? You really intend to go to Ginonhive?"

"Of course I do. This is Delacroix—ahem, *High Countess* Delacroix we're talking about. To accept her invitation and then later renege would be such an affront that she might very well go to war against us. Even I do not wish to lose the house I've only just married into. It would be a bitter pill to swallow."

Jorah's shoulders only slumped even more, but by that point, Priscilla was hardly paying attention to him. Her crimson eyes were looking to the sky, over the horizon where the sky dragons had disappeared—her thoughts on the sword-slave island that must be out there. The thought of it brought a swell to her still-flat chest. Even Priscilla could not predict what was waiting for them there. And yet—

"It matters not. For the world bends itself to suit me."

6

"Ahh!" Al sat bolt upright in bed as a shock of something akin to fear ran through him. He looked quickly this way and that, but there was no one and nothing there.

"Al! Hey, man! What was that all about? You playin' around?"

"Gah-ha-ha-ha-ha! Ain't it enough for you to be on display up top?"

The other sword slaves, enjoying some drinks nearby, were more than happy to give him a hard time about it. In the same way that there were prostitutes on the island, there were some down here who knew their way around cooking and brewing.

Al glared at his soused companions, running a hand through his black hair.

"*Hellooo*, Al? *Allll*! Don't tell me you're all *upseeet*," one of them said.

"Spare me your Hornet impressions. It's like a waking nightmare," Al spat. Then he slowly got to his feet. His mood was never going to recover if he sat there arguing with drunks. He shuffled off, hoping to find somewhere he could be alone. He had to be careful, though—he wouldn't want to accidentally stumble across the Hornet or Ubirk. The thought made him realize that the only person on this island he could really relax around was Orlan, and *that* thought made him unbearably depressed.

Al wandered along until he found himself emerging from the suf-focating underground, out in the night breeze.

"___"

Directly connected to the underground space dedicated for the use of the sword slaves was a small staging area for the patrols that policed the island's outer walls. Since the drawbridge was the only way on or off the island, security was somewhat lax about making sure people on the inside stayed indoors. Of course, that led a few morons to try swimming across the massive lake...

"But that's not much of a plan when the lake is crawling with demon beasts that live in the water. Only thing you get that way is killed," Al said to himself.

Thus, despite the laissez-faire approach to security, not a single person had ever yet succeeded in escaping from the sword-slave island. In a place like this, to even dream of freedom was the height of foolishness.

The thought reminded Al of Ubirk's ridiculous chatter from earlier in the day, and he clicked his tongue angrily. It was just babble, and usually, he would have been able to let it roll right off his back, but today, it nagged at him.

"Dreams are for when you're sleeping, not when you're awake. Damned idiot," he grumbled. He looked up at the sky to see a half-full moon. It looked awfully large, yet what drew his attention wasn't the moon itself, but the stars that stippled the night sky around it. Pinpricks of light beyond counting. Al stared at them for a long moment, then bit his lip.

"Bad stars. That's what's behind it all."

The "celebration" to be held on the island was getting very, very close.

7

Fierceness personified—that was Priscilla's first impression of High Countess Serena Delacroix. She was an incredibly tall woman, her

slim arms and legs obviously toned. And yet it didn't look unrefined; she still had a feminine shapeliness, which alleviated any
impression that she was simply a woman who had given herself to
soldiering.

One might even characterize her as a beautiful but wild beast.

Waves of rusty-red hair cascaded down her back, and she wore not
a dress, but a cloak like a captain of a merchant vessel might have.
Some said she didn't look much like a noble—but only behind her
back, because in the Volakian Empire, the powerful and the capable
could comport themselves however they wished.

Who, then, could possibly criticize any action of Serena Delacroix, who was sometimes even known as the Scorching Lady?

"It's been too long, Count Pendleton. Have you been well?" Serena
said as she smiled—but it was impossible not to notice the old scar
that ran down the left side of her otherwise impeccable face. It was
a sword wound, large and white, given to her by her father when
she had taken the reins of the family for herself. Her nickname, the
Scorching Lady, had come about because at the conclusion of that
family power struggle, she supposedly burned her father alive.

"Serena! I'm grateful to say I have. And you seem in good health.
That's wonderful." Jorah's simpering smile contrasted sharply with
Serena's easy, confident greeting. Priscilla was used to her "beloved"
husband's meekness by now; it was just how he always was and not a
sign that he was intimidated by Serena's rank.

A count and a high countess, a man and a woman, one of them
forceful and the other weak—the two of them seemed different in
every possible way, and more than twenty years of age separated
them, yet they seemed to be friends.

Still, confronted with a fifty-something-year-old man and his
twelve-year-old spouse, even Serena couldn't help being a bit surprised. "You must be the new wife I've heard so much about," she
said, allowing her gaze to settle on Priscilla. "I'd been told you were
quite young, and I wondered if maybe that was why he'd been single for so long..." While her husband doubled over, Priscilla stood
beside him looking entirely in her element. "But I'm reminded that

rumors can't always be trusted. I see Miles and Balleroy gave me an accurate report."

"Hoh, they reported on me, did they? And what fine phrases did they use to flatter me?"

"They said you possess a gravitas beyond your years, as I recall. And if I recall correctly, you were 'sassy,' and they wished they could 'teach you some manners.'"

"Hoh…"

Priscilla had taken the liberty of speaking to Serena without so much as properly introducing herself, but the high countess seemed willing to shrug it off. Priscilla narrowed her crimson eyes and looked at the two men standing behind Serena—Balleroy and Miles, the high countess's sometime messengers. Miles ducked away from her glare, but Balleroy grinned stupidly and waved at her.

"I suppose it goes without saying which of them is the senior," Priscilla remarked.

"I wouldn't be so sure. Miles may not look like much, but he's very perceptive. Both of them are important pawns to me. I'm sorry to say you can't have them, even if you have taken a liking to them."

"Nor do I need them. The only ones who may stand by myself are those who excel me in beauty, or at least some clown entertaining enough not to bore me. Frankly, even my husband doesn't meet either of those standards."

"Wha?! Wh-what do I have to do with any of this?" Jorah exclaimed, his voice even thinner than usual.

"Oh, stop sniveling." Priscilla sniffed, linking her thin arm with his.

At the moment, Priscilla and Jorah had left the mansion where they had grown accustomed to living as husband and wife in order to accept the invitation of High Countess Serena Delacroix. It brought them far into the western reaches of the empire. Namely, to the sword-slave island of Ginonhive, where there was to be a great celebration marking the accession of the new emperor.

"Strictly speaking, there's no necessary connection between the Rite of Imperial Selection and the sword-slave island," Priscilla said. "It's simply a convenient excuse for them to draw a large crowd."

"Sharp tongue you have, young mistress. You don't like these sorts of shows?" Serena asked.

"Hmm? They're fine. I'm simply saying it has no specific relevance as a demonstration of loyalty to the emperor. But I'm not so narrow-minded that I would censure the common people for losing themselves in such entertainments. Besides…"

"Yes?"

"…watching others fight for their lives, and evaluating their performance, is something I particularly enjoy." Priscilla produced a folding fan from her dress, using it to cover her mouth as she spoke.

Serena's eyes widened slightly. "Ha," she laughed. "I like her! A fine catch you've made, Count Pendleton! I think I could really *talk* with this young lady. It's only a shame she's too young to share a drink of wine."

"Please, you'll make my head hurt… And, Priscilla, you mustn't speak so frivolously…"

"Fool. Of course I'm acquainted with the taste of wine. Who do you take me for?"

Jorah almost choked. "Priscilla?!" But Serena only looked more and more amused.

The high countess smiled, distorting the white scar on her face. "Oops. As much fun as this conversation could prove to be, I think we had best get moving while we enjoy it."

"It will be a pleasure, I'm sure," Priscilla said. "Now, as I recall, Ginonhive is accessible by a drawbridge, yes? I suppose it will be quite crowded in light of the festivities."

"Don't worry. As your host, I'll certainly see to it that you don't get bored," Serena said. Jorah cocked his head in confusion, but Serena snapped her fingers, and at the signal, Miles and Balleroy jumped into action.

"——" Each of them put his fingers in his mouth and whistled loudly, summoning…

"My goodness!"

"Ah, sky dragons."

Jorah stared in amazement; Priscilla merely fixed her eyes upon the shapes that came floating down out of the heavens. Two sky dragons, flaring their wings and kicking up a gale as they landed.

If they had merely been a couple of sky dragons, they would have been no different from what Priscilla and Jorah had seen Miles and Balleroy ride off on recently. What warranted surprise was that these pulled a ship behind them.

The so-called sky-dragon ships, secured to the creatures by chains, were an unusual sight even in the Empire of Volakia, where sky-dragon tamers existed.

"I doubt even you have much experience with something like this. I know it's a little late, but please consider this my wedding present to you," Serena said, grinning proudly as the ship floated in the air behind her.

Jorah was struck speechless by her boldness, but Priscilla smirked; it was indeed a fitting nuptial gift. "Very good," she said. "Well chosen. I think I like you, High Countess Delacroix."

"—" For a second, Serena didn't say anything to the fearless Priscilla but only scratched her cheek in some embarrassment. Then she could be heard to mutter, "Yes, Count Pendleton... A very fine catch indeed."

8

"Did you hear, Al? They say a sky-dragon ship is here! A sky-dragon ship!" Ubirk exclaimed, distinctly excited, just as Al was placing a hand on the wall and trying to stretch the ligaments in his leg.

Another day's work, another day risking his life—that was how it was for the sword slave Al here in this awful place. The entire country might be celebrating the coronation of a new emperor, but Al still had his job to do.

"In fact, that celebration means the spectacle's gonna be bigger than ever around here," Al muttered.

"I can't believe I missed the sky-dragon ship!" Ubirk said. "You're lucky to see one of those once in a lifetime! I must be the unluckiest person in the whole world! Al! Are you listening, Al?"

"Shut up already! Can't you see I'm tryin' to stretch?!" Al was busy making circles with his hips as Ubirk flitted around him.

He felt bad for Ubirk, he really did, but in Al's opinion, Ubirk was at least lucky enough avoid ending up in death match after death match. Al was constantly in danger and fighting for his life, put on display until his luck finally ran out. That was how a sword slave lived and, ultimately, how he died. Ubirk might have wound up on this island, but he hadn't been sucked into that murderous system, and that seemed good fortune enough to Al.

The ingratiating smile disappeared from Ubirk's face, and he said quietly, "That doesn't change the fact that I'm forever getting either tortured or ignored. From where I'm standing, I don't think I'm luckier than you at all, Al."

Al likewise dropped his voice. "A male prostitute, acting like he's the same as one of us sword slaves! Hell!"

It was the kind of brutal remark that could have kept two people from ever speaking on civil terms again, but Ubirk only grinned. "You're ruthless," he said, scratching his head. "I guess as long as I don't know how to use a sword, I'll never be able to be your friend, huh, Al? Guess we'll be just acquaintances our whole lives."

"Don't assume you'll never swing a sword in your lifetime. You might get by on being all cute and personable right now, but you never know if it'll last. Think about where you'll be ten, twenty years down the road."

"What about you, Al? You plan to be here another ten years? There's perseverance, and then there's playing real hardball."

It rankled to hear it, but Ubirk was right. The idea of surviving ten or twenty years on this island was outright ridiculous. Al was likely to fall long before he reached those milestones. Maybe next year, maybe next week. Or maybe his time would come today.

"So why not, Al? Before you end up like…"

"——" Al didn't answer.

"If the best you can do is sit here and wait to die, why not take up arms against your destiny? If you joined us, Al, you would be worth a hundred men!" Ubirk must have noticed something in Al's narrowed obsidian eyes, because he spoke with fresh fervor.

He was rambling about his baseless, senseless revolution again. *Don't just stand there! Arm yourself! Fight oppression!* It probably felt good to him, whipping people into a frenzy with that kind of talk. But as for Al…

"Thanks but no thanks, kid. I've got nothing to do here but fight like hell and survive."

"Al…" Unusually—indeed, perhaps for the first time—Ubirk began really, truly arguing with him. "Okay, but then *why* do you fight? If you win, that means someone else loses—and dies doing it. I don't think that makes any sense!"

"It makes perfect sense. I just ain't got any reason to die." Al's voice was cold.

Ubirk looked like he wanted to say more, but they could see someone coming from the direction of the lobby to collect Al for the fight. It was Al's guard, Orlan. If he was here, that meant it was time.

"I'll be back. Or maybe I won't. Just in case, you go ahead and eat. Don't wait for me."

"You'll be back, Al. I know it."

"You sound like the perfect heroine. 'Course, if a *girl* said anything like that to me, I wouldn't know what to do…" Al was careful to act nonchalant, lest he wind up on the Ubirk dating-sim route.

Orlan chaperoned Al to the arena, Ubirk and the various sword slaves he knew watching him go. He wore the handcuffs on the way—he had to—but as soon as his beloved sword was in his hand, Orlan said, "Stay alive out there, Aldeberan. Like you always do."

"You know the one problem with you? Your memory sucks," Al said, smiling grimly as he stepped out into the arena. He'd told Orlan not to call him that.

The moment he entered the arena, he was showered with shouts and cheers from the spectators enjoying their dark little hobby. Al gave a deeply sardonic bow, but he wasn't above playing to the audience. He would never be their friend, but having them on his side couldn't be a bad thing. Just one of the survival strategies Al had learned during his ten years as a sword slave.

"Gotta say, this place is pretty lively today... Might be just another death match, but maybe there's something to this new-emperor stuff after all."

The entertainment offered by the sword slaves on Ginonhive was exactly the same as it always was, but it was clear the audience was significantly larger than usual. All the more reason to stir them up, get them to give him whatever help they could in his bid to survive.

"Ladies and gentlemen in the house seats, all our dear guests in the VIP rooms, and everyone watching from the roof, please make sure you've got your biggest handkerchiefs ready...yeah?" Al smirked, then calmly brought his liuyedao sword into a fighting stance.

From the tunnel directly across from him, his opponent emerged— a large, bald man clasping a broadsword in each hand. His body was covered in visible sword scars, showing that he, too, was an experienced sword slave.

You never knew who you were going to fight until the day came. Honestly, Al had always wondered when he would be pitted against the Empress of the sword slaves, the Hornet. He was just as glad that death sentence hadn't been handed down today.

"Eh, neither of us is lucky. Nobody's fault. Blame the fuckin' stars."

9

The bald head went flying through the air, a spray of blood arcing behind it. At the same moment, the watching crowd gave its greatest shout of the day, applauding the battle—no, mocking the loser and, for that matter, the winner as well, even as they cheered for him.

"Gosh, that's quite something. I'd heard they put on death matches here, but I didn't know they were real, all-out killing. Wonder why."

"It shows off the worst in people. I don't understand the people who like watching this stuff."

Serena's subordinates, Balleroy and Miles, shared a moment of appreciation—or perhaps lack thereof—for the spectacle they were witnessing.

Balleroy appeared to use some sort of polearm, while Miles claimed to have no fighting ability whatsoever. In much the same way, their views of the sword slaves' battles seemed to represent two extremes. Well, what with them being like brothers, it could be charitably said that each had what the other lacked.

"What about you, Priscilla? Are you enjoying yourself?" Serena asked. "I see your dear husband is white as a sheet."

"It's not bad. The idea of those who have nothing risking all in the fight is an intriguing one," Priscilla said. "Although, the way that clumsy brute fought just now was not particularly amusing."

"Clumsy? Ah, you mean the one-armed man." Serena brushed the scar on her face and flashed a smile that reeked of blood.

Priscilla was talking about the winner of the battle that had gotten the crowd so worked up. The black-haired man had taken the victory, but it had been an unsightly one. He'd played with his big, bald opponent before finally chopping his head off, but the way he had done it had been incredibly unrefined. There was no *elegance* to his fighting style. Not that she had expected to see any transcendently skilled fighters among the sword slaves, but still…

"I didn't even detect any attachment to his own life. What in the world is he fighting for?" Priscilla crossed her arms as she rendered her verdict on the ugly man with his ugly style.

It was a reality that many of those imprisoned here on this island were forced into battles they did not wish to fight. And yet each had their own reasons for fighting, winning, and surviving, or so one would expect. Maybe they sought to be reunited with a friend or loved one, or perhaps they were simply after a vulgar kind of fame. Even survival in and of itself could be a motivation in its own right. But someone who didn't even have that—that was unusual. Someone who didn't even care for his own life but murdered merely to deal with what was in front of him. It was so deeply…

"Uncouth," Priscilla said, at the same time as Jorah gave a

nauseous gurgle. She glanced over to see the pale-faced count looking studiously away from the arena, his neck and forehead drenched
with sweat. Well, she'd known very well that he wasn't suited to
spectate any blood sport. That he had taken advantage of Serena's
invitation to gratify his wife's wishes to come here was as much as
could be expected of him.

"You are a man most unfit for the Volakian nobility," Priscilla
informed him.

"I... I'm sorry... Even I thought I would be able to endure a little
more than this, but— Hrk!"

"Your timing is perfect. I was just thinking I'd like to get some
air. Come with me," Priscilla said, and then she took her blanching
husband by the arm and got to her feet.

The seats prepared for Priscilla and her party were at a height that
provided an ideal view of the fighting, but it was not so high that the
stench of blood and fat—the stink of *life*—didn't reach them. Jorah
was never going to recover his wits while they remained in such an
environment.

"Use the outer passageway. Balleroy, stay with them," Serena
instructed.

"What? Why me? I have so much to learn from these death
matches— Ouch!"

"Don't talk back to the high countess! Get out of here, before you
embarrass me any worse! And mind your manners around Count
Pendleton and his wife!" Miles said.

"Yessir," Balleroy replied, resigning himself to the task. Then he
followed Priscilla and Jorah away from their seats, carrying a long
object wrapped in a cloth.

They emerged onto one of the observation decks that looked down
on the lake surrounding Ginonhive. Outside, away from the swirl-
ing fervor of the arena, the three of them were greeted by salty air.
The sun was already sinking, replaced in the sky by a moon red like
blood. The dark lake surface reflected it, so that two moons, one in
the water and one in the sky, seemed to frown out at the world.

"*Sigh*... Thank you for your consideration, Priscilla. I'm sorry again. And young Balleroy, I apologize for obliging you to accompany us. You seemed to be enjoying the fights very much," Jorah said.

"Aw, don't mention it. No worries at all. I wouldn't say I was enjoyin' the fights, not really. Just learnin' a lot."

"Is that so?"

"Sure. Anyway, sure not enough reason to stick around there if it would only upset you, Count Pendleton."

Balleroy had supposedly entered Serena's service only recently, but he seemed quite willing to speak his mind. It didn't particularly bother Priscilla, but Jorah constantly seemed anxious that Balleroy might say something the count would be expected to punish. Priscilla spared a glance at her husband, who was as reluctant as ever to exercise the privileges of his nobility, then stared out at the lake.

"——" She didn't speak but reflected privately that the sword-slave island was something rather less than she'd expected. She'd been almost excited to discover exactly how significant it was, but seeing the real thing had diminished it in her mind. Although unlike Jorah, she didn't abhor blood, nor did she feel any contempt for mortal contests.

"In fact, it might be the only thing that gets my blood rushing," she said. For better or for worse, Priscilla, too, was Volakian nobility. In fact—although she couldn't speak publicly about it—her blood was as Volakian as anybody's.

Priscilla didn't believe personality resided in one's bloodline, but she, at least, would not look away from the fighters gambling their lives in the arena. It was simply that two bugs fighting in a cage was not enough to excite her.

"Say, Ms. Wife, you've got a lot of guts for someone so young," Balleroy said. "Even my brother Miles was wincing a little, but you didn't so much as blink even when that head came flying off." Balleroy glanced over at Priscilla where she stood at the railing looking down at the lake. He leaned against the railing and kicked his legs in the air—hardly the behavior of a servant.

Priscilla, however, didn't remark on it; she simply replied, "What are you trying to say? That I would be cuter or more lovable if I squealed and shrieked like a common village girl and wailed each time a loser died?"

"Naw, naw, nothin' like that. Hey, anyone who came out to this island just to burst into tears every time someone kicked the bucket, I think they'd be in real trouble. Besides..."

"Yes?"

"...I've got a thing for strong women. Like High Countess Delacroix."

That remark was even more disrespectful than his posture, but still, Priscilla didn't say anything about it. There were several reasons why not. She could see that there was no malice in Balleroy's words or actions. She had judged that he was something special, a vessel it would be a shame to break here and now. And besides—he was, after all, her assigned bodyguard at the moment. As relaxed and nonchalant as he acted, Priscilla noted that Balleroy still regularly scanned the area with an alert glance. Priscilla had known many fighters, and she could see that although young, Balleroy belonged among the best of them. If he was allowed to continue to mature and grow, he might well become a warrior known throughout the empire.

"___"

Then there was Serena, who'd assigned this man to guard Priscilla and Jorah. Given that it was she who had invited them to the island, one could say it was only natural that she would seek to ensure their safety while they were here.

At the moment, Priscilla did not have a bad impression of Serena. She even treated Jorah, mocked by so many other nobles, as an equal. Priscilla saw no reason to view her with hostility. As such, she thought it would be just as well to play along with Serena's plan for the time being.

"That's odd," she said, arching a shapely eyebrow.

"What's odd?" Balleroy asked with a wink.

When Priscilla spoke again, she sounded less like she was answering him and more like she was continuing to talk to herself. "When did they raise the drawbridge?"

10

Guess I was a little too optimistic about things.

"——" Al calmly accepted his circumstances even as he heard the shouting bouncing off the walls of the passageway behind him.

Until a moment ago, literally minutes before, he'd been in a fight for his life. The big man with the two broadswords had been a pretty good fighter; for the first time in a long while, Al had needed a double-digit number of attempts before he was able to wrest victory from his opponent. Securing his survival had worn him down dramatically, and although it would be wrong to say he was triumphant, the tension certainly drained from his shoulders as he returned to the living quarters—only to find himself asking…

"Is this your idea of a joke, Ubirk?"

"Joke? You should know I've never made a joke once in my life, Al. Haven't I been saying? Didn't I tell you this place needed a revolution?" The pretty boy grinned at him, showing that he was still the same old Ubirk. Except that at his feet lay the guard Orlan in a spreading pool of gore, his lifeblood having spilled out from a deep gash on his neck.

It was obvious at a glance what had happened: Ubirk had killed Orlan. A sword slave had killed a guard.

"Killing a guard is the ultimate taboo," Al said. "This won't get chalked up as some passing problem. We've got a disaster on our hands."

"Yes, if you look only at what's happening *here*, you're right. I'm not just a sword slave; now I'm a criminal facing serious consequences. If things don't go my way, I might even be forced to fight a death match as punishment…pitted against the Hornet or something. Ha-ha. Guess I'm as good as dead."

"And you're *laughing* about it?!" Al exploded with indignation at Ubirk's failure to understand his situation. He stood with his liuyedao at the ready, facing down Ubirk, who held only a crude dagger dripping with Orlan's blood. He must have been hiding it on his person. It was dwarfed by Al's thick blade. If it came to a fight, it was obvious it would be no contest. They both knew…

"You can't beat me, kid. Even you ought to be smart enough to see that."

"Yes, I know. I know all too well. I'm not under any illusions that I can fight you, Al. After all, even this man here— I had to really get his guard down first, if you know what I mean." Even as he spoke, Ubirk tossed the dagger on the ground and raised his bloodstained hands. He appeared to be surrendering, but Al frowned, still not sure what he was really up to.

"Al, no matter how many times you turn me down, I'll keep asking: Won't you help us? With your strength on our side, I'm sure the revolution would succeed."

"It won't. We can't just sit here on this waterlogged rock and dream stupid dreams. The fact is, nobody gives a shit what the likes of you and me have to say."

"No, that's not true! If *you* were with us, Al—"

"Don't you ever shut up?"

Ubirk was clearly out of ideas, but he refused to stop trying to bring Al into his fold. Al was hell-bent on getting him to be quiet.

Sorry, Ubirk, but a revolution is a dream. It's beyond a dream.

Al had no intention of joining Ubirk on his sinking ship just because of a little blathering. Instead, he took a step forward, swinging his liuyedao at Ubirk with all his strength. "I don't wanna kill ya," he said. "I'm just gonna chop off an arm, and then when you and I have that in common, I'll find the other guards and—"

"Throw me to them? I'm afraid I'd really rather not." Ubirk's expression drooped; he looked at Al with genuine sympathy. "It's such a shame, Al, it really is."

Al tried to bring the blade directly across at him, as if to slice the look off his face, but then he stopped. Well, really, his blade stopped. Technically speaking, his blade *was* stopped.

"Wha—?"

His diagonal stroke was interrupted when his weapon bounced off a massive sword. He could have given himself a pat on the back for managing to hold on to the hilt, but the sight that greeted his eyes left him no chance for such self-congratulation.

"What the hell is this? Another one of your awful little jokes?" Al swallowed hard, his hand buzzing as he tried to adjust his grip on his sword. A tall figure had moved to protect Ubirk—a terrible, overwhelming figure. The most beautiful and vicious of all the sword slaves on the island with her cruel weapons… "Hornet?!"

"Oh my goodness, what a scary look. You're supposed to be my sweet little Al. How can you be so cold?" The Hornet laughed cheerfully. The black-haired woman looked down at Al; with her long legs, she stood so tall that he practically had to crane his neck look up at her. Her weapons, those gigantic blades, were already secured to the stumps of her arms; she was truly the definition of a human weapon.

The Hornet was the famed Empress of the sword slaves, a woman whose wiles and fighting spirit had enraptured many, even though she was enslaved on this island. If she was protecting Ubirk, the implications were staggering.

"So you're on his side? You're on board with Ubirk's little rebellion? You're just full of surprises."

"Oh gosh, you think so? Did you think I was one of those boring, conservative ladies? That makes me so saaaad."

"I know better than to call you *boring* if I want to keep living. But it's a good point. I'm still surprised. It seemed like you had everything you could want on this island."

Every other sword slave respected her, and even the guards had bowed to her—the Hornet practically ruled Ginonhive. She loved to fight, and she was undefeated in the arena. She was all but a monarch here. Life on this island had been good to her, and she seemed more suited to it than anyone.

So what was she doing supporting Ubirk's ridiculous fantasy of a revolution?

"You wanna talk about conservatives, I'm practically the poster boy. Why would you throw away a stable livelihood for some wannabe revolutionary? Have you actually lost your mind?"

"Oh, come now. That's just rude. But that's one of the things I find

charming about you, my sweet little Al. And you're being so mean…
You've finally done what I always wanted you to."

"What could you want from me?" Al winked at the Hornet, even
as he felt the battle lust rising, like a burning point between his eyebrows. He couldn't imagine what she might have been expecting of
him.

"Ha-ha-ha!" The Hornet chuckled. "What I wanted most wasn't
for you to join us, Al. I think it's much more interesting to have you
as an enemy."

"——!"

An instant later, two massive blades that couldn't have weighed
less than two hundred pounds each came slicing through the air at
him. The Hornet was a force to be reckoned with; Al couldn't have
lifted one of those swords even if his life depended on it, yet she
wielded them both as easily as if she was swinging a couple of twigs.

The passageway was something less than spacious; there was
hardly anywhere to dodge her attacks. Al crouched down to avoid
the first stroke, then leaped backward.

"Ohhh, we can't have that," the Hornet said, following him and
delivering a brutal thrust to his chest. It flung him farther back, his
heart and stomach and other internal organs veritably rearranged
by the blow.

The second blade bit into his body, battering him from side to side
before he could catch his breath, cutting him cleanly—or rather,
gorily—in two.

Death was hard to avoid, and it was coming for Al…

"Ohhh, we can't have that," the Hornet said, stepping forward and
thrusting with one giant blade. Al dodged it by the skin of his teeth.
"Oh," the Hornet said, surprised; Al tried to use his liuyedao to hit
back, striking out on pure instinct since his opponent was behind
him now that he had spun away from her strike.

The Hornet ducked his counter with astonishing speed for someone so tall, allowing Al's attack to pass over her head. The next
instant, he took a kick from below, his feet leaving the ground. He

could no longer avoid what was coming; the massive blade slammed down from above, cleaving him in two…

"Ohhh, we can't have that," the Hornet said, stepping forward and thrusting with one giant blade. Al met it with his liuyedao at an angle, forcibly blocking its path. "Oh," the Hornet said, surprised; Al was already shouting, lashing out at his opponent's weighted leg with a sweeping cut.

The Hornet leaped gracefully over his move. But having his opponent in the air was the perfect chance for Al—he instantly turned and started running down the hallway. "Yaaaahhh!"

This was the first time he'd ever fought the Hornet, but they didn't call her the Empress of the sword slaves for nothing. Al knew all too well that in a hundred rounds with her, he would die a hundred times. As much as it pained him, he knew he had to escape the battlefield entirely.

He wasn't the kind who was obsessed with the idea of always winning every battle he fought. By his logic, survival was as good as victory. Meaning…

"If I can get out into the arena…get the audience on my side…"

"Al! Please don't make me give up faith in you! Just think about it for a minute—you know this is right!" Ubirk called to Al's retreating back. Al didn't want to listen. But he couldn't stop Ubirk's voice from slithering its way to his eardrums. "The moment I got our friend the Hornet on my side, I knew I had everyone I needed. I just really, really hoped you would join us…"

Al didn't want to think about what Ubirk was saying, but he had to listen. For before he could come up with a response, he saw it.

"___"

He had reached the arena somehow, but everything had changed.

Until moments before, the spectators had been cheering and jeering at the death matches, but they were distanced from all of it; it was always someone else fighting the life-and-death struggles, never them. Now the wild passion was gone, replaced by palpable tension and fear that pervaded the building. And no wonder—there were now armed, rebellious sword slaves milling about in the spectator seating, tying up frowning audience members, taking the place over.

A few people had tried to resist, probably, but Al was sure the revolutionaries had swiftly made examples of them, any would-be heroes reduced to corpses by the sword slaves' merciless blades.

Al was stunned, but he understood.

"Don't tell me... He really..."

Take over the sword-slave island and fight the empire.

The dream was coming true.

11

During the celebration, traffic between the sword-slave island and the mainland was copious and frequent. Priscilla thought she had heard that for that reason, the drawbridge that was the one means of connection between the two would be left down for the duration. So when she noticed that it was raised, she began to have questions. And then when she, Jorah, and Balleroy rushed back to Serena...

"Looks like your guess was dead-on, Ms. Wife," Balleroy said. He stood beside her, taking in the sight. They had come back, wondering if something terrible had happened, to discover a scene of chaos. Just not the chaos of spectators shouting and cheering at the death matches.

"G-gracious... Are those sword slaves *outside* the arena...?" Jorah asked. It was taking him a moment to catch up with the situation, but his succinct summary was accurate enough. As the now-pale-faced man had observed, the sword slaves had spilled over out of the arena into the audience seating, and they were now menacing the formerly relaxed patrons with their weapons. The fact that those who had attempted to oppose them were already lying in pools of blood made clear that this wasn't a game and wasn't part of the show. No, this had to be—

"A sword-slave rebellion, eh?" Priscilla said.

"What?" Jorah gasped.

But the only answer to his question was an enraged voice shouting, "Where is High Countess Serena Delacroix?!"

A group of obviously brutal men were working their way through the seats, acting very much in charge. Evidently, they were looking for Priscilla and Jorah's host. It seemed unlikely that they were rash enough to kill her on sight, but—

"Stop hiding and come out here! Otherwise, we'll kill everyone in this damn stadium!"

Priscilla corrected herself—she doubted they were *that* short-tempered, but they were more short-tempered than she had imagined. They didn't seem smart enough not to actually carry out their threat. Priscilla smiled, thinking about how this would go.

"Priscilla, g-get behind me," Jorah said, mustering what little fortitude he possessed when he stepped in front of the young girl. (What did Jorah make of his wife's expression at that moment?) It was enough to earn her husband a raise of the eyebrow from her. Even Balleroy, despite the clear and present threat to his mistress, had time for an impressed "Huh!"

However, Jorah's movement also attracted the aggressive men's attention.

"What's this? Hey, you lot, won't do you any good bein' up there. If you think you can get away—"

"I myself am the woman you seek—Serena Delacroix," Priscilla announced, interrupting the man and causing her companions to look at her with considerable shock.

"Hngh?!" choked Jorah.

"Well, now!" observed Balleroy.

Priscilla's voice echoed through the tense arena, naturally drawing the attention of both the ruffians and the captive spectators— among them, the real Serena Delacroix. Her eyes widened slightly, but she seemed to grasp Priscilla's intention. Of course she did. Serena was no mean operator herself. However...

"She still doesn't approach *my* abilities, of course," Priscilla muttered to herself.

"*You*, kid? You're High Countess Delacroix?" a man in a black outfit asked, sidling up to her. His hair was done in a strange fashion, long on the right side of his head and totally shaved on the left. At his hip, he carried a sword with a curved blade, and it was obvious that he knew what to do with it.

The man looked Priscilla up and down, unmistakably skeptical. "What I heard was that High Countess Delacroix was a real piece of work of a woman, so bad they call her the Scorching Lady. Little girl like you, you look like you could barely warm a cold room, let alone scorch anybo—"

"That nickname was most likely invented by commoners who witnessed my fiery-red hair. In any case, I care not what the chattering masses call me. You may observe me with your own eyes."

"——" The man didn't respond.

"What do you think? Do I look like some young fool playing at being a high countess? Or like someone who needs the validation of some common nickname when I am already a member of the nobility of the Volakian Empire?" Although the man loomed over her, Priscilla held her head high and looked him square in the eye as she spoke.

The man stiffened. He must have taken the young woman for what she first looked like: a little girl who would fly away if he so much as blew on her. But in Priscilla's expression, he saw not a trace of fear, not a hint of any weakness of spirit. If this man was a sword slave, then he must have stared death in the face many times on this island. And yet Priscilla's audacity was enough to cow him.

"I'm sorry, High Countess. You're going to have to come with us. Our leader wants to meet you." The man was trying to be polite— at least, as best as a commoner like him could manage. But he had accepted Priscilla's claim to the title of high countess. He glanced at his companions and prepared to lead her off. Priscilla didn't intend to fight him.

That, however, left Jorah, who was still trying to assert his now-unhelpful manliness. "H-hold, you! If you're going to take her, then take me as well!"

The man in black looked like he was noticing Jorah for the first time. Perhaps he was; Jorah had spent the entire conversation saying nothing and trying to shrink into himself. "Didn't hear anything about you being here with your dad…," the man said.

"I am not her father. I am her husband!"

"Her *husband*?" The man looked more skeptical than ever, glancing back and forth between Priscilla and Jorah. Chances were he was less shocked by the difference in their ages than the difference in the force of their personalities.

However, it would be all manner of trouble for Priscilla if Jorah was to be cut down here and now, so she said, "It is true—that man there is my husband. He cannot be my father, for my father was burned to death before my very eyes. More than reason enough to call me the Scorching Lady, I should think, quite apart from my hair."

"Point taken. But if that story's true, then your husband—"

"Bring him. Otherwise, he'll simply shout and struggle and make life difficult for you. He'll be much more pliant if he's with me. And if you strike him down now— Well, you wouldn't want me coming after you later, would you?"

Priscilla, of course, wasn't the type to piously follow her dear departed husband into death; she was not compelled by such romantic notions. But the men were already convinced that Priscilla was very much the picture of the Volakian nobility.

And then something happened to rob them of what little composure they had left. Piercing the uneasy silence that had fallen over the arena when Priscilla had drawn the men's attention, one of the ruffians looked down into the coliseum and exclaimed, "Hey! Is that the Hornet?"

Everyone turned and looked into the ring to discover that the death matches, interrupted by the outbreak of rebellion, had resumed. Not the officially scheduled ones, but a real, true fight to the death, one that had started of its own accord.

"Though with a skill difference like that, it's more like an execution," Priscilla remarked.

One of the two sword slaves who had entered the ring was more than six feet tall, her missing arms replaced with two massive, crushing blades. It was obvious at a glance that she'd produced a mountain of corpses in her time, shed rivers of blood—she must be the one who had evoked such fear when the voice had said her name. She was facing a one-armed swordsman who, sadly, possessed no obvious advantages. His skill level was clearly nowhere near the Hornet's, and it seemed as if at any moment—no, even at this very moment—he would be taking a critical blow.

"——" The one-armed man grunted and went flying with a spray of blood. His body struck the ground and rolled along, winding up by a ditch at one edge of the stadium that was used for disposing of blood and bodies after a fight. The Hornet strode up to him and kicked him with her long legs, sending him, still alive, down into the pit.

"Guess he turned down the Hornet's invitation. What an idiot." The man with the curved saber sighed as he witnessed the spectacle of the woman's overwhelming strength. Perhaps the sword slave who'd just been cut down was an acquaintance of his. The man appeared to be some foolish fellow who had refused to join the rebels, although Priscilla couldn't see the advantage of turning them down at this moment.

"To assert one's will requires a certain degree of power. From that perspective, perhaps it was only natural that man should have died. You there, did you come here just to stand around looking stupid?"

"Awfully chatty, aren't ya, High Countess? Think we won't lay a hand on you? That why your mouth's so big?"

"Do you truly believe that, you cur?"

"...Ahem..."

"Am I understanding it correctly that you think my high-and-mighty attitude springs from the conviction that you won't lay a hand on me?"

The man saw something in Priscilla's gaze that caused him to swallow whatever he had been about to say. He jerked his chin at his companions, and they led her and Jorah away.

"What about me, Ms. Wife?" Balleroy asked, making to follow them, but Priscilla stopped him with a word.

"Surely, you don't expect me to claim that *you're* my husband, too. There would be no job for you to do even if you did follow us. Be a good boy and wait—bide your time until your moment arrives."

Even a fighter of Balleroy's caliber couldn't prevail against all the sword slaves here. Making a last stand against a hundred grizzled warriors would serve no purpose; that was clear enough. But Balleroy was young and inexperienced—and a bit impetuous.

"That's easy for you to say, Ms. Wife, but I've got my pride to— Hngh?!"

"Cram it, dumbass!"

Balleroy was just taking the wrapping off his spear when he was struck in the back of the head with a bottle by Miles, who had snuck up behind him at some point. The impromptu weapon made a nasty *thump*, and Balleroy's eyes rolled back in his head as he collapsed. Miles gave him a kick. "They're going to start thinking we're all morons like you! And what good will that do us, huh?!"

"Who're you?" one of the men asked.

"Nobody, nobody. I'm not interested in fighting with you," Miles said, tossing the bottle aside and showing every sign of compliance. "You said you've got the high countess? Fine, take the girl and her husband and get going. We're not here to cause any trouble."

The men looked at each other, but they were no longer stupid enough to take what Miles said quite at face value. They checked to make sure Balleroy was really unconscious before they resumed leading Priscilla away. Just before they left the spectator seating area, Priscilla caught a glimpse of Serena. The high countess's lips moved, silently saying, *Sorry. And thanks.* Priscilla didn't respond but followed the men out with appropriate majesty.

"Pri—ahem, Serena, what are you planning?" Jorah whispered.

"So you're at least smart enough to realize I had a plan. If I hadn't identified myself as I did, we would likely have spent this entire rebellion without ever seeing the face of their leader. And that would be no fun."

Jorah was all but struck dumb. "N-no *fun*?"

Priscilla didn't know what all-powerful answer her husband had been expecting, but her mind was not to be changed. It was unclear what this "leader" wanted with Serena, but if she had been stuck in the spectator seating, Priscilla would have lost her chance to discover what was going on here. It would have been no different from curling up into a ball at the foot of the stage.

"And that is the last thing I want," she said.

"——" Jorah met this with a tense silence.

"Relax. It doesn't matter what position we find ourselves in—for this world bends itself to suit me," Priscilla said. Jorah's only response to his wife's rather bold philosophy was to stare in wonderment, although his shoulders slumped a little. It was not a particularly inspiring reaction, but Priscilla didn't have time to take him to task over it.

"We're here," one of the men said. After a few minutes of walking, they had arrived at a room with a remarkably heavy door, through which they were now led. Priscilla, who had been making a mental map of the island as they went, estimated that this room must be at the highest point on the sword slaves' island—in other words, it probably belonged to whoever ran the place. That would explain the lavish furnishings and expensive carpet, which otherwise would have seemed out of place on an island of captive gladiators.

It might also explain the blood on the carpet, and the corpse of a portly man who lay there like a gutted pig.

"I-is that...?" Jorah began.

"The master of the island, I presume... The one formerly in charge of entertainments here. The slaves he was putting on display rose up in revolt. It shouldn't take more than half a brain to figure out who they would slaughter first."

The man had brought it on himself by failing to sufficiently gauge the danger despite the hatred he had earned. Then again, perhaps the sword slaves had proven even smarter than the man's sense of danger...

Priscilla's thoughts were interrupted by a man who came trotting up with an ingratiating grin on his face, stepping over the corpse of the former master of the island. "Well! A pleasure to finally lay eyes on you, High Countess. I'm sorry to greet you like…well, like this. I would have liked to meet you in a cleaner room." The overall impression he gave was one of slimness; he was something of a pretty boy.

Unlike the unmistakably rough and ready ruffians, this young man didn't look like he belonged on the sword-slave island—but Priscilla knew at a glance that he must be the leader of the rebellion.

"It's you, isn't it? The host of this banquet," she said.

"Banquet? Ooh, I like that word. I love lively get-togethers—that's why I didn't hate life on this island, you know. Even if some parts of it were difficult to endure." The pretty boy smiled but cast a contemptuous glance down at the corpse on the floor. It was enough to tell Priscilla how he had survived on the island: not by wielding a weapon, but by wielding his body. Of course the master of the island had died. That was a foregone conclusion.

"And what is it you lot want, then? You decided to kidnap me— ahem, the high countess. I assume you saw that leading somewhere."

"Ah, they don't call you the victor of a hundred battles for nothing… Although I must say, you seem a little young to have been in so many fights. Oh well, it makes things easy. High Countess Serena Delacroix, the famed Scorching Lady… You are one of the most prominent nobles in the empire."

"*One of*? Don't be a fool. There is no replacement for me. To even compare me with those other villains is a mark of disrespect."

"Sere—!" Jorah almost choked on the name, but he managed to shake his head vigorously. Priscilla furrowed her brow at him but only leaned into her performance as Serena. From the way the young man had begun, it was fairly obvious what he was planning.

He wanted to use the high countess as a hostage.

"And you hope to negotiate with the empire for something. What?"

"It's very simple. The sword-slave island is to be given independence, and all the slaves are to be freed. I want to get out of this puddle, High Countess Delacroix." The pretty boy chuckled darkly, even as his proclamation made the entire empire his enemy.

12

The sword-slave island had been taken over by the sword slaves themselves, and the substantial crowds of spectators were now hostages. That included more than a few Volakian nobles, High Countess Serena Delacroix not least among them. The rebels were hoping to use these hostages to bargain for their freedom.

Such was the report that had been sent to the heart of the empire, and one would have expected it to shock the country just as its newest emperor had ascended the throne…but that shock never came.

"Muster a response force immediately and send it to that island. I have no intention of negotiating," commanded the new emperor, Vincent Volakia.

The emperor's will was given primacy in all things, and so an extermination unit was immediately formed. There were about five hundred sword slaves on the island—but the imperial force consisted of two thousand handpicked troops. Even tested, experienced fighters like the sword slaves wouldn't be able to withstand such numbers. What was more, the emperor's orders regarding the fate of the island dwellers consisted of just two words: "Crush them."

These two thousand troops made no pretense of being there to rescue hostages. They had permission to use overwhelming force to annihilate the opposition.

"Still, it'd only make more headaches to abandon Delacroix."

"Then His Majesty lied…?"

"Don't say that, kiddo! Not if you value your life. It wasn't a lie. It was just…expedient. That's a better way to put it. A way to clean things up with no mistakes. That's the truth of it," said an old white-haired man who was scratching his neck and not bothering to hide his annoyance.

He was short to begin with, and that was only exacerbated by the fact that his back was bent with age. It was exceptional for an ordinary human, and not some long-lived demi-human, to reach his nineties, as this one had done. His vigor was also quite impressive considering his years. One might doubt one's ears if one was told that this wise and old man, his eyes all but hidden beneath his inordinately long eyebrows, was one of the Nine Divine Generals, fighters famous throughout Volakia.

Securing a place among the Nine Generals could only be done by demonstrating supreme martial prowess. Yet this white-haired old man—Orbart Dankelken—was one of them. And speaking with him was a young woman with brown skin, much of it exposed, and an eye patch over one eye. Orbart smiled at her from under his ample eyebrows. "Your name. Remind me, it was…"

"Arakiya. I believe I have told you several times."

"Ah, yes, of course. Arakiya, that's right, Arakiya. This time, I'm going to remember!" Orbart snapped his fingers and gave a wheezing laugh that made him sound rather ill. Arakiya merely sighed at him and gazed with heavy-lidded eyes across at the distant island.

At the moment, Orbart and Arakiya were stationed with the handful of imperial troops dispatched to the Ginonhive region, taking stock of the island.

"Quickest thing would be to pile on in there, but the drawbridge would have to be down for that," Orbart said.

"Can we not use boats?"

"Boats, boats! Yeah, we thought about it, but—you know. That lake is swimming with aquatic demon beasts. They were released into the water to keep the sword slaves from escaping way back when, but now they own the place. So with no drawbridge, we can't get in, and the rebels can't get out. Tough nut, no?" Orbart laughed his wheezing laugh again.

Arakiya turned her attention to the lake and found that in the dark night waters, she could see shapes drifting, floating, and swimming like fish. Except they weren't fish. They were aquatic demon beasts. Many land-bound creatures found it difficult to fight underwater, so it wasn't uncommon for many to consider these beasts even more dangerous than some of their land-dwelling counterparts. It wasn't surprising that Orbart might laugh off the idea of boats as impractical. And so…

"I will go," Arakiya said.

"Hey now, this is more than just a little swim we're talking about. You'd be down a monster's gullet before you got anywhere near that island, eh? I'm old and haven't much time left, but to watch a young girl with her whole future ahead of her throw her life away—it's too much!"

"It's...all right. I will simply become the water."

"Hoh!" Orbart's eyebrows shifted in what was definitely surprise. As he watched, Arakiya stripped off her already minimal clothing until she was completely naked. Then she crouched by the water, extended a hand to the lake surface, and went "*Nom!*" She scooped up a water spirit, a little lesser spirit, and popped it into her mouth.

As a spirit eater, Arakiya could ingest the spirits in the atmosphere around her and make their power her own. She could only use that power until the spirit was fully consumed, but because spirits were everywhere if you looked, she never lacked for fuel.

This was the ability that enabled her to ingest the water spirit, making its qualities her own. She glanced toward Orbart and said, "The drawbridge—it just needs to come down, right?"

"Yes, that'd do it. Anyway, if I went back to His Majesty and said that a little girl like you had given her all while my old bones had sat and done nothing, he'd kill me on the spot. Go about your task, my dear!" He gave her a perfunctory wave good-bye. It didn't bother Arakiya, who simply nodded and dived into the water. She set out with a speed that rivaled any aquatic demon beast.

The actual aquatic creatures didn't notice Arakiya, who had practically *become* water thanks to the power of the spirit. No beast would deliberately snap at empty water. Thus, Arakiya managed to do what no one had done since the foundation of the sword-slave island—cross the lake alone, and easily at that. It had taken her less than ten minutes.

"—?" Suddenly, she noticed something that caused her to drop her otherwise steady pace. She had spotted a small island between the shore and the main island. In fact, it was really too small to be called an island; it was more a collection of rocks. She'd noticed it because partaking of the water spirit made her more sensitive to slight changes in the current and flow of the lake water.

She also registered blood in the water. She changed direction and headed for the spit of rocks, following the smell of blood until she made landfall. Now she could see traces of gore, leading into a little crevice among the boulders. And when she followed it...

"Hell, I don't even know what's goin' on anymore. I must have lost so much blood that I'm seein' things."

"——" Arakiya squinted to see better.

"One thing's for sure. I know a naked, silver-haired girl didn't just drop in and find me on these rocks... Not with my karma..."

In the crevice, she found a man who was missing one arm. His black hair was soaked, and across his chest was a wound that was obviously serious. It was his blood she had been following, and it was clear that if the man—presumably someone somehow connected to the island—didn't get help soon, death would not be long in coming.

Arakiya thought for a moment. Her orders were to retrieve the imperial nobility on the island. To do that, she had to lower the drawbridge so that Orbart could get across. And to do *that*, it would be helpful to have some knowledge of the island's inner workings.

"You don't...want to die?" she asked.

"——" The man didn't respond.

"If you don't want to die... Mmm. I will help you. In exchange, you will talk to me."

Arakiya modeled the terms of her negotiation based on the way her former mistress— No, in Arakiya's heart, she still served the young woman. But this was the first time Arakiya had ever tried to negotiate for anything in her life, and when the man on death's doorstep heard her, he answered with a quiet laugh.

"You think I'm afraid of dying, after all this? Shoulda tried that... before I'd died a million times..." Blood flecked the man's lips as he spoke. He sounded like he was pronouncing a curse.

13

The sword slaves of Ginonhive had rebelled and were demanding to be freed from the island. All the spectators who had come to Ginonhive to celebrate the enthronement of the new emperor had been taken as hostages. That was the plan anyway, explained the pretty boy who appeared to be the leader of this armed rebellion. Priscilla Pendleton, posing as Serena Delacroix, narrowed her crimson eyes.

She was a girl of just twelve years old, but the glint in her stare, the hard edge of knowledge and cruelty, was enough to convince everyone that she was the esteemed high countess. No one in the room dared to doubt her claim.

Of course, if they ever figured out the truth, Priscilla's life would be forfeit, along with that of her husband Jorah, who had accompanied her…

"Independence for the sword-slave island? Exactly the sort of myopic dream I would expect of people who live tiny lives on a cramped rock in a lake. Not surprising. Not *interesting*. A true waste of time." Priscilla sniffed.

"Oh—," Jorah interjected, pale. Naturally, none of the sword slaves standing around looked particularly pleased, either. Only the pretty boy standing directly in front of Priscilla reacted differently.

"Heh-heh!" He laughed as if the entire thing was very funny to him. "You do have a way with words. A ruthless way. I'm not upset… Although, I'm not sure I can speak for everyone here."

"As if I care what mindless incompetents make of *my* words. Clearly, you gave them a pretty speech or two, and it was enough to have them eating out of your hand."

"Well! Did I say something strange?"

"I should say so. You seem like one of the less stupid people here, which means you ought to appreciate that the chances of achieving independence for this island and freedom for the sword slaves are exactly zero."

The boy shrugged, but he didn't so much as flinch at Priscilla's pronouncement. The ruffians with him certainly did, though.

"Hey, what's this about?" one of them demanded. "You said that if we took the high countess here hostage, those bastards in the capital would—"

"Listen to you? You live in Volakia. Surely, you know that ridiculous saying: *Citizens of the empire, be strong.* Would a high countess who got back to the capital by fearing for her life be strong? And what about you, who have taken hostages in hopes of gaining an edge in negotiations? Are *you* strong?"

"___"

"I can tell you what the capital's response will be. When he hears that you're demanding to speak with him about your freedom, the emperor will act quickly to destroy his enemies. I expect it will involve the Nine Divine Generals, who serve His Excellency directly."

That name, *the Nine Divine Generals*, sent a shiver through all the ruffians and Jorah as well. They were Volakia's nine strongest warriors who served directly under the emperor. The sword slaves on this island had some justifiable confidence in their abilities after surviving so many fights, but the Nine were on a different level.

In this world, some were blessed with specific talents, natural abilities; and some were not. The gulf in power between the two was despair-inducing—and the Nine Divine Generals demonstrated this. It was not a title one could gain by virtue of status or pedigree, but only through the glory of triumphant violence.

A lively confusion broke out among the sword slaves when they were told that the Nine might be coming for them. The man who had led Priscilla here laid into the pretty boy: "This is no laughing matter, Ubirk! Is that true, what she said?! We didn't hear anything about this!"

"Please, please calm down, Gajeet. Just imagine how frightened *I* would be if the likes of them showed up! I hardly know how to hold a sword!"

"This is no time for games, you little…" The man called Gajeet, the one with the saber, grabbed the pretty boy—Ubirk—by the collar, but Ubirk continued trying to calm him down.

"It's obvious what the high countess wants," he said. "She's hoping to rattle us, just like this, so that we'll fold and surrender to her. But I… No, no, *we* won't be taken in by her little plan. Persistence and even greed are our bread and butter. Am I wrong?"

At that, the other man clicked his tongue—"Pfah!"—and released his grip on Ubirk. The other sword slaves likewise looked pained but no longer angry.

Priscilla found the entire thing idiotic, to put it in a word, but she knew they could hardly stop now. They had already done the deed. They couldn't surrender at this point, apologizing and saying that their assumptions had been wrong. It was impossible. They were already beyond the point of no return.

That was why they couldn't back down.

"Pri—Serena, what is he planning?" Jorah whispered.

"Huh. So my husband has actually found use for his head besides quaking in fear. Color me surprised."

"Pl-please don't mock me, this is an important matter." Jorah's voice shook, but he took a breath and said, "I agree with you about the emperor's judgment. We can't expect him to recognize Ginonhive's independence. We can't expect help."

As she listened to her husband quietly poke holes in the sword slaves' plan, Priscilla narrowed her crimson eyes, encouraging him with her silence to continue.

"I am a count of this empire myself, even if not much of one. I know how this nation operates. Even if the new emperor is a person of deep compassion—"

"The traditional ways of our empire would never allow him to show anything even resembling weakness. The only end this armed rebellion can have is destruction," Priscilla concluded.

"I can't imagine *he* doesn't know that," Jorah said, his gaze turning slowly toward Ubirk, who was still trying to fire up his ruffians. Priscilla quite agreed with Jorah's assessment. If Ubirk had eyes to see or a mind to think, he would have realized this rebellion was over before it had begun. And yet he had done it, and he had talked these sword slaves into it with a verbal smoke screen. This situation was of his making. Why?

"Independence for this island is just a cover. He has some other goal," Priscilla said. She was loathe to see it succeed—and just as uninterested in continuing to roll along with the situation. Priscilla had never been one to simply do as others told her. No matter who she was dealing with, *she* would decide how she lived.

Thus, Priscilla looked around, quietly waiting for her moment. Her chance would come, and when it did, she would not miss it. For...

"The world bends itself to suit me."

14

"That will help. You won't die now. Probably."

"Yeah, than— Hngh!" He was trying to thank her when he was hit in his freshly cloth-wrapped wound and cried out in pain.

The first aid she'd given was, well, not terribly confidence-inspiring, and each time she'd touched the wound, tears had sprung to his eyes. The irony was that it might have helped keep him alive—it kept him awake at a moment when falling unconscious meant likely death.

In any case, the man—Al—finally looked at his nurse and said, "Maybe it's a little late to be sayin' this, but you don't embarrass easily, do you? Gotta admit, I never thought I'd ever be lucky enough to see a gorgeous gal like you just show up in front of me in her birthday suit."

"—? Did I do something strange?" asked the brown-skinned girl currently scratching her cheek and cocking her head at Al (all while buck naked). There wasn't an ounce of unnecessary flesh on her gorgeous form, but she seemed totally oblivious to any sense of shame about her state of undress.

Al guessed the girl was about twelve or thirteen years old, an age when he would have expected her to be getting sensitive about such things. "Guess it all depends on where you were born and how you were raised. Me, I like a dynamite body—you know, *babababoom!* Lucky thing, too. Looks like both our lives were saved today."

"It's you whose life was saved. Me...just normal. I think?"

"Hey, you're the one askin' the question. But anyway, here I am seein' a silver-haired girl when I'm about to die... Any chance I'm in hell?" Al suddenly shivered, and not because it was cold. He smiled pathetically.

The girl, Arakiya (that was what she'd called herself when he asked her name while she was working on him), touched her hair. It was sopping wet, water dripping water. She narrowed her crimson eyes and said, "My silver hair... Is it strange? It's pretty. That's what the princess always said."

"Aw, no, no. Just talking to myself. It's my own problem. Nothing to do with you, kid—I've just got some bad memories about silver hair. It reminds me that I'm a useless piece of trash."

"—?" Arakiya simply cocked her head again at Al's self-directed tirade; she didn't understand. Al's smile only grew more bitter; he couldn't believe he was unloading on this young lady right after she'd saved his life.

He heaved a very long sigh, as if he might be able to breathe out the knot in his chest. But of course he couldn't. "It's...Ya know. There was someone important to me, and I wasn't able to help them when it mattered most."

"Oh... I understand that. I'm the same. I couldn't help the princess." Arakiya's head drooped, and her fingers brushed her left eye. She'd fretted at the bandage on it while she was tending to Al. Her right eye appeared to be a bright red, but he suspected that under that covering, her left eye had lost its light. That one blind eye seemed to be the key to the memory of her regrets.

"Yeesh. Guess I can't say anything right," Al said. He felt bad for the girl; he shouldn't have brought up what he had. It was sick, a middle-aged guy getting a youngster with her whole life ahead of her wrapped up in his own feeling of powerlessness.

He'd spent enough worthless, empty time on that island to think this sort of self-reproach was appropriate.

"Hey, I'm sorry. I'm just talking funny talk now. Guess it wouldn't be very nice to ask you to forget I said anything, but maybe you could ignore it. There must be something you're here to do, right? Otherwise, you wouldn't be out in a dangerous lake like this."

"Mm-hmm. The island… It's been taken over, right?"

"Seems like. I didn't really see what happened myself." Al felt bad not being able to speak with more authority, but he hadn't exactly been able to slow down and take it all in. All he knew was he'd suddenly found himself in a fight to the death with the most powerful woman on the sword-slave island. The truth of it was, he considered it nothing short of a miracle that he hadn't sustained a fatal injury— and even that had been a near thing. He'd come within an inch of his life for that miracle.

"And while I was busy finding out if I was gonna buy the farm, Ubirk and the Hornet took over the place with everyone who bought into their spiel, huh? …And what's your part in all this, young lady?"

"The drawbridge. I will lower it. Because without that, the soldiers cannot get to the island."

"That ain't gonna be easy."

"Hmm," Arakiya said, annoyed at how quickly Al poked a hole in her plan when he heard what she was after. It was an adorable reaction, very much expected of a girl her age, but unfortunately for her, what Al said was true. She would not find it easy to do.

As long as the drawbridge between the island and the mainland was up, the troops from the capital wouldn't be able to assault Ginonhive. In other words, that drawbridge was the lifeline of the sword slaves currently occupying the island, and they would know it. Which meant only one thing: "The strongest card they have in their hand is going to be played there. And the strongest card on this island is a monster named the Hornet. We call her the Empress of the sword slaves."

"The Empress…of the sword slaves? Is she strong?"

"Remember how you found me mostly dead? She did that to me," Al said, pointing to himself.

"—? Does that mean she's strong?" Arakiya's question was not really answered. Al's prowess was likely a matter of debate in her eyes. He only had one arm, he'd been clinging to life when she found him, and Arakiya herself was probably no slouch in a fight. He couldn't blame her if she didn't think much of him. But there was no question about the Hornet's strength. There was no one on the island who could stand against her, and even the strongest warriors in the empire might have their hands full in a straight fight. Even Arakiya, who appeared to be stronger than Al, was likely no exception.

"Might be a different story if you put it off a while, grow up strong and healthy first. You got a few years to kill before you need that drawbridge down?"

"No… I have things I must do." Arakiya shook her head and gave the obvious answer.

"Figures." Al smiled ruefully but got to his feet, supporting himself against the wall. He still felt a little light-headed from blood loss, but he thought he could move if he focused on it.

Arakiya watched him stand, then blinked her large eyes. "What are you going to do?"

"What've I *got* to do? You need to get to that island, right, young lady? You'll need someone who knows their way around the place if you want to get that drawbridge down. That's why you helped me—right?"

"…Oh!"

"Don't tell me you forgot! …Ooh. Yelling makes a guy's head spin…" Al smiled at Arakiya, realizing she was the type to get lost in whatever she was doing at that moment.

Here was the reality: Going back to an island bristling with enemies was suicidal no matter how many lives he had. But going with Arakiya? That was another story.

His life might hardly be worth a grain of sand, but he owed it to her. "And ain't no one gonna accuse me of being ungrateful. I'll guide you around that island. But…"

"Mn. That will help. Fighting… That is my job."

He stopped short of saying that when the enemy showed up, he was going to run away with his tail between his legs. If Arakiya, who actually *had* a tail, was so determined, Al could hardly go around whining.

With their minds made up, Al squeezed out of the crevice among the rocks and looked at the accursed island, the home of the sword slaves, where a bunch of spectators were being held hostage, and a bunch of people who were either very brave or very stupid had declared war against the empire…

Al tilted his head from side to side to get the water out of his ears. "All right, so we know we're going. But how do we get there?" he said, frowning. He was confronted with the same thing that made it necessary to lower the drawbridge in the first place: the lake that surrounded the island, chock-full of demon beasts. The lake they had to cross if they wanted to make it to land.

That was the first hurdle. The first thing between him and repaying his savior.

15

"Hey, how much of what you said was true?"

"——" Priscilla pensively closed an eye as she looked at him from her place in a luxurious chair, where she was waiting for time to pass, bored. The speaker was a man with a strange haircut—he'd shaved off his hair, but only half of it. He was the saber user, the one Ubirk had called Gajeet. She assumed he had a certain authority, here where proven ability was valued above all. She suspected he could handle himself in a fight. The fact that he seemed to be acting as spokesman for the others made that clear. Although, the fact that he only acted when the true leader, Ubirk, wasn't present showed that Gajeet's bravery was something of a sham.

"Don't be coy with me, noblewoman. Do ya understand the position you're in? Eh?"

"Spare me your yammering. I think *you* fail to understand the position *you're* in. The very ground beneath your feet is unstable."

"What was that?" Gajeet demanded.

"You've let that rabble-rouser dictate every little thing. You're unwilling or unable to use your own head. And if you can't use your head, that means you can't use the eyes, ears, or nose that go with it. The lot of you got here by covering your eyes, blocking your ears, and plugging your noses, simply letting yourselves be led along by the hand. Am I wrong?"

Priscilla's attitude never changed despite Gajeet's attempt to intimidate her. Beside her, Jorah was looking distinctly nervous. As for the thoroughly berated Gajeet, he couldn't hide his displeasure, but he didn't look like he was going to do anything rash.

The sword slaves in general appeared to be coming down from the high of taking over the island. A rush of blood to the head was all well and good for starting a rebellion, but now the question of what came next seemed to be looming. Hence why they turned to Priscilla—or rather, High Countess Delacroix—the one person here with the most experience dealing with the empire.

"The capital will do exactly as I said. The Nine Divine Generals will come—precisely how many fingers of the emperor's hand fall upon you is up to him, but when the generals arrive, this little uprising will be quashed in a matter of moments."

"Listen to you talk. How many people do you think we have here?"

"It doesn't matter. And you know it."

"——!"

No matter how much of a brave front they might try to put up, anyone who had lived their lives in the empire, anyone who had made their living there by the sword, understood this very well. Gajeet and the other sword slaves had no illusions that they could go toe-to-toe with the legendary Nine Divine Generals. They would understand that when they cooled off a little.

"And yet you did this... Why?" Jorah asked, looking at the blanching sword slaves. The question was not quite one of pity, nor of sympathy.

Gajeet gave a listless sigh. A frail man like Jorah could never understand the feelings of men who possessed greater yet still middling strength like himself. A man blessed with wealth and status could never understand the despair of men trapped on an isolated island. Nor could Priscilla. Even if the two of them could be made to imagine it, they wouldn't *understand*. And Gajeet didn't intend to take the effort to try to make them. Thus...

"You curs may take one of two paths. You may continue to let that agitator lead you around by the nose and allow your lives to be snuffed out trying and failing to challenge the Nine Divine Generals. Or..."

"Yes? Or what?"

"Or you may struggle against your destiny and win back your lives with your own hands."

The sword slaves swallowed heavily, every one of them enraptured by Priscilla's words. The road ahead of them at this moment could only be a dead end. It was foolishness and nothing else that they had trapped themselves like that, cut off their own way back. But to abandon all hope that there might be some way to break out of that dead end was to forego any other possibility but death.

"___"

"Try using those heads of yours, which have gone untested until now. Your destiny is your own," Priscilla said, but as she watched the men try to quicken wits they didn't have, she could only shrug.

Just as an extra furrow was forming in Gajeet's brow, a voice called out. "High Countess Delacroix. Won't you join me on the balcony? You can see the shore quite clearly." It was Ubirk, who had come back into the room.

"A mundane invitation. But better than being *here*, I suppose." Priscilla rose to accept the pretty boy's offer, but as she did so, she turned to her husband and said, "You stay here. I need no strange suspicions arising."

"Wha?!" Jorah goggled, but Priscilla ignored him. She'd taken this dangerous role upon herself, and she would see it through to the end. With Jorah's anxious eyes on her, she followed Ubirk out onto the balcony, where the night breeze brushed past them. The drawbridge remained up, as it had since several hours before, cutting Ginonhive off from the outside world.

But there was something that was different from how she remembered it, too. Namely...

"It looks like the emperor's troops have camped out on the far shore. You can see little lights over there," Ubirk said, shading his eyes with his hand. And indeed, fires could be seen twinkling on the distant mainland. When word had reached the capital of the events on Ginonhive and the sword slaves' demands, the army had evidently been dispatched to surround the lake. The breeze carried a sense of almost palpable anticipation as the soldiers prepared for battle.

"I saw you talking to Gajeet and the others. Not very quick to act, are they? I know how you must feel, I really do. I spent five years convincing them to stop dragging their feet."

"Don't venture to compare your sophistry with my grandeur, commoner. It's disrespectful."

"Sophistry? You wound me," Ubirk said. But then he chuckled. "So I'm a disrespectful commoner, am I?" He leaned against the balcony railing. He was making himself awfully vulnerable. Yes, there was a guard some distance away, but if Priscilla sprang into action, the guard would never reach them in time. As Ubirk himself said, he was no warrior. Plucking the pretty boy's life away from him would have been simple for Priscilla. But then...

"It wouldn't mean anything, would it? We've come this far. Taking my head now wouldn't stop it. I just gave things a little push."

"Hmph. A push. And whom, exactly, did you give this push to?"

"Oh, whoever happened to be around. Anyone who didn't seem to have much on their minds." Ubirk laughed aloud. Then he took the hem of his own shirt and began to raise it up. It was the simple, rough-hewn outfit of every captive on the island, and as he pulled it upward, it revealed his thin, bony body.

Priscilla frowned, but she soon realized that he wasn't stripping simply for the sake of it. He was showing her something. Something that explained how he'd managed to fan the flames of this rebellion.

There, in the middle of Ubirk's chest, was a third eye, closed at the moment.

"The Demon Eye Clan."

"Precisely. A rare sight, right? There aren't many of us left. I'm one of just a few survivors." Ubirk let his shirt drop back down and raised his hands in a teasing *I'm gonna get you* posture. Priscilla didn't react at all, but she crossed her arms, resting her elbows in her hands.

Even among demi-humans, the Demon Eye Clan possessed exceptionally rare abilities. They had a third eye, commonly known as a Demon Eye, somewhere on their bodies, and it could grant them a range of powers. It was similar to a blessing—seen another way, the Demon Eye Clan could be said to be a people who always manifested a blessing.

Blessings were not quite magic, and a people who was always born with what was effectively a blessing was a mouthwatering prospect to those who wished to use such powers for their own ends. There had been more than one battle in Volakia's history to control the Demon Eye Clan. And many members of the clan, treated like treasures to be stolen back and forth, perished in the wars...

"Now the Demon Eye Clan is supposed to be all but extinct," Priscilla observed. "They're considered almost as rare as Demons."

"You're well-informed. Yes, I'm a member of that rarest of clans. Although, ahem, the reasons the master of the island liked me had nothing to do with my Demon Eye."

"You're a prostitute."

"Embarrassing, but true." Ubirk scratched his cheek, and for the first time, it sounded as if he was really speaking from his heart.

Priscilla, however, dismissed his shame with a "Hmph. What need is there to be embarrassed?"

"What?"

"All life seeks to carve a place for itself using the abilities it has. And if you carved yours without a weapon, then you must have done it by wits. And that shows that you are not a beast, but a human being."

To achieve victory when both opponents were baring their fangs at each other was to prove oneself physically strong. But to use intelligence instead of one's fangs—that showed not physical but intellectual strength. Not that either one was inherently better than the other. Each had its place.

"I see… You're quite a clever one," Ubirk said.

"Of course I am, fool. Who do you take me for?"

"Well now, that's a tricky question." Ubirk smiled sadly at Priscilla. From the way she talked, the way she puffed out her chest, he suspected she knew what he was going to say next. If Ubirk had manufactured this situation in hopes of capturing High Countess Serena Delacroix, then he would have noticed by now. "Whoever you really are… It's not High Countess Serena Delacroix, is it, miss?"

"Don't waste time stating the obvious. Are you just as empty-headed as all your cronies?" There was no particular malice in Priscilla's answer.

Ubirk's shoulders slumped. "I thought you might try to play dumb. Instead, you owned right up to it…"

As far as it went, it made no real difference to Priscilla that Ubirk had seen through her lie. She hadn't expected the cover to last very long. For his part, Ubirk, who was being careful to keep this conversation out of earshot of the guards, didn't seem to plan on telling the other sword slaves who Priscilla really was.

It was, in a sense, a negotiating strategy on his part. He knew she wasn't who she claimed to be, but he wouldn't tell anyone. And in exchange…

"I need you to stay out of my way for a little while, miss."

"You benighted little boy. Even you must be able to see that your trivial rebellion will be crushed in short order. Drawbridge or no, those forces you see assembled on the far shore will figure out a way to cross the lake sooner or later. It's only a matter of time."

Ubirk smiled and said softly, "Yes. And time is exactly what I want."

At that moment, from the swirl of Priscilla's questions emerged an answer that made sense to her. "So that's what you're after," she said. She saw now why Ubirk had instigated this uprising, knowing perfectly well that it would be quashed. She knew why he wanted to buy this time so desperately.

He looked at her in surprise. Her murmured words had given away that his plan was now known to her. "Well, well. Is that all it took for you to figure out what I was after? And—and! The strange thing is, I don't doubt that you're telling the truth. You're weirdly persuasive that way."

"—I don't much care whether or not you find me persuasive. The question is, what are you going to do? Now that I've figured out your plan, what comes next?"

"This is a pickle. Here I thought I had the upper hand," Ubirk said, scratching his head and smiling with a touch of bitterness. Under his shirt, the Demon Eye in his chest was fixed on Priscilla. If it was the Demon Eye that had allowed him to cause this rebellion, then its power must be related to sensing the emotions of others—a dangerous ability.

Ubirk, though, shook his head and said, "No. My Demon Eye doesn't do anything so convenient. And I doubt it would work on you. So I suppose the wisest course of action would be to silence you…"

"——" Priscilla didn't speak.

"…but one nagging doubt won't let me do that. And so." Ubirk summoned the guards with a snap of his fingers. Two men appeared, a large one in full body armor and another, smaller, with his torso exposed. "Please escort the lady to a separate room from her husband. And try to be courteous about it."

"Courteous. That's a good one," the smaller man said, a grating laugh that sounded like a buzzing insect issuing from his mouth. "That's all we ever are around here. *Courteous.*"

"Well, she is our trump card." Ubirk turned and looked at Priscilla. His eyes were so deep. It was impossible to tell what emotion they held. "I'm going to have to ask you to stay with us for a while. Although, I admit that might seem like hubris when I consider that the Nine Divine Generals are going to reduce this place to dust."

"Hoh. So you have a plan? Something that will foil the emperor's own generals?" Priscilla raised an eyebrow.

"Let's just say that you have your emperor…and we have our Empress."

The word *empress* caught Priscilla's attention. If there was someone on this island referred to by a word like that, she was either the world's most ridiculous clown or…

"…someone strong enough to challenge for the imperial throne."

16

Glub glub, glub glub—the scenery went shooting past them at incredible speed. Well, that wasn't entirely accurate. Really, there was nothing striking enough to be called "scenery" anywhere nearby, and it wasn't what was around them that was moving, but they themselves.

Just a one-armed, middle-aged man named Al being dragged through the water of the lake at a fantastic rate.

"Blrgh?!" he exclaimed as the swim came to an abrupt halt. Unable to completely kill his momentum, Al came flying out of the water and rolled across a hard surface. He came to a halt lying on his back on the cold ground, where he greedily filled his lungs with as much oxygen as he could get. "Hoo…hoo… I thought I was a goner!" Al panted, reflecting that he had been scared to death as well as almost just plain dead. One reason for that was, of course, that he couldn't breathe underwater—but the second was that he'd found himself locking eyes with more than one demon beast swimming through the lake.

It was literally a different world down there, and it belonged to those guys, who called the water home. The very fact that Al had survived to be washed up on the tiny rock where Arakiya had found him was itself only thanks to a small series of miracles.

It's ridiculous, thinkin' how many times I should've been torn to pieces by those creatures.

There was a splash as Arakiya followed him out of the water. "We've arrived."

"Thanks, I can see that. And here...put this on." He scowled at the still-naked (and still-not-embarrassed) young woman and tossed her his own ratty shirt. It was soaked with water, covered in blood, and boasted plenty of holes, but it would sure beat walking around with a naked girl. Arakiya, in deference to Al's feelings, tore the shirt in two, wrapping one piece around her chest and the other around her waist, thereby eliminating the most problematic things about her lack of dress.

Having solved the logical problem, Al then cocked his head and said softly, "Back home, and it's only been a few hours... Place feels eerie, though." He gazed up at the sword-slave island, over which a shroud of silence had fallen.

He and Arakiya had made landfall at the waste-disposal site on the lower part of the island—a simple landing from which trash, garbage, and anything else unnecessary that was generated on the island was thrown into the lake to feed the demon beasts. Despite its direct access to the lake, there were no guards here on the lookout for any imperial soldiers trying to sneak in this way. The aquatic demon beasts were guards enough—usually.

"They gotta figure no one'd be crazy enough to try to come up this way."

"This place. What is it for?"

"It's where they pitch the island's trash. Rotten food, human shit—and any person who's become waste themselves."

"A person who's become waste?"

"I mean corpses. The demon beasts take 'em away. It's real...eco-friendly, ya know?" Al said. Arakiya looked deeply disturbed.

Regardless of what she might think, Al felt it was an eminently sensible way of handling things. After all, as long as sword slaves had to fight one another for the entertainment of spectators, the island would continue to generate bodies. The whole island was dedicated to the fights—they couldn't set aside land to bury anyone. Besides, who would go visit the graves even if they had them?

Hence, it was the most efficient way to take care of the dead.

"'Course, you get the occasional spectator with, uh, funny tastes who'll buy one of the corpses."

"The corpses? What do they do with them?"

"Hey, not every sword slave is a big, ugly brute like me. Sometimes, you get handsome guys, even the occasional attractive woman passing through here. But everyone dies when it's their time. If they die pretty, there are people who'll pay for 'em."

He'd even heard of people who purchased the bodies of rare demihumans in order to have them stuffed—more than a few people from unusual tribes came through the sword-slave island.

In any event, excepting those few poor souls who continued to find themselves debased even after death, most corpses were flung into the lake, where they became nutrients for the demon beasts and entered the food chain.

"Not sure if one's any better than the other after you're dead," Al said. As far as he was concerned, he didn't think it would make much difference to him after he was gone whether his body was turned into a plaything or fed to the beasts. Dead was dead; there was nothing left after that.

There was nothing left—but there was a proper cycle of nature.

"Hmm? What's up, young lady? You keep starin' at me."

Arakiya, quite ignorant of Al's thoughts and feelings at that moment, did indeed have him pinned with her gaze, with one eye in which a spark burned and one in which the light had gone out.

"Not bad...I think," she said.

"Hmm? What's not bad?"

"Your face? Your face. I do not think you're an ugly brute."

Al found himself lost for words—of everything he'd thought she might say, that wasn't it. He was surprised, for one thing, that Arakiya even noticed a guy's looks—and more surprised that she'd kept on the subject out of consideration for him. Or maybe it wasn't really either of those things; maybe, in her own way, she was simply saying what was on her mind—but even that would be surprising in a way.

Al wasn't a big fan of his own face. In fact, he kind of hated it. He almost would have preferred to just keep it hidden, if he could.

"—The drawbridge. The thing that makes it move—where is it?" While Al was still trying to figure out whether to say thank you, Arakiya was already on to the next subject.

That made the decision for Al: He stopped worrying about words of gratitude and jerked his chin upward. "That's it. You see the big tower right by the drawbridge? That's the control tower for the bridge mechanism. If you can get in there, it shouldn't be hard at all to let the bridge down."

"——" Arakiya looked where Al had indicated, squinting to get a better view of the tower. If she got up there and lowered the bridge, the imperial troops would come piling across from the opposite shore, and this armed rebellion would be squelched in a moment. The sword slaves who'd let Ubirk talk them into being a part of his wild idea, his reckless fight, would be crushed, probably still half dreaming.

"And that means everyone I know's likely to disappear all at once...just like they did four years ago," Al said. "Hey, hold on. Are they gonna blame *me* for this, too? Wipe me right out?"

"It's all right... I will talk to them. I will probably not forget. Certainly."

"That's a little vague for comfort! Anyway—" But then Al stopped talking, for Arakiya was giving him a strange look despite his grimace.

As hard as it was for her to admit, Arakiya had no assurances that she would safely link up with her companions. In fact, she could expect that the control tower would be guarded by the Empress of the sword slaves, the Hornet—the one Al had said it was impossible to beat.

"——" Al wasn't trying to pretend that his own strength was something to scoff at, but the Hornet was the most powerful fighter on the sword-slave island. In his mind, it seemed incredibly plausible that she could even battle the Nine Divine Generals, the empire's strongest warriors, on equal terms. If Ubirk's plan had any hope of succeeding, it meant having someone with combat prowess who could match the generals when they came to the island. To actually bring the Volakian Empire to the negotiating table, they would need the strength not to be crushed by the government's spectacular violence.

The Hornet had to be the key to Ubirk's plan. From that angle...

"I really don't think you can beat the Hornet, little girl."

Arakiya was stronger than Al, or so he suspected. But the Hornet was stronger than *a hundred* Als. There was no way Arakiya could overcome that monster.

He thought they should beat a retreat, go get those Nine Divine Generals, who were supposedly waiting back on the far shore. Arakiya could drag them over here through the water, the same way she'd done with Al.

"I think...swimming would be hard. Over a short distance, it might be all right, but..."

"Guess it's not really realistic to tell them to hold their breath for ten or fifteen minutes, huh? But I'm not sure it's any better to think you can beat the Hornet."

"I'm thinking. If I can't win...then I won't fight."

"What?"

Al looked shocked, but Arakiya grabbed something out of the air—a lesser spirit, glowing dimly. Without a moment's hesitation, she stuffed it into her mouth, chewing the incorporeal being.

"___"

She'd told Al she was a "spirit eater." She could consume the countless beings known as spirits that floated through the air, taking them into her body and acquiring their characteristics. That was how she had become like a lesser water spirit in order to safely cross the lake. In fact, it wouldn't be an exaggeration to say she had become water itself, swimming at a speed that far outstripped any normal person. How could Al not buy her explanation? She'd dragged him through the lake at a tremendous speed.

So in order to cross the lake, Arakiya had consumed a water spirit. In that case, in order to reach the control tower and lower the drawbridge, she would consume...

"A wind spirit."

"Hey, hold on, you can't be serious…" As Al watched, Arakiya's body began to transform into wind. Meaning she gradually turned invisible. If he squinted, Al could just see Arakiya's silhouette, but only because he knew what to look for. "Wow, you can do anything with those things. Convenient stuff. I think I'll start living on spirits from now on."

"I don't really recommend it… You can end up disappearing."

"Ahh, it's that sort of thing, huh? You can't maintain your identity, and then—poof!"

It sounded to him like in order to merge with the spirits as a spirit eater, an absolutely unshakable sense of self was required. And if sense of self was the key, well, she was right: He wasn't cut out for it. Al was practically the poster boy for not knowing who he really *was*.

"It's gonna be a riot if you get up there and find out the Hornet isn't even inside." After all his warnings about how powerful she was, if the Hornet herself wasn't in that control tower, it would really be anticlimactic. Even if it would also make it a lot easier for Arakiya to accomplish her goal.

Arakiya, though, didn't so much as smile at Al's little joke. Instead, the translucent young woman looked up at the tower and said, "No. She's there."

17

Al and Arakiya, full of doubt and vigilance, arrived back on the island in short order. They were headed for the control tower—although it was purely circumstance that made Al stick with Arakiya. He wanted to pay her back for saving his life, but once he felt he'd fulfilled his debt, he planned to part ways with Arakiya. To live a different life.

By this point, he'd already told her how to lower the drawbridge, helped her get around the island, and given her enough clothing that people wouldn't just dismiss her as a pervert. He thought that all amounted to quite a bit of help. He didn't have much debt left to pay off.

"Hrgh!" As Al watched, the short-haired man before him crumpled, blood gushing from his head. Another man who had been talking to him reacted with shock at the sudden and violent death of his conversation partner. But it wasn't Al's job to tell him what had happened—or to soothe his wounded heart. Instead, he snatched the knife the startled man had at his waist, grabbed it in a reverse grip, and stabbed the man in the heart with it. Then he twisted hard.

The two guards died without a sound, within five seconds of each other. Maybe they could continue their conversation in the next life.

Al made an impressed sound as he wiped the blood off the knife on his shirt. "Phew. Turning invisible. Now that's an unfair advantage."

"And you... You're stronger than I thought. Even though you have only one arm," the barely visible Arakiya responded. He thought maybe her assessment was a little too honest, but he chose to take it as a compliment.

Whatever the case, the guards' outfits were too bloodstained to be wearable, so it looked like Old Man Al was going to have to continue this stealth mission in his half-dressed state. "Man, they really did take over this island, didn't they?" he said.

"You thought I was lying?"

"Let's say I hoped I was...dreaming."

Al hadn't loved anyone on the island—he hadn't even had any friends. No, that wasn't true. The guard Orlan had been his friend. Al mourned his death from the bottom of his heart. But that was it. After ten years as a sword slave, Orlan was about the only person Al felt any affection toward. Otherwise, there really wasn't anything here for him. The reason he'd hoped it was a dream was because of the way everything had been turned on its head, including Orlan's life.

"Wonder what I'll do next..."

To at least some extent, there would have to be changes on the island once this was all over. The one thing he'd wanted to stay the same had already changed, and there would be more changes to come. If they were unavoidable, then why would he stay here? What had he even accomplished in the decade of his life that he'd spent on this rock?

"Jack shit, that's what. I ain't done jack, and I probably won't in the future, either." He'd spent his days like grass blowing in the wind, like a leaf scudding across a pond at the behest of the breeze. He'd never even had the imagination to picture what might be waiting for him at the end of it all...

As Al stood by the guards he'd taken out, Arakiya suddenly spoke. "There."

Al held his breath and looked in the direction she was pointing. He saw flagstones, the control tower surrounded by walls both natural and man-made, and standing at the foot of them...

...was a very, very large figure, her back to them.

"——!" Al almost choked, seized by a feeling like his heart was caught in a vise. He hurried to hide in the shadows by the wall. He'd only poked his head out for a second. There was no way someone with their back turned could have noticed him, never mind Arakiya. But imagine if she'd been looking in their direction at that instant.

"*Huff...huff...*" Al became aware of his own ragged breath as he put a hand to his chest, which suddenly hurt again.

He had looked death in the face time and again and lived to tell about it—yet at this moment, he was overwhelmed by an almost irresistible terror of death. It wasn't that he was afraid of experiencing suffering and despair over and over. He could face them hundreds, even thousands of times so long as he knew they would end eventually. But what if it never ended? Al—Aldeberan—knew that in this world, there were some enemies who could not be defeated. Some walls that could never be scaled.

The Empress of the sword slaves was one of them.

"...Ha!" With that thought, Al laughed mockingly, getting his frozen thoughts back into motion. What made him so certain that she couldn't be defeated, couldn't be overcome? Al wasn't the one who had to fight her. He'd told Arakiya that there would be a moment when he'd done enough to pay her back. The time for him to run with his tail between his legs had come.

He knew that if *she* saw him, she would come to kill him again. He didn't want to spend another second within range of her poisonous fangs—he wanted to get out of here.

"Hey... Young lady... I'm real sorry, but this is as far as I go."

"——" Arakiya didn't say anything.

"She's already almost killed me once... Hell, more like a hundred times. I can't find it in me to do anything about her."

That was how Al told Arakiya that he was leaving the battlefield, fully expecting her to berate him as an ingrate. But even if Arakiya attacked him in a fury here and now, it would be better than going up against that monster in another death match. That monster might be an impassable wall, but Arakiya—he thought he could find a way to beat her.

It turned out Al's nerves were for nothing. Arakiya said simply, "Mmm. Understood. Thank you."

Her plainspoken response left him blinking, but he detected no change in Arakiya's attitude. She accepted his cowardice as naturally as anything else and simply factored him out of the fighting strength she had at her disposal.

This also, however, indicated that she wasn't going to back down in the face of that beast...

"Listen, kid, give it up. No one'll blame you. 'Least, I won't. You hear me, right?"

"She is probably strong."

"No *probably* about it. She's the real deal. She's at least the third or fourth strongest living creature I've come across in my lifetime."

"What are the first and second?"

"Don't wanna think about 'em."

They had one thing in common—all those monsters had made his heart feel as if it was freezing solid in his chest. Just thinking about facing them made him die a little inside. After all, it had been impossible. No matter how many times, no matter how many hundreds or thousands of times he battled them, it would still be impossible.

For he knew that in this world, there were some walls that were impossible to pass.

"Listen, kid—," he began, but his middle-aged-man sermon couldn't stop the rash young woman with a future.

"Bye," Arakiya said, and then her almost-invisible body merged with the wind as she made for the control tower, literally as quick as the breeze. The lanky fighter ahead still had her back to them; she was gazing out at the lake. Arakiya was just about to slip by her when—

"Weeell, now. What an odd breeze."

Arakiya was not going to simply slip past. Some people were superhuman; they lived in a world beyond ordinary experience. The Hornet was one of those people. What subtle shift had she detected in the wind? Whatever it was, she turned and brought her blades—her very arms—straight through the breeze. The swipe looked broad, undirected, but it struck Arakiya square in the chest. It would have cleaved her in two if she had taken the blow undefended. But she detected the aura of oncoming death and floated into the air, dodging the blow.

That was not, however, the end of the dance of death.

"Well! Well, well, weeeell!" The Hornet almost seemed to be singing as she continued her danse macabre, the evil rolling off her.

"———!" Arakiya, one with the wind, could move better and faster than could possibly be expected, but the Hornet pressed her with merciless strokes of the swords that were her arms until Arakiya was nearly cornered. She tried desperately to evade the spiral of death—she was obviously fighting a monumental battle, but the Hornet was still only playing.

Which was not to say she wasn't enjoying the fight. Murder was her hobby, torment one of her favorite pastimes. Thus, the exchange of attack and defense that enabled her to corner Arakiya was all part of a ritual for her pleasure.

"I...," Al started, but he couldn't bring himself to say it out loud. *I told you so.* She'd been rash, yes; it had been obvious that this was what was going to happen. But it had been Al's choice not to stop the young woman by force.

Of course, there was a distinct possibility he wouldn't have been able to stop her even if he'd tried—but that was how people who only had one chance at life thought about things. It didn't apply to Al.

If he'd wanted to, he could have stopped her. And yet he hadn't.

Al had no desire any longer to spend himself trying to bend the wills of others. That was why he'd watched the girl go to a battle in which he knew she would die, why he only observed the fight knowingly, and why he would watch as the girl met her blood-soaked end.

"___"

Something deep within him ached; it was like a tremendous weight was going to crush his heart. If this was a symptom of the stress of facing something deeply difficult to bear, then why was he standing here, watching something he didn't want to see? Not for any heroic reason like wanting to see out the consequences of his choices. He wasn't a big enough person to have important reasons like that.

He was just a middle-aged man with a pitiful excuse for a weapon and a lifetime of somehow avoiding any mortal wounds—though he still bore the scars of so many others. His spirit was broken. He couldn't even dream.

He had no reason to fight and nothing that would drive him to win. No motivation at all to struggle against anything.

And yet Al—

"Oh."

"Well!"

The great blade came down in a strike that was impossible to avoid. Blood danced into the night sky.

The half naked girl's bond with the wind was broken; she stumbled backward and collapsed on the flagstones. The Empress of the island of the sword slaves looked down at the blood-spattered girl and gave her a sweet smile. "You are just the cutest little thing, aren't you? I don't recognize you... I wonder how you got here."

"____"

The Hornet cocked her head in curiosity, but the girl said nothing, only fixing her with a single scarlet eye blazing with hostility. The Hornet smiled even wider.

Dripping blood turned the girl's lovely silver hair red and stippled her brown skin, which seemed to pulse with the fight.

The Hornet raised her blades, savoring what she was going to do next...

"All right, that's enough," someone said just before she could bring the weapons down. Who was interrupting her fun?

Her annoyance vanished, though, when she saw the owner of the voice. "Well, well, well!" Her eyes widened as she registered the moonlit figure with pleasure.

Like her, he lacked his full complement of limbs; like her, he had that unusual black hair; and like her, he had managed to survive in this place of death...

"Aldeberan!" she said.

"Don't call me that," he spat. "Bah, who cares? I've got a feeling like I want to die." He leveled his dagger at the Hornet. A short, crude weapon, its reach much shorter than the huge sword he usually used. And thus, the man who had fled from her in the arena, the man who had only just avoided being critically injured, came at her again.

"Well! This is unexpected. I didn't know my sweet little Al was such a hot-blooded man!"

"I'm not a hot-blooded anything. The girl's just too pretty to let her die so young...and the sight of her blood on that silver hair made me sicker than I expected. And..."

"Yeeees?" the Hornet said, drawing out the question.

Al scowled, but then he chuckled darkly. The Hornet smiled back, a pleasant thrill running down her spine.

As they stood there grinning at each other, Al said, "The stars were... Naw. It's my *temper* that's bad today."

18

"The poison should be taking effect by now," Priscilla murmured from her chair.

"Whazzat?" said the small, half-dressed man, his eyes widening. He was one of two guards who had been assigned to Priscilla after her conversation with Ubirk on the balcony, when she and Jorah had been put in different rooms. The other guard, a big man in full armor, was silent, but she had his attention. Both of them were troubled by what she'd said.

She held up a finger with a flourish so that they could see. "It's not difficult. Let me explain it so that even you dim-witted fools can understand: The poison is figurative. There is no *actual* poison coursing anywhere. Although, there is something that eats away at the life, stealing vitality even as we speak."

"The more you talk, the less sense you make. But I know when I'm bein' mocked!"

The room Priscilla was in currently left something to be desired in terms of opulence compared with the island master's chamber. The small man, having drawn a boring guard duty, now grabbed a dagger in each hand and glared at Priscilla. His anger with her words was written on his ugly face, as was the fact that he wanted to take that anger out on her.

However...

"If you're hoping to threaten me, you're much too late."

"Yeah? Let's see how long you can keep up that talk, ya little—"

"Nah, I think she'll be talkin' like that until the day she dies," someone said, interrupting the howling little man. He jumped back, ready to fight, but he was caught by a spear blow, a single strike that stabbed him through the face and took his life. He fell on the spot.

At the exact same moment, the big man sank to the red carpet with an earsplitting clatter of armor. That was thanks to the man with the saber and the strange haircut—Gajeet, who had killed another sword slave. Accompanying him into the room was...

"You do know how to keep a woman waiting," Priscilla remarked.

"Aw, I hurried, y'know, I really did. But first, Miles needed to give me a good thrashing, then the high countess told me to bide my time…"

"Enough excuses. You at least have my praise for arriving before the poison finished its work." That was the most appreciation Priscilla would offer the slump-shouldered Balleroy. Then she turned and looked at Gajeet.

He was one of the drops of poison Priscilla had sown. Now he flicked his companions' blood off his saber, giving a click of his tongue when he saw her looking at him.

Presumably, it all showed that he had chosen to fight against his circumstances in order to take control of his own destiny. If Gajeet was on the move, it most likely meant that the sword slaves in the room with Jorah had made up their minds as well.

"Although, there's a possibility they're all dead—along with my beloved husband."

"Aw, don't say that, you're scarin' me. The high countess told me to protect Count Pendleton too, see."

"Then we had better get about it," Priscilla said with consummate detachment. She stood up, straightening her dress as she rose. She had already tired of the transient amusements of this upheaval, and she had a fair idea of what its leader, Ubirk, was up to. All of which meant she couldn't expect the situation to save her from boredom any longer.

Thus, Priscilla Pendleton had but one thing to do—

"For its final act, I must grace this boorish performance with the flower that is myself."

19

With the pale moonlight at his back and the drawbridge control tower ahead, he faced off with his most potent enemy.

"___"

It was pretty dramatic, if he did say so himself, Al thought ruefully. A one-armed swordsman with a blood-soaked young girl beside him. It was like something out of a heroic legend or a saga—if they both got out alive, that was. If not, well, then it could be one of the great tragedies so often found in these stories. If it hadn't been him there, but some more powerful and more handsome warrior, the moment could have been the subject of a painting, no doubt.

"Heh, I guess this moment could be a picture, too. One of those pictures of Hell," Al said bitterly. He fought off a pang of remorse as he pointed his dagger forward. In a situation where even his beloved liuyedao would have put him at a disadvantage, being reduced to relying on this sorry excuse for a weapon was even more depressing.

Al was quickly beginning to have second thoughts about his decision. Meanwhile, the Hornet flashed him one of those brilliant smiles. "A bad temper, eh?" The Empress of the sword slaves offered him a mocking chuckle. Between her tall frame and the two massive swords proceeding from the stumps of her arms, she almost looked like three people standing next to one another. Al found himself thinking once again what an extraordinary figure she cut.

A truly strong opponent is someone you can take one look at and realize you have no chance of beating them. The Hornet certainly met that definition. Two missing arms might normally have been considered a handicap—but the Hornet had neatly turned it into her greatest strength.

"Hee! Hee-hee! Ha-ha-ha-ha-ha!" The Hornet laughed, seeming to hug her arms with their great blades tightly, quite uninterested in Al's appraisal of the situation. She seemed downright delighted, notwithstanding the fact that she was turning her weapons against a longtime companion.

"The hell's so funny?" Al said.

"Oh, my dear, sweet Al, you ought to know. I've always wanted to try a fight to the death with you."

"Not a fact I ever wanted to know, but yeah, I got an inkling. We *had* a fight to the death, and I lost like an asshole. You kicked me into the corpse gutter, remember?"

"I *dooo*. And yet here you are. Which can only mean one thing."

"Yeah? What's that?" Sadly for Al, he couldn't fathom the thoughts of a battle-crazed fighter like her. In ten years on the sword-slave island, he'd never once enjoyed a fight. That said, if he was going to be forced to keep battling against his will, surely it wouldn't have done him any harm to enjoy a victory toast once in his life.

But Al couldn't do that. He didn't have it in him to be happy at taking the life of another. And he doubted he ever would. That was why…

"…I'll never understand you in a million years, Hornet."

"We don't have to understand each other, Al, sweetie. If I can have a little fun, that's all I want."

What a self-interested, unilateral view of the world. How very fitting for an Empress. For the empire.

If, of course, he himself didn't end up sacrificed to that worldview.

"Ugly…brute," Arakiya mumbled.

"Oh, pipe down and watch me work, young lady. I really took it to heart when you told me I wasn't an ugly brute," Al said.

"——" Arakiya looked back at him, unable to hide the sting of his riposte. She didn't show much emotion in her one eye, but it was clear as a burning flame that she knew Al was at a disadvantage here.

"An overwhelming disadvantage. Believe me, I know it better than anybody," he said. No one had to tell him the odds on the frankly idiotic challenge he'd accepted.

"All right then, sweetie, here we go! Don't die *too* easily, all right?" The Hornet's voice was veritably sugary—then she let loose with her blades, and a storm enveloped the bridge. Al immediately crouched down, raising his knife in hopes of enduring it.

"—!"

But he found his weapon swept away—along with his torso—and Al died. Very easily, as it turned out.

20

"I believe the real aim of this disturbance is the emperor's head," Priscilla said, picking up the hem of her dress as she stepped over the body of the sword slave who had been standing sentry in the hallway.

"Damn, that's some guess," Balleroy replied, eyes wide. Just a second ago, he had been thrusting his spear through the sword slave's heart.

The young man had to rush to clear a path for Priscilla, who proceeded ever more fearlessly, but he never voiced a word of complaint. With the tip of his spear dripping blood, he looked around and said, "It's one thing to start a rebellion on the sword-slave island and demand their freedom in the face of the empire. They've actually done it, so I guess you can trust them on that. But how does he go after the emperor himself? You don't think he'd demand the emperor's head in exchange for releasing the hostages, do you?"

"No, I most assuredly don't. Nor do I believe the emperor would make any decision that would put his own life in danger, unless perhaps it was the only way to take his opponent's head…"

"Gosh, I dunno. I think maybe even that's going a little far," Balleroy said, scratching his cheek and smiling a little at Priscilla's pronouncement. The bold girl's words had force in them; if one listened to her without thinking very hard, it would have been all too easy to just start nodding along, to find oneself helplessly agreeing with her.

Still, the way she talked as if she knew the emperor personally really seemed like a bridge too far.

"Don't you think that's a bit of a leap of logic, Ms. Wife? The best they can hope for is to draw out the Nine Divine Generals—military representatives of the empire. I guess to be fair, it sounds like they may really be over there on that shore…"

"I see you're at least able to put what semblance of intelligence you do have to work. Try this one, then: If the Divine Generals do show up, what happens to the island?"

"Well…I guess the rebellion fails, and the sword slaves are beaten into submission."

Balleroy's companion, the sword slave Gajeet, looked pained by how readily he said this—but it was a fact. The Nine Divine Generals, who stood at the zenith of the Volakian military, were not chosen like military commanders in other nations. Neither family background nor personality entered into the equation—in true Volakian fashion, only strength mattered.

As such, the sword slaves would be annihilated, every last one of them. That much was obvious.

"Yes, that's a foregone conclusion," Priscilla said. "Why, then, did their leader plan a rebellion he knew would be crushed?"

"Well, uh…he knew the Divine Generals would come out, and they would definitely destroy him…"

"Most definitely. However, that means that at that same moment, the generals will *not* be by the emperor's side."

"——" Balleroy's eyes widened again at what Priscilla was saying. He swallowed in spite of himself, chewed over the meaning of her words. Then he shook his head and said, "Naw, naw. I mean, I follow the logic, but one or two generals stepping out for a few minutes wouldn't be enough to compromise the emperor's safety. There's nine of them—that's why they call them the *Nine* Divine Generals! So why…?"

"Very well. Then suppose an upheaval were to occur that required the dispatch of all nine. Suppose something were to happen beyond what's occurring on the sword-slave island."

"You're not sayin'…?" Was this a joint operation, meticulously planned in conjunction with something or someone else? "But that's ridiculous," Balleroy said, but once the possibility had been shown to him, he couldn't get it out of his head.

The fact was that he and everyone else on this island was cut off from any information about what was going on in the outside world. Maybe there were insurrections like this one occurring elsewhere; they would have no way of knowing.

The emperor, though, would. If there were other outbreaks of rebellion, he would commit the forces necessary to subdue them. He would dispatch the nine generals who served him personally.

"The emperor is not a careless man, nor are his bodyguards. I doubt he would send all nine generals away at once. But nonetheless, they would be fewer in number than usual, and thereby, an opportunity might arise."

"So all the sword slaves on this island are just a big sacrifice play?" Balleroy asked, licking his dry lips with a shudder.

A plan that took no account of the harm inflicted on those involved was more than worthy of praise. Someone had conceived a masterstroke, one that would require a tremendous number of sacrificial lambs to achieve its goal. But if Balleroy couldn't hide the shiver that went down his spine, it was inspired not by the plan in motion, but Priscilla's perspicacity in spotting it. How, he wondered, did the world look to those crimson eyes?

He was sure of at least one thing: that this young girl was condescending if she consented to be the wife of Count Jorah Pendleton.

"Hey! This is no freakin' joke!" If Balleroy found Priscilla's logic irrefutable, the same could not be said of one of the very pawns involved, Gajeet. His lips trembled, and his eyes blazed with anger. "The emperor's head?! Who gives a shit about that? We just want—"

"To escape from the dead end you find yourselves in? Your prosaic motivations made it a simple matter to manipulate you. You should have tried using your heads first," Priscilla said mercilessly.

"Hrn! Why, you little…!"

Gajeet turned his unsheathed saber on Priscilla's neck. It was a powder-keg moment, but Balleroy just shrugged and said, "C'mon, now, that's enough, Brother. Ms. Wife isn't the one you should be angry at. Won't get you nothing doing that."

"Shaddap! So it won't get me anything, will it? If you're right about all this, then *nothing* will get me anything! Trying to free the island, that was one thing, but kill the emperor? We're accomplices to *that*?!"

"Naw, the lady's just guessin'. She doesn't know for sure."

"I told you to shut up, spearman. I know you're just trying to talk me down. But I…I believed the runt earlier!"

This time, Balleroy didn't answer the increasingly panicked Gajeet. The truth was, privately, he agreed with the sword slave:

Priscilla's perspective was likely the correct one. The enemy was probably out for the emperor's head. And that meant that, whether they had known it or not, Gajeet and his companions had aided and abetted a conspiracy to assassinate the emperor. This wasn't going to end well for them. The death penalty was almost a certainty.

"____"

As much as he sympathized with Gajeet's position, though, Balleroy closed an eye as he sank into thought. If he really tried, he could reach Gajeet with his spear from where he was standing. If he hit something vital—Gajeet's neck or his chest, say—Balleroy could end his life with a minimum of suffering. But considering Gajeet's skill level, there was a chance that he would escape a critical injury and have the opportunity to harm Priscilla in response. And Balleroy wanted to avoid any harm to Priscilla. Partly because those were his master Serena's orders—but partly because of his own judgment.

He absolutely did not want anything to happen that would cause him to lose Priscilla.

His thoughts were interrupted by a sharp "What are you dawdling about for? What are you mulling over, Balleroy Temeglyph?" It was none other than Priscilla who spoke his name. She showed nothing less than total composure despite the blade at her neck. In fact, the flames still burned in her eyes as she said to Balleroy, "This world bends itself to suit me."

"____"

"As such, your own choices cannot harm me. I urge you to remember that."

She was saying she was the very center of the world—and she said it so easily. Balleroy and Gajeet both swallowed, struck by the pronouncement. And the next instant—

"Hrrrahhh!"

"Gagh!"

—there was a husky shout, and a piece of rubble came flying in, striking Gajeet in the side of the head. He exclaimed with the impact, which was swiftly followed by a leaping figure holding another chunk of debris that slammed mercilessly into the sword slave's head. Gajeet went down hard, his saber clattering as it skipped across the floor of the passageway.

"Huh! Turning a weapon on the high countess. I've never heard of such insolence!"

"M-Miles? Brother?" Balleroy said in shock. And it was indeed Miles who had just triumphed over Gajeet.

It was startling to see him there when he had been guarding Serena in the spectator seats. But Miles only glared at his astonished younger brother and said, "Fine work you did, standing around like an idiot! What if Count Pendleton's wife had been hurt while you were dithering? What then, ya great bozo?"

"I'm not an idiot or a bozo, Brother...," Balleroy said, his shoulders slumping. His older brother might have been shouting so angrily that spit was flying from his mouth, but at the same time, his presence started to relieve the sense of isolation that had been gripping Balleroy. The thought banished the clouds that had made it so hard to decide how to deal with Gajeet.

"They say even the biggest containers have lids that will close them," Priscilla remarked when she saw how relieved Balleroy was. "Although I must say, your lid is a rather unpleasant-looking one." There was a smile on her lips as she spoke.

Miles, joining them in what amounted to the middle of the conversation, didn't understand what she meant, but Balleroy did. And she was right. His "older brother" had always made up for his own shortcomings.

"Never been much of a thinker. I've always let Miles be the brains," Balleroy said.

"Hmm? What are you talking about? Bah, who cares! Young mistress, are you all right? The high countess has been worried!" Miles, mostly ignoring Balleroy, hefted Gajeet up off the ground and tried to see if Priscilla was unhurt. Gajeet was evidently still alive, for he groaned quietly, but his conviction had fled him.

"She sure is," Balleroy said, grateful to Miles for intervening. "Not a scratch on her. Just like the high countess wanted!"

"Shut yer hole! I wasn't asking you! Why should I trust you

anyway? You were just standing there watching the enemy! The one who saved the young mistress from danger was me! Miles!"

"You are as bad as he is. This is no time to be squalling like a cat in heat," Priscilla said, ending the debate. "I am not hurt. Now let's go." She promptly turned around.

Miles and Balleroy were about to follow her, but then Balleroy realized she wasn't going in the direction of the island master's chamber—the room where Jorah was being kept.

"Er, Ms. Wife? You won't find Count Pendleton over there..."

"Don't be ridiculous. My beloved husband can wait. Our enemies' true aim might be the death of the emperor, but *our* most salient crisis is here on this very island. First, we must end this rebellion."

"What's that? They want to kill the emperor? W-wait— They want to *what*?! What are you talking about?!" exclaimed Miles, who was just catching up.

Balleroy ignored him. "All right, so what, then?" he asked Priscilla. If she was acting not to free Jorah, but to quell the uprising among the sword slaves, how did she plan to do that? Where was she going?

The answer was simple.

"That sword slave earlier gave us a fine demonstration. All we need to do is alert them to their situation."

21

The island of Ginonhive offered a variety of entertainments featuring its sword slaves. The simplest was a straightforward one-on-one death match. Sometimes, there might be team battles, three-on-three or five-on-five. Sometimes, a massive demon beast might be brought in, and the sword slaves would be forced to fight it in a "raid"-style battle. Anything to sate the spectators' lust for blood and gore.

On the sword-slave island, any battle could be permitted if it would slake the audience's thirst for violence. But even in that context, it was hard to call what was happening now a battle. After all…

"Don't die *too* easily."

…Al could only withstand the tempest that came after those words for so long. He could never hope to overcome it. The storm of blows rained at him from above, below, left, right—the manifestation of a relentless force that could destroy the world. It didn't matter if he jumped back, parried with his dagger. It didn't matter if he moved to the side, forward, or diagonally. Wherever he went, he died.

His head was crushed, his torso split open, his legs cut off, his arms broken, his innards spilled all over the ground—no matter how many times he tried, he couldn't evade some such future.

It was a slaughter. Just a tragic slaughter. Of course, there were some in the island audience who would have been pleased even to see a fly being swatted, but most of the spectators would have been disappointed with this outcome. If the *only* thing they wanted was to see someone dying, most of those with the clout to come here on leisure could have just stayed home and ginned up a bit of bloodshed in their own lands. No, what they wanted to see was a contest of survival, people fighting for their very lives.

From that perspective, this spectacle would have been an utter disappointment.

But Al didn't care what anyone might have thought of him after he'd been split open.

"*Dooonaaa!*"

Around scenario twenty by his count, he tried a desperate burst of magic. No aim, just an incantation, the spell sending the flagstones atop the bridge flying. Specifically, flying toward the Hornet, giving her something to swing her swords at other than Al.

Al seized the instantaneous opening, taking his life in his hands as he rushed in, just barely dodging the first riposte. Then he had some distance, and knowing he had cleared the first deadly hurdle, he—

"Hrgh!"

—was about to let out a sigh of relief when a blow from above crushed his head.

"Don't die *too* easily."

"*Dooonaaa!*"

Starting from the moment he'd intoned his magic, he jumped backward, coordinating his movements with those of the stone debris. Then without so much as taking a breath, he leaped to the side.

A howling blow slammed into the floor, making it seem as if the whole bridge was shaking violently. The Hornet, with one great blade lodged in the ground, twisted, closing in on Al with a strike that smashed through the hallway. Al jumped over the crushing blow, and then his thrust reached the Hornet. Unfortunately, she batted away his most powerful attack like he were a biting insect.

"*That's* what I wanted! Oh, my sweet Al, I knew you could do it!"

"You think? I've been fightin' this whole time with my life flashing before my eyes. I think I'm out of my league!"

With apologies to the suitably pleased Hornet, she and Al were all but living in different worlds. She might see him as someone who dug deep and found the ability to rise to an occasion when there was a real crisis—but in Al's opinion, the longer the fight went on, the more worn down he got; that was how it always went.

Whenever he found himself confronted with the truly strong like this, he had the same thought: *I could never be like them.*

It wasn't because of his one arm, and it wasn't because of his age. It was more fundamental, something to do with his basic makeup as a living being.

There was a famous proverb that went *Why is the tiger strong? Because she's a tiger.* It was just like that. The strong were strong because they were born strong. The weak were weak because they were born weak. Nothing more, nothing less.

And so...

"I'm not done yet! Let's have a little more fun!" said the strong one, the Hornet, gleefully bringing her blades to bear. And Al, the weakling, would most likely be crushed, trampled underfoot many more times—tens, hundreds, thousands.

22

Arakiya intently watched the battle unfold between the terrible woman with the gigantic swords and the one-armed swordsman. It had only been twenty or thirty seconds since the fight had started, yet she'd seen a staggering number of volleys and exchanges—attack, defense. The girl was on the edge of death, and yet she was transfixed.

"____"

The one trading blows with the user of the huge swords, the Hornet, was the man who had brought her this far. Apparently, his name was Al, given that the Hornet kept referring to him as "my sweet little Al."

The fact that Al somehow continued to survive against the Hornet looked to Arakiya like nothing short of a whole series of miracles. Sad to say, in her eyes, Al's abilities were no more than secondrate—if she was being generous.

Having spent his life on the sword-slave island, he must have survived many battles for his very life. But he couldn't hope to improve his abilities further, even with more of these mortal contests. The man named Al had reached the limits of his natural abilities, and it left him with a gulf to the Empress of the sword slaves, a chasm of power, talent, and skill, that would be difficult to bridge. Arakiya judged that if she'd felt like it, even she could have taken Al out in a matter of seconds.

And yet she was confronted with the reality she saw before her.

"Amazing..."

It wasn't that her estimation of Al's skill had improved, but rather Al's fighting style—the way he would parry or dodge the Hornet's attacks by a hairbreadth, then attempt a pitiful counterattack—that gradually turned Arakiya's opinion.

He should have been dead by now. With those skills, he shouldn't have lasted two seconds against the Hornet. And yet here he was, still alive and even trying to fight back. Unlike Arakiya, who had hoped to slip past unseen—an underhanded tactic—Al faced the Hornet head-on, and he kept fighting.

And he did all this—taking on the Hornet—to protect Arakiya.

"—!" She gritted her teeth and forced strength into her arms and legs.

She hadn't exactly been cut by the blow from the giant sword; it was more the impact itself that had threatened to crush the young woman. She suspected she had a number of broken bones, not to mention a range of internal injuries. She was using the power of the water spirit she'd ingested to speed up her recovery, but she wouldn't heal quickly. What was more…

"*Ding*," the Hornet said warningly, turning toward Arakiya. Even as she'd been fighting with Al, she'd been keeping track of what Arakiya was doing. If Arakiya had tried to make a break for the control tower, the Hornet would no doubt have broken off her fight to stop her. And as much as she hated to admit it, unlike Al, Arakiya couldn't fathom any way to dodge such an attack. She would be buried by the blow, and there would have been no point to Al's jumping out to help her.

So what was there that Arakiya could do? Arakiya, who hadn't been able to repay the most important person in her life even the slightest bit…

"Princess…," she murmured, casting her eyes to the ground at the thought of the one who had been like a second self to her. Someone who had been by her side since birth but who could be by her side no longer. The imperious young woman who had looked as if she ruled the entire world and who had certainly ruled Arakiya.

"Hear me, you sword-slave rabble!"

A voice dripping arrogance echoed around the island, startling Arakiya and stopping Al and the Hornet in the middle of their battle.

They both looked around questioningly, but Arakiya's amazement was greater than theirs. For they were surprised by the suddenness of the voice, but Arakiya was astonished because she *knew* the voice.

"There is no future for your uprising. Your leader seeks the emperor's head; this talk of freedom for the sword slaves is nothing but a diversion. You've been had. You are nothing but pitiful headless soldiers.

"Only death awaits you fools. However, your new emperor is not without mercy. If you show the proper attitude, he may reconsider your fate. I advise you to use the wits in those missing heads and determine how you will act.

"Now, O headless soldiers! If you want any hope of getting your heads back, this is your last opportunity!"

With that, before Arakiya could even overcome her stupefaction, the condescending voice cut off, having said what it wished to say.

It had been broadcast through communications devices peppered around the area—metal tubes that carried the voice—and Arakiya, Al, and the Hornet were not the only ones who had heard it. It had reached every corner of the island.

Arakiya was so shocked that she barely had space left in her brain to consider what the voice had actually said. Al and the Hornet had different reactions, however.

"Dunno who that was, but I guess they're lookin' to turn the tide on you," Al said.

"Yes, I guess so. And I'm sure the cowards among us will turn traitor. Even if we might have pulled it off, depending how things went."

"Heh, don't be ridiculous. You can't believe it was ever going to work."

"Tee-hee-hee!" The Hornet hugged her swords to herself and laughed, her body producing a creaking sound as it spasmed.

"Hey," Al said, looking at her with genuine distaste. "I know it's crazy to talk about having a stable life in this place, but did you

really take Ubirk so seriously that you were willing to ditch what you had? Tell me you're not *really* trying to kill the emperor."

"Ohh, of course not. The emperor lives above the clouds, and I couldn't care less about him. If he was a great warrior, I might be interested in having a fight with him, but it doesn't sound like it."

"Yeah, that's what I hear, too. So what you were after was a test of your strength. You take over the island, then try your hand against whichever of the Nine Divine Generals they send after you. You're nuts, lady," Al said, but the Hornet never stopped smiling.

She didn't deny it—which meant he was right. Her goal had been to fight the Divine Generals, and her wish would come true if they lowered the bridge.

"Why not let us put the drawbridge down, then?"

"Good question. Oh, but the sweet temptation of fighting my dear Al called to me. Not to mention all the other sweet little sword slaves I've never got to battle. I just thought—"

"Okay, hold on, time-out. I don't think I want to hear the rest of this…"

"I thought first I would kill everyone on the island, and when I was out of people to fight, *then* I would lower the bridge."

"I *just said* I didn't want to hear it." Al scowled, disgusted by the Hornet's blasphemous notion. She planned to kill everyone on the island— the sword slaves, everyone connected with the sword slaves, all the spectators who had come to watch the sword slaves—and then when she'd had her fill of their blood, she would throw herself into battle with the Nine Divine Generals. A sort of grand take on suicide.

"You don't really believe you're the strongest in the whole world, do you? The strongest person *I* know about in this world is walkin' around Lugunica with an elementary schooler's backpack right about now."

"I'm not under any illusions that I'm the strongest. No, no, not at all. I'll run out of strength sometime during the fighting and die."

"——" Al said nothing to that.

"But that's all right by me, you see? Falling gloriously in battle is what I *want*. By my family name, I swear I'm going to put on a show for them before I go."

The Hornet licked her lips in anticipation of the battle as she described the manner of her death. She was showing that her mind was made up, that she had no intention of retreating. Al screwed up his black eyes as he watched this warrior make her mad pronouncement, then took the feeble dagger in his hand and scratched his own neck with the blade. Then he said, "Everyone reads too much into dying. It's ridiculous."

"——" This time, it was the Hornet's turn to say nothing.

"Death isn't salvation, and it's not a treasure. It's just painful and sad. Why don't you understand that?" He looked at her coldly, with disgust. He felt nothing but contempt for her.

The depth of feeling in Al's dark eyes was cruel enough to freeze the heart of any who saw him. There was an abyss within them, a place tenebrous and deep into which none had ever gazed. It was such that even the Hornet, who had never looked other than in control, found herself lost for words, stymied by his assertion that the thing she had lived and would die for was trivial, ridiculous.

"I will...fight, too."

"Hey, young lady, I don't think you should push yourself too hard. Just stay there and rest."

"No... I can't do that."

Into the lull in the conversation came Arakiya, crawling forward on all fours before rising to her feet. Her mauled shoulder had re-formed itself, and her bones had begun to knit, so that at least she no longer looked like she might fall apart every time she moved. She was still far from fully healed, but she couldn't let Al fight this battle completely on his own. How could she ever face the princess again if she allowed someone to die after he was drawn into a fight because of her own incompetence?

"The princess..."

The voice she had heard during the announcement belonged to the most important girl in Arakiya's life. It proved that she had not changed at all. She was still arrogant, still firmly convinced that she held the world in the palm of her hand. That had been the voice of this world's ruler.

Hearing that voice, Arakiya's soul had burned within her. She was still under that girl's control.

"I still…belong…to the princess!"

Knowing that, feeling it in her bones, made Arakiya happier than anything else. When Al saw the flare of her crimson eye, he seemed to decide it would be no more use arguing. Instead, he got a fresh grip on his weapon and faced forward again, he and Arakiya pincering the Hornet, with him in front of her and Arakiya behind.

"All right, Hornet. We'll grant your wish and finish you. Because there ain't anyone who can beat me."

23

Holding the communications device with one hand, Priscilla leaned back away from the broadcasting unit. She could tell that her announcement—that the armed rebellion on Ginonhive was really just a prelude to the attempted assassination of the emperor—had inspired a fresh hubbub around the island. Just as she'd hoped, infighting had begun among the sword slaves.

"Those who believe in the success of this rebellion and those who have the slightest bit of sense in their heads have begun to embrace different objectives. Thus, we have two groups with opposing goals—and both of them are armed. They're also both accustomed to brutal fights to the death, so it goes without saying that whoever attacks first will have the advantage."

"Sure looks that way," Balleroy said. He'd been listening very carefully and probably had an even better grasp of the situation on the island than Priscilla. He was putting all five of his well-honed senses to work. "Mm." He nodded. "It looks just like you said, Ms. Wife—lots of arguing and fighting starting here, there, everywhere. If we leave 'em to their own devices, they'll probably tear each other apart."

"You really think it'll go that well? These people aren't bugs or fish. They'll realize they're in trouble as soon as their numbers start to noticeably drop. Though, I agree we can probably just keep our heads down until then," Miles said.

"No, we cannot," Priscilla responded. "Once they're reduced to chiefly those who can use their heads to some extent, it will be time to implement the next phase of our plan. The initiation of new negotiations, with the powerful people as hostages *without* relying on their ringleader."

"Ah!" Miles saw what she was getting at; Balleroy, meanwhile, continued to look perplexed. Priscilla saw that Serena had been quite right: The two of them complemented each other nicely, Balleroy with his slightly lacking wits and Miles making up in intelligence what he lacked in fighting strength. Miles fell somewhat short of Priscilla's standards, which prized physical beauty as well—but taking Balleroy by himself wouldn't be worthwhile, either.

For her beloved husband's sake, she would consider this a victory if she could maintain relations with the high countess.

"Miles, Brother, do you get the weird feeling that we're bein'… evaluated?"

"Well, you don't have to say it out loud, moron. Still…for a kid so young, she's sure got some presence. Noble and imposing. You just wanna *discipline* her."

The brothers leaned toward each other for a whispered conversation, but Priscilla's special ears easily picked up their secrets. Miles's sadistic remark was technically disrespectful, but so long as he didn't act on it, Priscilla didn't feel compelled to consider it an offense. A man with a desire for her was a man who would put himself in her service.

"——" Feeling their eyes on her, Priscilla continued down the hallway at a brisk pace. If anyone attempted to bar her way, Balleroy quickly dispatched them. Even the experienced warriors of the sword-slave island were no match for his spear skills.

Finally, Priscilla arrived untouched at the room she had been looking for.

"I advise you to move aside, peasants. I am here to retrieve my husband."

"Wha?!"

The men in the room were amazed to find Priscilla kicking down the door and making demands, but the most startled of all was

Jorah, who was seated in a chair in the center of the room. "Priscilla?!" he exclaimed at the appearance of his wife.

Priscilla clicked her tongue at the way Jorah forgot that she was going by an assumed name. "That's the trouble with my dear husband—losing his mind just because he turned fifty," Priscilla muttered as she grabbed a vase of flowers by the door and flung it into the room. Her aim was true; the vase struck the back of the chair Jorah was sitting in, knocking it over along with its occupant. It meant that just for an instant, the men in the room didn't know where Jorah had gone. And in that instant...

"Go, Balleroy."

"Yep. As you wish, m'lady."

Commanded by name, Balleroy was off like a shot, piercing to the center of the room like a beam of light. The men had been slow to react to Priscilla, but they responded to this new intruder by drawing their weapons. The six of them all moved at once to meet Balleroy.

They were too slow. In the space of a second, his spear described a great half circle.

"Ya think a spear's just for stabbing? Think again. It's good for sweeping, too." Balleroy winked one eye—and then the three men whose stomachs he'd slit open spilled their innards all over the floor. The trio pitched forward, adding themselves to the piles of their own guts.

"Yaaaah!" Two of the surviving sword slaves leaped over the corpses of their three companions, trying to make a move against Balleroy. One was a hand-to-hand fighter with hobnails pounded into his fists, and the other, a beast person with a hand ax in each hand. Neither had the reach of a spear, but if they could get in close enough, they would have a distinct advantage.

Indeed, they did manage to get close and were trying to press their gains when—

"*Spear users can only use spears.* Is that what you're thinking? Another lil' misconception there."

Balleroy's left fist came down at the face of the fighter, costing the man his consciousness as well as his front teeth. Balleroy had tossed his spear to his right hand, leaving his left free to strike.

The unconscious man fell backward—directly into the line of the beast person's ax attack. There was a dull *thump* of the ax connecting with the back of the man's head, depriving his absent consciousness of anywhere to return to. The beast person, unfazed, attempted to push clear through his companion's head to smash Balleroy's slim frame. The sheer physical strength this demi-human wielded was something to behold, but—

"I'm still faster."

Balleroy let go of the spear with his right hand, lashing out with a spear-hand strike. His two extended fingers caught the beast person in the face, jabbing into his eyeballs and blinding him.

The beast person gave a howl of pain and stumbled backward. That he exposed his neck while doing so was the ultimate mistake. Balleroy stepped on the man's windpipe with one foot, caught his spear up in his left hand, and rammed the butt into the man's throat. The beast person fell back, choking on his own blood, twitching, unable even to utter a death rattle.

With that, five of the six men in the room were dead. As for the last one, he had gone not for Balleroy, but for the toppled Jorah.

"Don't move! If you take one step, I'll—"

It was a decent idea, but it was all the man could do to hold his dagger to Jorah's neck.

"Now, Gaius!"

"—Hkk!"

From behind Priscilla, Miles, standing in the entrance, shouted—and the ceiling of the room came crashing down, a winged dragon sticking its head through the hole and latching on to the head of the man threatening Jorah. He was dragged helplessly upward and out, only his scream echoing behind him. A copious shower of blood poured through the eviscerated ceiling, drenching Jorah, who was directly below.

"Gah?! Blood? This is blood! Priscilla, I'm done for..."

"Fool. It's not *your* blood. It belongs to a commoner." Priscilla sniffed at the sight of Jorah losing his mind over a bit of gore. She glanced up and found herself looking into the eyes of the sky dragon peering down through the ceiling.

She recognized the creature. It was one of the winged dragons that had brought them to the island on the dragon ship. Given that it had obeyed Miles's order, she presumed it was his pet.

Priscilla said, "A fine performance. However..."

"That's everyone in here, ain't it? What about that, uh, ringleader?" Balleroy said. A quick glance around the room confirmed that the pretty boy, Ubirk, was not among the dead. Priscilla narrowed her crimson eyes as she looked at the corpses; beside her, Balleroy rested his spear on his shoulder and seemed to be searching for the same thing. But Ubirk was nowhere to be seen in the island master's chamber. No—perhaps it was more than that.

"Perhaps he's fled the entire island," Priscilla said.

"But the drawbridge's still up. Ain't no way out of here."

"No *easy* way. But it might still be possible to get around. Even the emperor in his capital has access to hidden devices akin to magic that allow one to move instantaneously to a distant location."

"Yikes! I feel like I could be killed just for knowin' that," Balleroy said. He was, though, at least tutored enough not to ask where Priscilla had gotten the information.

Once again reevaluating her opinion of Balleroy and Miles, Priscilla went and looked out from the room's balcony, letting herself sink into the distant clangor of battle.

"Priscilla? Ahem, I think it may be dangerous to stay here for very long..."

"Things are already settled for the most part," she said, silencing the annoying background noise that was Jorah's voice. "All that remains is for the sword slaves to decide where they stand. As for the drawbridge, there are any number of ways to bring it down." She closed her eyes. "For the moment, I'm enjoying listening to the breeze."

The clash of swords could be heard from every corner of Ginonhive— the sound of everything being shattered, destroyed. The most noticeable crash of all came from the direction of the still-raised drawbridge.

Along with the great gusts of wind and the clamor of fighting, she heard a small sound, something like a rat struggling desperately for its life. However—

"They say a cornered rat knows how to bite. I wonder who will be consumed in the end."

24

Arakiya's participation changed the face of the battle against the Hornet. Now worrying not only about his own death, but also Arakiya's, Al felt like his head was going to explode from the massive surge of thoughts rising from within.

"I don't know your quirks, I don't know anything about you—how are we supposed to fight together?!"

"Just move in tandem…"

"You think I'm quick-witted enough for that?!"

Arakiya was a spirit eater; she could consume spirits and use them to manifest special powers. She was *too* special, in fact; Al had never done any "simulations" about how to work with someone like her. The way she fought on all fours, even using her teeth, made him think of some wild animal, but seeing a beautiful but underdeveloped girl like Arakiya do it had something sordid and erotic about it. The impression was only reinforced by the fact that their opponent was another beautiful woman, this one without arms.

"Would've liked to record this match, if I could've been a spectator watching from a safe distance," Al said.

"Well! It's an honor to get a compliment from *you*," the Hornet replied. There was a broad smile on her face as she lashed out with her swords, the start of a combo move that saw Al avoid death by a hair; he'd seen the attack enough times over their dozens of rematches to have discovered a way to survive it.

He felt the impact through his entire arm, clutching his dagger as hard as he could to keep it from being wrenched out of his hand. It might not be much, but a weapon was a weapon. If he lost this thing, he could expect to lose his other arm shortly thereafter.

"Hrn! *Dooona!*" he cried as he stumbled backward under the blow; his incantation lofted several chunks of rock from the ground.

The Hornet calmly guarded against any attacks from the dead

angles created by the stone, but she seemed annoyed by the little twig who'd stuck her nose into their battle. "You *are* troublesome," she said with a snorting laugh, and then she jammed both of her blades into the flagstones. From there, she deftly dodged Arakiya's flame-clad charge, and then the Empress poured her strength into her arms and began to spin—tearing up the floor.

With the ground beneath their feet suddenly giving way, Al and Arakiya were sucked into the storm of destruction. They each gave a short shout as they dropped from just in front of the drawbridge toward the lowest levels of the island. Al fell helplessly, but Arakiya kicked off a passing wall and grabbed him, stabilizing them.

"Gah! Th-thanks, kid. Ya saved me…"

"It is all right. But I haven't saved you. That is yet to come."

When they finally landed in the deepest depths of the island, Al and Arakiya squinted, trying to see beyond the dust cloud they'd kicked up.

What they saw was the Hornet, easily slicing through the eruption of dust. She rubbed her blades together, creating an earsplitting shriek of metal, and laughed. "Now we have a little more space for our fight. Oh, my sweet Al, I hope you'll show me a good time."

"…If I hit at your feet with a twig, there's about a sixty percent chance that you'll destroy the bridge."

"——? What did you say?" the Hornet asked, perplexed by Al's words. The smile froze on her face. But Al wasn't done talking to the confused Empress of the sword slaves.

"When the bridge comes down, the girl saves me a hundred percent of the time. She's a loyal one. When I charge in the moment you start your little sword dance, my head gets crushed. If I just watch you, I get sliced up, and even if I try to run away, a little over seventy percent of the time, the girl and I turn out not to be on the same page."

"____"

"It's all trial and error, seven hundred thirteen times. You've killed me seven hundred thirteen times tonight."

"____"

"Huh. Actually, if we count that first battle in the arena, I guess it's seven hundred ninety-two times."

The Hornet, struck dumb, could only listen to Al calmly explaining…something. Al was honestly impressed that she didn't interrupt him or burst out laughing about how ridiculous he sounded. It suggested the Hornet understood that he wasn't trying to threaten her and wasn't out of his mind. That must mean…

"You can see it, too, can't you? The god of death I'm stuck with."

"…I can't see anything at all, including what any of this babble means. I haven't managed to kill you even once, Al, sweetie. But…" She paused, her eyes filling with bloodlust and desire. "Getting to kill you eight hundred times sounds like a dream come true to me."

The Hornet leaned forward easily, her face flushing with excitement.

It was the first phase of her deadliest sword dance. It could lead to any of several patterns, but all of them ended in death. The only thing that could be done was not let her start in the first place. In order to protect himself, he had to…

"All right, sweetie, we're done with all this worthless chitchat. Get ready."

"It wasn't worthless."

"____?"

"Everything I've done was to buy time."

The Hornet frowned at that—but then Al saw the effect of his work.

"Wha…?" the Hornet rasped and fell to her knees. Her eyes were bloodshot, and her breathing grew noticeably quicker. But the faster and deeper she breathed, the more her life was eaten away.

The Empress of the sword slaves looked around with her reddened eyes, trying to understand what had happened. Al stood over her, and as he looked down, he understood that he found no pleasure in making another person kneel before him. Thinking of what he owed her for that battle against the demon beast four years before, he decided to fill her in.

"It's poison," he said.

"Ah… —ison…" The Hornet looked at him, her face a mask of disbelief and pain.

"Got the idea from an old movie. They say poison's killed more people than any other weapon."

"Poi...son...? When did I...take...?"

"I mixed it up right here. Here where they put the bodies."

Shaking his head, Al explained to the Hornet that here in the deepest reaches of the island was where they kept the corpses. He'd mentioned this to Arakiya—the idea that certain spectators with particularly twisted tastes liked to buy the bodies of those who had lost their lives in especially spectacular fashion. They each had their reasons, whether it was because the fighter came from somewhere special or was uniquely beautiful, or so that the buyer could dissect a person's most unusual skills. Any number of things.

Among the corpses collected for this purpose was the one Al wanted. Specifically...

"A bit back, I fought a guy, a shinobi, who had the Poison Hand. He must have been soaked in the stuff to the bitter end. I asked the young lady to burn him up for me."

"H—"

"The poison carries on the wind. And you breathed it in."

The Hornet pitched forward on the floor, her eyes bloodshot and wide. The way her body shivered and twitched made it look almost like the Empress of the sword slaves was begging forgiveness from Al and Arakiya. The Empress of the sword slaves, who had made so many kneel before her, now found herself in the reverse position.

"Sure glad that poison gas worked. And it took a *lot* of trial and error to get you right over this spot when the floor smashed in. Glad it went off without a hitch."

"N-no... Wait. P-poison? You used...poison? On *me*? It's not... fair..."

"Fair? You're freakin' joking, right? There's no right or wrong when it comes to surviving on the sword-slave island. Or did you not even know that, *rookie*?"

The Hornet could call him whatever she wanted as she wept tears of blood, but Al was merciless. Though the Hornet had dominated the island with her prowess, bending it to her will, she had misunderstood something: It was not the strong who were the victors here. It was whoever won.

Inundate the opponent with poison gas, use a second fighter to corner them—it didn't matter. If you won, you won.

"If the gas hadn't worked, it would've been pretty tricky. Would've had to bring down the whole island, maybe, or crush you with the drawbridge... I probably didn't even have ten more ideas up my sleeve. And no clue if any of 'em would've worked," Al said softly.

"——hhh..." The Hornet, her eyes clouded by the bloodred tears, was afraid of him. She understood that this was no lie, this talk of ways of winning that he hadn't tried. Even if the poison hadn't been available, Al had still had ways of killing her.

The Hornet would never get to realize her dreams of entertaining herself with murderous contests. The moment she had chosen to fight Al to the death, that possibility had winked out of existence.

"——" Chewing over that reality, the Hornet discovered her own sort of acceptance within the agony; whoever won, whoever survived, was stronger. It was a very Volakian way of acknowledging one's defeat. And so finally, she crawled up to Al. "Al... Sweetie... Finish me...off..."

She begged him to finish what he had started with his own hand, to give her an end worthy of the Empress of the sword slaves. Al winced. And then...

"What, ya want me to at least deal the final blow? Hey, I get it, but..."

"Ah..."

"But you never know what someone might do if you get too close to them at the last moment. I'm gonna stand right here and wait for you to die." With his teeth, Al freed the dirty rag that had been securing his dagger in his hand and got a little more distance from the Hornet. She'd used the last of her strength to crawl forward like a potato bug, but he had denied her request to be her executioner, and the despair of that fact gripped her afresh as he stepped away.

So the Empress of the sword slaves would not have the fitting end she desired—Al scratched his chin with his free hand as he contemplated the desolation this brought to her face, which had always before been full of self-assurance. Next, he scratched his head, turning a look of pity upon his acquaintance, who could no longer hear him.

"I told ya, Hornet. I said it'd be boring to fight me."

25

Once the drawbridge was lowered and the troops on the far shore came across, defeat was assured. Although, it should be said that defeat was largely accomplished the moment the voice of the young girl on the announcement system revealed the plotters' true intentions. The Divine Generals and the rest of the relief troops found themselves handling a simple mop-up operation.

And it was going quite well...

"Heeey, Arakiya. Old Gramps won't let you get away with this—a strange man so much older than you! How much older *is* he anyway? Can't keep him around—I suppose we'll just have to kill him."

"...What are you talking about?" Arakiya asked.

"Gah-ha-ha-ha-ha! This is just how old men talk. You don't think it's funny? Oh... You don't. Right, right, it's not a pretty sight when an old man does that sort of thing. My mistake, my mistake."

The source of the raucous laughter was a diminutive, white-haired old man—Orbart Dankelken. Arakiya was somewhat bemused by the behavior of the man who claimed to be number Three of the Nine Divine Generals, but Al, who had been hauled in front of the old guy, was even more confused.

Al was exhausted through and through; he wanted nothing more than to fling himself down somewhere and go to sleep. Of course, he wouldn't say that to Orbart if it killed him (literally). After all...

"You're the one, aren't you? You helped lower the bridge. You were a big help. Especially seeing as if I didn't get this all squared away in a hurry, His Excellency would've killed me."

...After all, Al's instincts were warning him urgently that despite the old man's comical demeanor, his power was even greater than that of the Hornet, whom Al had only escaped after hundreds and

hundreds of attempts. Al had definitely considered the Hornet the third or fourth most powerful person he'd encountered in his life—but that ranking was quickly changing.

"The world's a big place…but this little island has been enough for me," he said.

"No worldly desires, is that it? You're…well, not quite young enough to be called a youngster, I guess. Though, most people are youngsters from my perspective! And young people are supposed to have dreams, aren't they?" Orbart asked.

"Dreams, huh? Already had myself a good one." That was Al's response to Orbart's heedless outburst as he glanced at Arakiya, who stood beside the venerable man. He reached out and patted her head, with its dusty silver hair. Arakiya still looked a bit confused, but she accepted his gesture. "I dreamed I was able to protect a beautiful, silver-haired young lady. It was *the* thing I had to do in all my lives."

"Hey now, are you serious? I won't let you have Arakiya, y'know. That's a dream too far!"

"I'm fond of her. That don't mean I'm romantically interested. Silver hair's my one dealbreaker." Al pulled his hand back as he tried to placate Orbart's simple wariness.

Arakiya, more or less divorced from their conversation, looked at Orbart and said, "Um… This ugly brute. What will happen to him?"

"Those piercing words! And she doesn't even mean anything by them! My heart…"

"Him? Nothing. If he wants a reward, I'll give him one if my authority can make it happen. And if he wants to get out of here, I think he's earned it." Orbart glanced over at Al, who found it a little grating to be effectively asked indirectly what he wanted, but he nodded at Orbart just the same. The old man hadn't survived so long for no reason; a lifetime of experience told him what was in Al's heart.

"That's right. I don't need anything. Got no plans to leave here, either. If I had to pick something, I'd just ask that there was still a *here* to be."

"Don't think you need to worry about that. The empire's got no shortage of villains, and this little episode just got us a whole heap of new criminals. We'll replenish the numbers here in no time! Gah-hah-hah-hah!" Orbart guffawed again, pounding Al on the shoulder.

Then the old man turned to leave, and Arakiya was about to follow him. Al watched the small figure for a moment, and just as he was about to make his own exit, she stopped. She didn't turn all the way around—just turned her head to look at him. "Thank you," she said simply.

Al just shrugged at that. "*Douitashimashite*, kid."

"...I don't know what that means."

"That's all the thanks I need. Full marks. Oh man, I'm getting goose bumps... Have a long life, kid."

Arakiya knit her brow for a second, but then she nodded, and this time, she did follow Orbart off. Al watched her go, then gave a great stretch. The uprising on the sword-slave island had been quelled, and most of the people he knew, including the Hornet, were dead. There was just one exception—rumor had it that the chief culprit, Ubirk, was gone without a trace. A bit of a surprise considering his plan had supposedly encompassed not only Ginonhive, but also rebellions all over the empire that were only a prelude to the ultimate murder of the emperor.

Well, the emperor was still kicking, and Al told himself that Ubirk was probably fish food or something. A fitting fate for a worthless, stupid fugitive who had no right to be screwing around with the destinies of others.

"Huh. Guess *I* changed that Arakiya girl's destiny, though."

Because of him, Arakiya would live on, maybe find someone, have kids, have grandkids and great grandkids. Maybe a whole new family line would spring from her. That could revolutionize the world in unimaginable ways.

It might turn out to be one of the few marks Al had left on the world.

"I can just imagine how badly my teacher would beat me if I started talking like that," Al said, scratching his head. He turned to go back into the sword-slave island. No matter who was no longer there, no matter if no one wanted him, this was his place. The one place his existence was permitted, a paradise for black sheep like him.

"'Headless soldiers,' huh…," he mumbled, suddenly recalling the voice he'd heard over the announcement system. "Headless soldiers" had been the girl's contemptuous description of the sword slaves who had risen up in armed rebellion thoughtlessly—but Al wasn't so different from them. She'd told the fools to get their heads back.

"A cruel woman, her."

Confronting people with the truth wasn't always enough to save those who lived in lies. Shivering at that bloodred declaration, lacking every hint of kindness, Al licked his dried-out lips.

If he hoped for anything, it was that he and the owner of that arrogant voice would never meet as long as he lived.

26

"In a way, I rather enjoyed myself on this little excursion. Allow me to thank you on behalf of my husband," Priscilla said, her arrogance undiminished, as they sat in the parlor of the Pendleton mansion. She brought a cup to her lips as she spoke.

Across from her, that most distinguished woman, Serena Delacroix, smiled and accepted Priscilla's expression of gratitude. "As your host, it is a burden off my shoulders to hear you say that. And speaking of your husband, I don't believe I see him. Where might he be?"

"He's been indisposed in the days since our trip. Overstimulated. He's a weakling, you see."

"If what Miles and Balleroy told me is true, I can't blame the count for feeling overwhelmed. But in any case, I'm glad to hear that he's safe."

Priscilla smiled quietly; such decency was unexpected from the Scorching Lady, known for the depths of her brutality.

Just as Priscilla had predicted, armed uprisings and large-scale rebellions had taken place all over the empire, not merely on the sword-slave island. Each, however, had quickly been subdued by the

Divine General sent to deal with it, and the capital—which was theoretically the objective of the entire exercise—remained blissfully undisturbed.

In the end, the enemy's true aim remained unknown. Ubirk, who had started the trouble on Ginonhive, had vanished, and the entire incident left an unpleasant irritation behind it.

"It seems our new emperor can relax, despite having just assumed the throne. I will watch with great interest to see whether he can really handle the task he so eagerly took upon himself," Priscilla said.

"So you take that tone even with regards to His Majesty the Emperor. You are indeed quite something, young wife. And…"

"And what?"

"It's nothing. I owe you a debt, I'm afraid. I put you in danger." Serena shrugged. She was referring to how Priscilla had assumed Serena's identity—and the danger that went with it—on the sword-slave island. From the outside, it might have looked as if Priscilla had been trying to protect Serena from the disaster that threatened to befall her. But the two women themselves knew full well that Priscilla's motives were nothing so admirable.

Serena would have heard reports from Balleroy and Miles, who had been with Priscilla. It was hard to say what Balleroy might have noticed or said, but Miles would certainly not have minced words when describing Priscilla's actions. What was more, what Priscilla had achieved had gone well beyond merely acting like a body double, and Serena apparently valued that service highly. What they were doing now was a sort of ritual to highlight that.

"I don't like owing people," Serena said. "I want to repay my debt as quickly as possible. Is there anything you want? Aside from my subordinates, whom I'm afraid I can't part with…"

"Don't make me repeat myself. If I desired your lackeys for myself, I would not bother to ask for your permission. They would come to me of their own accord."

"Is that so? A frightening prospect in itself. Very well. This debt is to remain, then?"

"For the time being, yes."

Serena frowned and looked at Priscilla, who noticed again the white sword scar that ran along the left side of the woman's face. She winked her own left eye but looked squarely back at the high countess.

One of them was substantially older than the other, but they shared this—they were both masterful women who could make men quiver before them. Thus, Serena, her intuition whispering in her ear, might even have guessed that the entire reason Priscilla had impersonated her on the island had been to create this debt.

Priscilla, of course, would not say precisely what the facts were. However…

"One day, I will call in this favor you owe me. In the meantime, you may savor the anticipation of when and how that will be."

"Heh. It seems I've incurred quite a serious debt indeed." The girl before her was so young and yet so lovely. The Scorching Lady could only swallow at the prospect of one day having to make good on this obligation. She let out a sigh.

27

"Here, Aldeberan, take this."

"I *told* you not to call me that."

The cuffs—purely for formality's sake—were removed, and he was handed his liuyedao instead. The conversation was practically a ritual by now, but Al was sharing it not with that rare person on the sword-slave island whom he had permitted into his heart, but rather with the sour guard who had replaced the dead man.

He still missed the deceased Orlan sometimes. Maybe part of his motivation for taking on the Hornet had been some measure of revenge, trying to make up for what had happened.

"Heh. Yeah, right… The assassination attempt on the emperor failed, we got a whole bunch of new faces on the island, and life here goes on as usual. Not a lot of difference in the grand scheme of things."

Everything changed; nothing lasted. Not Ubirk's sedition, not the Hornet's evil, not the sword slaves' fervent wishes, nor Arakiya's loyalty, nor Orbart's cunning. Not even Orlan's death. Everything would fade in time. The ants could wail and cry, but they couldn't stop the river's flow. The rebellion on the island had brought this realization home to Al. The thought was still in his mind as he stepped into the arena, greeted by the wild shouting of the crowd.

As his opponent for today's death match emerged from the opposite tunnel, Al's eyes went wide. "Gajeet? So you made it, too, huh? I thought for sure you were dead."

"Hey, so did I. But I survived and damned if I know how. Karma or something, I guess. Maybe it's the same thing that means one of us is gonna die here today."

It was the saber wielder with the half-shaved head. Al had heard he was one of the first on board with the rebellion, but he must have done something to gain clemency, because here he was.

And here Al was, facing off with him in a fight to the death. Everything changed. Nothing lasted. Nothing in the world. Not the world itself.

"Let's have at it, then. No hard feelings, eh, Gajeet?"

"Yeah, sure. We're sword slaves till we die. Even the Hornet eventually bit the dust. So will we one day."

"——" Al didn't respond to that. Instead, as Gajeet readied his saber, Al took up a fighting stance, preparing to let his liuyedao have the last word.

Everybody died. Everyone was going to die. It was something no one could escape. Except Al.

"At least for now," he muttered.

The frenzy of the crowd intensified, and a gong announced the start of the match. Gajeet crouched low and charged in, Al racing to meet him.

Gajeet wanted to chop his head off. Al would just have to chop Gajeet's head off first. It was how it always went. It was just...

"An unlucky star." That was all there was to it.

VERMILION PARTING

1

The days after the girl first pulled him in seemed to pass in the blink of an eye.

"You seem something of a sad excuse for a man."

"Wh-what?!"

A baroness, a local noble he'd known for a long time, had insisted that Jorah consider a marriage with her granddaughter.

Jorah Pendleton, approaching his fiftieth birthday, had imagined marriage to be an affair that had little to do with him, a world he would never occupy. As nobility, he felt the obligation to continue his family name, of course, but to that end, he'd been seriously considering *adopting* someone to be his successor.

When he came to hear the marriage proposal, therefore, it was chiefly so that the baroness wouldn't lose face. The granddaughter was all of twelve years old, after all. There was the proverbial woman "young enough to be your daughter"—but she was even younger than that! And Jorah had no desire to inflict the unhappiness of such a marriage on a young woman with her whole future ahead of her.

If necessary, he was prepared to offer to support her daily life and perhaps to find her a suitable marriage match.

All these ideas were shattered like glass at the actual meeting.

"You may call me Priscilla. Although, I used to be Prisca Benedict, a member of the Volakian Royal Family."

"Whaaaat?!"

Jorah found himself overwhelmed by a girl who acted far, far older than twelve. The discussion progressed rapidly, long before he'd been able to deploy any of the excuses he'd prepared. And then "Priscilla" had dropped the bombshell about her background.

Any Volakian noble, even one like Jorah, would have recognized the name *Prisca Benedict*. He promptly understood two things: that Priscilla's declaration was absolutely, incontrovertibly true; and what his old friend wanted from him about it. Thus, Jorah played the role that was expected of him, as the guardian who would protect this vulnerable young girl...

"Fool. You think that's the role I desire of you?"

"What? Well...but if not that, then why...?"

"Do you have to ask? I've heard that some very important old books rest within your family library." She said it as easily as she breathed. Her interest and hope lay not in Jorah's humanity, but in his possessions. This was an utterly self-assured way of being, one that took no notice or account of whatever situation the young woman was in.

Jorah took Priscilla, the young woman who lived like a fire, as his bride. He was deeply embarrassed, being in his fifties, but this was also the first time he had ever experienced someone desiring him intensely enough to sear.

2

Jorah Pendleton was a completely ordinary man with absolutely nothing to distinguish him as a noble of the empire. *Survival of the fittest; the strong consume the weak; rich nation, powerful soldiers—* such were the ideals that permeated the Empire of Volakia. There was scant place for a man with only his earnestness to recommend him.

In short, Jorah was the very epitome of the kind of person who was unsuited to be a member of imperial nobility.

Jorah himself was well aware that he was out of step with the empire's way of life; that was why he had, until now, lived quietly but pleasantly in the shadows, at pains not to make waves. He tackled no major challenges in his life. His job as he saw it was to safeguard the household for the next generation. Ironically, it was precisely this retiring attitude that had prevented him making a good match even until his late age.

But this was a miracle that bloomed precisely because he was still alone.

"Are you that amused by simply staring at me?"

Jorah's eyes widened when the girl called out his lingering gaze.

He had been stopped in his tracks by the sight of Priscilla—his wife—by the way she seemed completely absorbed in her reading, forgetting even to take a breath. Confronted by that fact, he let a finger wander to his bangs and fiddle with his hair. "M-my apologies. I was simply so...so taken with the sight of you."

The girl sniffed, uncrossing and recrossing her legs. "Hmph, is that so? Then I suppose you may be forgiven. People are transfixed by masterful paintings or precious gems because they contain a beauty that transcends logic. People find *true* beauty irresistible. How much more so might *I* draw the gaze?"

An arrogant pronouncement if there ever was one, yet Jorah didn't have it in him to argue with her—because in fact, she was very beautiful.

"___"

Throughout the course of their conversation, her crimson eyes never so much as glanced at Jorah. They remained fixed on the book on her lap, the pages of which she turned periodically, relentlessly devouring the story within.

When he thought about it, Jorah realized the young woman seemed to be reading a book every time he saw her. That must have been the wellspring of her overflowing knowledge: the piles and piles of books she had read in the course of her life. In other words, reading was something she found essential to storing up knowledge, carrying her to higher and higher places, raising and refining her very existence. In a word, it helped her come closer to her *completion*.

She'd said it was the way of people to be enraptured by beautiful things, even if it seemed irrational. If she was right, then that was surely why Jorah had welcomed her as his wife, why he found he couldn't take his eyes off her. Most likely, too, it explained why he seemed to be at her beck and call, why he wished to indulge her every whim. It explained everything.

And thus…

"Priscilla. Though it's been all too brief, the time I've spent with you has been perhaps the happiest in my life."

"——" Priscilla did not respond immediately.

"I am a cowardly man," Jorah continued. "To this point, I have used up the good fortune I was born with. Carefully, taking it a bit at a time, as if with a teaspoon. However…"

Having gotten that far, Jorah became lost for words. Not because he hadn't thought this far ahead or because his confidence had once again deserted him. Nothing so negative as that.

No, the reason was quite simple.

"——"

Priscilla was looking not at the book, but at him.

Her crimson eyes, as beautiful as rubies, were fixed upon Jorah. Without a word, they urged him to continue, and he swallowed heavily.

As ridiculous as it might sound, that was the first time he sensed—truly *knew*—that the girl before him, Priscilla, had given him words to say. A part to play as a main character in her life despite being a small man, a trivial man.

Thus, he was proud of himself for feeling no quiver in his heart. Not even when the shout came from outside his door.

"Count Jorah Pendleton! You're under arrest on charges of treason!"

3

Soldiers in golden armor surrounded the mansion of Count Jorah Pendleton. The glinting equipment that covered them from head to toe marked them out as subordinates of one of the Nine Divine Generals, who held a special position even within the Volakian Empire.

Each soldier carried a sword or spear, while others held an ax or bow, and they appeared to be a single indivisible unit—but that impression was mistaken. The troops with their golden armor felt no unity, not a shred of cohesion. In a unit where people measured each other's humanity in terms of their chosen weapons, it was impossible to keep the peace.

So if there was something that unified them, it was nothing so intangible as esprit de corps. It was something more obvious, more concrete. Namely: power.

"The troops are in position, General Ralphone."

"Mm, good. Everyone, fall back!"

The one receiving this report from one of the soldiers was a middle-aged man with a face covered in scars; he dipped his chin meaningfully. His huge, thoroughly muscled frame was covered in armor, every inch of him clad in golden plate. It seemed as if even his blood ran with a warrior's pride, and in fact, he considered it an honor to give that impression.

Goz Ralphone was the man's name, and he was one of the strongest people in the empire. He had been given the position of number One of the Nine Divine Generals, the apex of the Volakian hierarchy.

The troops surrounding the mansion, Goz not least among them, carried themselves soberly. And well they might, for they were there to arrest a traitor who plotted a rebellion against the empire. It could very easily turn into a battle, which was the whole reason troops had been sent. Even if it came to violence, though, it was not Count Pendleton's personal army about which they had to be most concerned—but rather the person he appeared to be harboring in his home…

"——" Goz closed his eyes briefly in a moment of genuine pity, but he swiftly shook his head, sweeping the feeling away. He straight-ened up to his full, imposing height and stepped forward from the line of his troops. He sucked in a deep breath and bellowed, "Count Jorah Pendleton! You're under arrest on charges of treason!"

With that, gold-clad troops broke down the front door. The charges were already laid; they would not give Jorah time to make a rebuttal. They would take him with utmost speed, and then he would be handed over to someone whose job it was to hear his arguments.

"And so we strike!" It was Goz who bore this particular burden. The task had been entrusted to none other but him.

No sooner had the golden troops entered the home than a furious clash of swords resounded from within. Evidently, Count Pendleton had readied his household troops, and battle was joined.

"I've no intention of giving you much time," Goz muttered, and then he picked up his own favored weapon, which had been waiting at his side. It was a manner of what was called a mace—a long, two-handed shaft with a large, round metal ball on the end. He hefted it easily, though it must have weighed over two hundred pounds; then in one great leap, he jumped over the heads of his soldiers, landing in front of them and lashing out with his weapon, the mace sweeping away the enemies who blocked his path.

"Stand down!" he cried. "We are here on His Excellency's orders. Any who stand in our way will be considered traitors along with Count Jorah Pendleton!"

"——"

His voice, loud enough to shake the air, sent fear through the count's troops. Considering Jorah's reputation, it seemed unlikely that his personal retinue was full of distinguished warriors. Cer-tainly, one assumed, none who would be willing to wield their weapon against number One of the Nines Divine Generals, Goz Ralphone.

But then...

"Goodness. I never expected you to come personally, General Ral-phone. Well, this is troubling..."

Footsteps sounded at the top of the stairs connecting the great hall just beyond the entranceway to the second floor, and then a slim figure appeared. Goz looked up and furrowed his bushy eyebrows. He knew that man—it was none other than the very person he had come for.

"Count Pendleton. How good of you to show yourself," Goz said.

"I know how people see me, but I am still a noble of the Volakian Empire, even if not much of one. I wouldn't wish people to say that I left my underlings to do all the work while I hid quivering behind them. Although…the part about quivering may be true." Jorah gave a thin smile.

His appearance in the midst of the battle surprised Goz. As far as he had been aware, Jorah was known only for being soft and indecisive, a weak man who possessed no love for war. For him to show himself in the middle of the fight…

"You've had some change of heart, then? I would be most interested to know what has motivated this," Goz said.

"With one of the Nine Divine Generals looming over me, I'm apt to tell you anything you want to know," Jorah said. "I am…a weak man. I have to be constantly working myself up to face things." He bit his lip, his voice trembling.

One of his soldiers knelt beside him and respectfully held up a sword. Jorah took it and drew it slowly from the scabbard. Was Jorah Pendleton an accomplished swordsman? Goz hadn't heard anything of that nature. And so it proved: It was obvious to see he was an amateur. Some people only knew the basic stances, but Jorah appeared not to even know those.

"I must warn you that so long as you have a weapon in your hand, I will not hold back," Goz said.

"Th-that's fine. The moment I chose this path, I knew it would come to this… I've already said my farewells to my wife."

"…Is that so? Then there is no further need for words." Goz nodded firmly at Jorah, who looked straight at him. Then he made sure he had a firm grip on his mace, and he shouted, both to fire the passions of his own soldiers and to break the will of the enemy: "I am Goz Ralphone, of the Nine Divine Generals of the Empire of Volakia! By His Excellency's command, I will root out any who would threaten the empire from within!"

"I am Jorah Pendleton, count of the Empire of Volakia, and for my wife's sake, with this feeble arm, I shall resist you."

4

"I know that bellowing. So Goz Ralphone is here. A bit much if all they want is to capture me and me alone. Not that I can say I'm surprised." Priscilla smiled ever so slightly—she knew that what she said was not quite true—and then resumed running through the woods. She held up the hem of her red dress, moving as easily as if the difficult footing were level ground or as if she were a wild girl born and raised in the natural wilderness.

Other than the way she handled herself, however, every last thing about her was the polar opposite of someone raised in the woods, making her current actions seem like a miracle.

"_____"

At her back, in the mansion she was leaving behind, her husband and his troops were engaging the soldiers of the empire. The smile Jorah had given her, that very last thing, was burned into her eyes.

"He's done a fine job."

Jorah had not been a man of many distinguished qualities. He was perhaps the least qualified person by the standards of the Volakian Empire's principles; he had left much to be desired as both a Volakian noble and as a man. And yet in that final moment, he had without question proven himself Priscilla's husband. His love for his wife had inspired him to sacrifice himself to buy her time, to secure her escape. Priscilla was not so base as to sniff at either the attempt or the success, nor would she let anyone else do so.

With those feelings in her heart, she all but flew through the woods...

"That's far enough, Princess."

"_____"

...until she was stopped by an unexpected voice. She came to a halt, turning her crimson eyes upward. There, in the high branches of a great tree, she saw a silhouette, which swiftly dropped down in front of her.

It was a girl, a girl wrapped only in some cloths that left much of her skin exposed. She was around the same age as Priscilla, maybe not quite a teenager. She was plainly in good health but hadn't quite developed the curves to be called alluring. She had one sleepy-looking red eye; the other was covered in a bandage that sported a flower pattern. Her hair was silver except for a single streak of red, and she had the unique, canine ears of the dogfolk.

In her hand, she held a pathetic twig she'd just plucked off the tree, and she fixed her single eye on Priscilla, her lips trembling. "Lady Prisca...," she said, using Priscilla's other name.

"____"

Priscilla exhaled quietly at the ancient moniker, a name she'd already abandoned. Time had passed—not much time, but still, time had passed. Strange, then, that the girl before her—the familiar face, the color of her eyes—looked as if she hadn't changed at all.

She served a new master now, supposedly, and yet she still turned a beseeching gaze on Priscilla. That was the proof that she was still the same.

"It's hard to escape the irony that it should be you appearing before me at this moment," Priscilla said.

"Princess. I—"

"Betrayed me and joined my brother. And it's brought you this opportunity to finish me off with your own hands. What do you have to say for yourself?"

"N-no, I didn't! I never...!" Though the young woman normally showed so little emotion, Priscilla's merciless assault still made her face twist in alarm. "Then just like now... Princess, for you, I..."

"——" Priscilla didn't speak.

"Today... Today, it's the same. Master Vincent said to me..."

"Fool. You mistake your form of address. My older brother is now the emperor of Volakia, and if you are a soldier of the empire, then you had best remember it. For—" Priscilla paused and crossed her arms. Then she stared down the other girl with her almond-shaped eyes and let her lips curl provocatively. "No… In truth, my brother has not gained the right to call himself emperor of Volakia."

"Oh…"

"Prisca Benedict is dead. My brother alone survives of all the candidates who participated in the Rite of Imperial Selection. Except *my* existence threatens that entire story, doesn't it?" If word was to get out, it would be the greatest scandal in the history of the empire. The emperor, who was expected to be the embodiment of the admonition to be strong, had acted contrary to the idea that only the strong survive."

"Lady…Prisca…"

"And get my name right while you're at it. I'm Priscilla now. Priscilla Pendleton—my token of respect for my husband's last act of service. I must insist you not mistake this, Arakiya."

"Pri…scilla…?"

"I grant it's merely a bit of playing with sounds. Wherever and in whatever circumstances I may be, I shall always be myself. As much of a headache as that might be for my elder brother." Priscilla winked at the girl, the one she called Arakiya, and then sniffed.

Arakiya straightened her small shoulders. "Prisca or Priscilla… The princess is my princess. Come with me. Master Vincent…I mean, His Excellency would speak with you. So…"

"I'm afraid I don't follow. He wants me to return now? To what end? My brother is the emperor, and he cannot abide my continued existence. If, in spite of that, he commands me to return to the capital…"

"Yes? If so…then what?"

"It's as good as declaring that he intends to seek my life once more."

"Oh…"

Priscilla's words were almost casual, but they left Arakiya shocked. She looked at her milk sister and realized it was true that Vincent hadn't explained the niceties of his orders. But it had been enough for Priscilla to guess what he was thinking. Why had he sent Arakiya to find her at this moment?

"The fact that he sent you to me was, in his own way, an act of love."

"What…?"

"Yes. Familial affection. My older brother does love me. And I have considerable fondness for him as well. But that is a separate matter from our respective positions. This time, my brother *must* kill me. And therefore…"

"——?!"

Priscilla's voice dropped on that last word, and then Arakiya's eyes widened, her small body flying backward. The reason was clear: a red flash. A sweep, a beautiful and a cruel strike that, had it connected with Arakiya's neck, would have seen her burned to cinders on the spot.

The source of the blow was a ruby-red blade that was suddenly in Priscilla's hand.

"The Bright Sword, Volakia…," Arakiya said.

"It must be most inconvenient for my brother that there are two of us who can wield this weapon. I doubt he has any need for such musty symbols of power, but without them, he would never be able to keep the likes of Belstetz in line."

"Princess, put your sword away, and—"

"Still, you urge surrender upon me? Then you leave me no choice but to carve my own path with this gleam in my hand."

The sword was too large for a girl who had not yet finished growing and too grand. But Priscilla burst with the confidence to use it freely and the competence to actually do so.

"Go, Princess." Arakiya lowered the twig she clutched in her hand. This made Priscilla breathe "Hoh?" and close an eye in amusement, taking the wind out of her sails. "Are you not defying the emperor's personal orders?"

"But Master Vincent…His Excellency bade me come here."

"——"

Arakiya, perceiving what she judged to be the *true* intent behind Vincent's orders, made her decision. Perhaps she was right, or perhaps it was simply an interpretation of those orders that was convenient to her personal wishes. Either way, it was a perceptible change in Arakiya, who had always before been loyal to the letter of what she was told.

When Priscilla saw that, she returned the Bright Sword to the air, where it disappeared.

"My princess…is the princess. But if Lady Prisca is dead…then this is the last. I beg you. Don't draw attention to yourself anymore. Like with the broadcast…on the sword-slave island…"

"Ah, but that was my own expression of love for my brother. With the resolution of matters on the island, he could keep his defenders at home in the capital."

In any case, ultimately, it had only been a matter of time before Priscilla's hiding place would have been discovered. She was a woman fundamentally unsuited to lying low somewhere and watching the world pass her by. Even her days with Jorah had been merely a detour—although, unexpectedly, not an unpleasant one. Pleasant enough, at least, that she had lost her resistance to using the name *Priscilla Pendleton*.

"Arakiya, I am grateful to you. But the next time we meet, you had best have your resolve set."

"…I hope we don't meet. Ever again."

"But we shall. At least, *I* believe so."

With that, Priscilla smiled—and at the same moment, there came a huge explosion from the direction she'd come, the direction of the mansion. The battle seemed to have reached some sort of climax. Arakiya glanced toward the sound for a bare instant, but her attention swiftly returned to what was in front of her eyes. However…

"Princess…"

…by the time she turned back, Priscilla was already gone. Arakiya looked everywhere, but she knew Priscilla was not so careless as to be found that easily. She was, after all, Arakiya's own milk sibling, and the Volakian emperor's only living relative…

"…I'm begging you…"

Arakiya dearly wished Priscilla would go away, as far away as possible, and live out her life. That she would forget about the brutal war of succession in the empire and go on as just another girl, living in some distant place.

But despite her wishes, Arakiya knew the truth. "It's absolutely… impossible."

The young woman, Prisca Benedict, would never endure that way of life. Sometime in the future, another day would come when, like today, Arakiya was brought face-to-face with her princess. When that day came, what, if anything, would she be able to do with Priscilla, or Prisca?

Set your resolve. That was what she had been told. And yet...

"Lady Prisca... You big dummy..."

And yet for the moment, that single murmur was all she could manage.

5

The rebellion plotted by Count Jorah Pendleton ended in failure. The count himself, mastermind of the scheme, was slain by Goz Ralphone, first among the empire's Divine Generals. Thereby, the foundation for a secure reign by the newly ascended emperor, Vincent Volakia, was assured.

The count had no blood relatives, and so the Pendleton family name, which had endured for generations, was snuffed out. Just two months before his rebellion, the count had married a younger woman, but the annihilation of the family was completed when she committed suicide. Although still so young, the girl, beset by grief over her husband's actions, took her own life.

That, at least, was the testimony of one Arakiya, who would later become one of the Nine Divine Generals of the Volakian Empire.

Thus, there were no fugitives. No one to threaten the swordwolf nation. The peace of the empire was secure.

No shadow would fall upon it. It would continue to carry on into the future.

AFTERWORD

The meek must fall; there should be no mercy! Hullo! Tappei Nagatsuki here! Who is also a gray cat!

Those opening words are something of a slogan among the people of Volakia, but they also sum up this book's content. Did you have fun spending an entire volume in Volakia?

This *Ex* volume reveals some of the background of the royal-selection candidate Priscilla, while also serving as an introduction to the ascendant Holy Volakian Empire, the stage on which Arc 7 of the main series is set. The place has some pretty twisted "common sense"; I think it would be fair to say it's number one on the list of countries you don't want to go to in *Re:ZERO*. At least, your author certainly doesn't.

Then again, forged by constant, brutal struggle, the Volakian Empire has become prosperous, maybe even more so than the Kingdom of Lugunica, and we can speculate that the people there are overall very satisfied with their lives. And they seem quite happy with the job the reigning emperor, Vincent Volakia, is doing.

The current state of the Volakian Empire in the main series is revealed in the seventh arc, which starts in *Re:ZERO*, Vol. 26. If you're interested, I urge you to pick up a copy. Meanwhile, I hope to continue being able to reveal pasts and perspectives that Subaru Natsuki couldn't have access to with these *Ex* books as well as the short-story collections. So keep an eye on them as well as the main series to maximize your enjoyment of the world of *Re:ZERO*!

Oops! With that, it looks like I'm almost out of pages, so let's move on to the traditional litany of gratitude.

To Editor I: I agonized about where to fit this volume of *Ex* in, but you saw that in terms of the main series, the timing could only be now, and you moved on it. Thank you. Let's run the race of the seventh arc together.

To my illustrator, Otsuka: Thank you so much for coming up with nine separate character designs in one go, even knowing that (given the book is set in the past) some of them were going to die in this outing. As times change in the empire, so do the fashions, and I really enjoyed seeing the different look of the characters! I look forward to having you with me for Arc 7!

To my designer, Kusano: Thank you for delivering another stupendous cover absolutely brimming with characters. Every character has a story, and I really appreciate the thought you put into these designs.

Over in *Monthly Comic Alive*, Haruno Atori and Yu Aikawa have been doing a great job creating an attractive, readable version of a very difficult chunk of plot as they work their way through the manga telling of Arc 4. Thank you both.

I also want to extend my deep gratitude to everyone on the editorial staff at MF Bunko J, and all the proofreaders, booksellers, and salespeople to whom I'm so indebted every day.

Above all, my most heartfelt thanks go out to my readers, who are so passionate about not only the main series but also these spin-offs. Thank you all so much!

All right, then. I'll see you in the Volakian Empire in the main series!

August 2021
(Eating ice cream while the rain and
thunder keep me awake at night.)

Miles

"So there ya have it! And here we are entrusted with that all-important bit, the closeout! Let's really go for it, eh, Miles?"

"Okay, hold on, just a second—are you serious? Why'd we end up with a job this big? Wouldn't you expect Count Pendleton and his wife, or maybe our master the high countess, to do this sort of thing?"

"I get the mild panic, Bro, I do, but big, important people like them are busy. And we've got some time on our hands, right?"

"I can't believe this… We're both dead in the main series, aren't we?!"

"Don't talk about the main series, it'll get confusing fast! But look, the buck's been passed—to us!— and I think this is a great chance to show everyone what we can do."

"Damn it, I'm getting a headache… Fine, all right, let's get to work! What've we got first?"

"Yeah! First up! Next December, Volume 28 of the main series should be coming out."

"So the story of the Volakian Empire goes on, eh? Guess they tried to cram this *Ex* volume in there to establish some of those relationships. Ms. Wife sure went on to big things."

"I always thought she'd grow up to be a beauty, but even I never imagined she'd be so lovely! Wonder if that merciless streak of hers has mellowed at all?"

"Good question. Really would've liked to teach her some manners when she was a kid… Next!"

Balleroy

"Sure thing! That same month, December, Shinichirou Otsuka's second collection of *Re:ZERO* illustrations will be coming out!"

"Just like the first one, it seems it'll include not only the pictures from the books up to this point, but a few extras, too... Sounds like a pretty sweet deal."

"Also like before, they're plannin' to throw in a collection of stories that started as store-exclusive bonus shorts—just another way to enjoy the world of *Re:ZERO* even more!"

"I think there's an annual event coming up in September, right?"

"Righty-o! There're going to be more commemorative events in honor of the annual observance of Emilia's birthday! Sad to say, I don't think you'll be seeing our faces on any of the stuff..."

"Missed my chance to meet that beauty. What a damn shame..."

"Y'know, Brother, I hear she's half-elf."

"I don't care if she's half-demon! The point is, she's gorgeous! Not to mention saucy— Ooh, it'd be a treat to discipline her!"

"Ha! I get it now. Miles, my brother, deep down, you're a real bully, aren't you?"

"Pipe down! Looks like our job's done, so let's get some wine in here! Drink with me, Balleroy!"

"You got it! You might be a bully, but you know how to look after a guy. That's what I love about you, Bro!"

Re:ZERO

−Starting Life in Another World−